LEAPFROG

STEVE HENDRY

Medallion Press, Inc.
Printed in USA

DEDICATION:

For Katie, my seven-year-old daughter,
who typed "The End" for me, but has been banned
from reading the book.

Published 2008 by Medallion Press, Inc.

The MEDALLION PRESS LOGO
is a registered trademark of Medallion Press, Inc.

Names, characters, places, and incidents are the products of the author's
imagination or are used fictionally. Any resemblance to actual events, locales,
or persons, living or dead, is entirely coincidental.

Typeset in Baskerville
Printed in the United States of America

ISBN# 978-193383650-8

10 9 8 7 6 5 4 3 2 1
First Edition

ACKNOWLEDGMENTS:

Special kudos to Mary, my wife, my proofreader, and for her constant struggle to keep me out of passive voice.

PROLOGUE

"WARNING! ALL PERSONNEL MUST REPORT to the cryogenic laboratory immediately. You have one hour, thirty minutes to begin processing. Repeat, all personnel must report to the cryogenic laboratory immediately," warned the starship's computer over the intercom.

Major General Thomas Bradford automatically checked his chronograph. *Yep, right on time,* he thought as the ship's interior lighting shifted from DayGlo orange to an eerie light pink. One more compartment to inspect before he would join the rest of the crew in deep frozen sleep. All the other ship's personnel had already reported to the cryogenic laboratory to begin final preparations for the required deep freeze inside the cryo-sleep capsules. The procedure of blood transfusion and slow freeze took just under twelve hours, after which the horrific main thrusters would activate. A person not frozen solid would certainly be crushed to death when the ship accelerated to cruise speed.

Thomas Bradford was, without a doubt, the most dedicated and talented general in the service. His dark blue, piercing eyes transmitted his intelligence to everyone who locked gazes with him. The general stood a little over two meters; he had light gray hair, was extremely fit, and looked like a poster board advertisement for CEOs, excluding, of course, his attire. He was dressed in a loose and baggy flight suit with two gold stars on his shoulders.

Saving the most critical area for last, Thomas made his way to the bridge. He was the supreme commander for the most important mission that humans had ever embarked upon and was meticulously thorough with all his responsibilities.

The computer biometrically recognized him as he approached, and the bridge's restricted access door automatically opened. The bridge was like a vast theatre with encircling lounge-type chairs, and each chair had a mini computer console attached to it. In the center stage sat the captain's console and just to the right and slightly elevated was the supreme commander's console, which controlled every function of the starship.

Something was wrong. The distance from the access door to the center stage and the dim pinkish light made it hard for Thomas to discern exactly what was out of place, but as he drew nearer, the silhouette of a human appeared from behind the supreme commander's console.

"Who the hell are you, and what the hell are you doing here?" the general demanded in a loud voice while picking up his pace.

"I have taken over this ship and relieved you of your duties," a familiar voice replied.

"What! Colonel Jackson? Have you lost your mind?" Thomas exclaimed as his eyes registered the colonel's distinguishing features. "I'll have you court-martialed for this."

"You'll do no such thing," smugly replied the colonel.

"Computer, abort," Thomas stated.

In her soothing, female voice the computer answered,

"You do not have clearance for the abort command."

In a voice laced with disrespect and bitterness, Colonel Jeffery Jackson spat out, "As I was saying, the ship's mission has been reprogrammed to my authority. We, the Federation Secret Service, have deemed this mission too critical for joint civilian tenure. The profile has been altered to better suit our needs."

Jackson had been a thorn in the general's side ever since the mission manning was plotted, but no matter how hard he tried to relieve the arrogant colonel of his duties, some guardian angel threw Jackson back into the fray. Now, it was pretty apparent who the "guardian angel" was.

"Bullshit!" blurted the general as he drew his stun gun. Confusion crept into his mind when he pulled his weapon clear of its holster, and Colonel Jackson simply sat there grinning like a Cheshire cat, not even making an attempt to defend himself or take cover.

Thump! A piercing sensation in his back followed by electrifying white light engulfed General Bradford's consciousness.

"That ought to take care of the old man for a few hours," Lieutenant Skip Carter commented as he crawled out of the maze of lounge chairs and consoles behind the prone general. The computer whiz, who had recently finished reprogramming the complex computer, had also just shot the general in the back.

This mutiny had been rehearsed many times under the intense scrutiny of Colonel Jackson. Although both men had received the same orders to liquidate General Bradford, Lieutenant Carter had wanted the general to be killed as quickly as possible, while Jackson wanted the gloating rights and insisted on the grandstanding.

"Double cuff him to the zero-g restraints," commanded Jackson. "I want this asshole to die slowly."

While rolling the general over and cuffing each hand to restraints located one meter apart on the floor, Carter said, "This will be a mess to clean up. When the ship depressurizes, he'll pop like a balloon."

"We'll worry about that a century from now. In any case, we'll be awakened ten hours before the others and can take care of cleanup before ship's company comes around." Jackson went over to the general and removed identification, crystal memory keys, and personal effects from the limp and secured body. "Now we'll see what kind of shape you're in," he said to the unconscious man.

Kicking the prone general hard in the ribs, he stepped aside and faced Carter. "Let's lock up the command console, reset the bio codes, and haul ass down to the cryogenic lab. We barely have enough time to set ourselves up. The launch window's approaching and if we miss it, we'll have to wait another twenty-two days."

"Aye, sir," was all Carter said in return.

"Warning! Warning! Biometric life form detected. Manually abort countdown! Abort countdown!" A loud clanging of bells followed and the computer repeated its last message.

"Wha . . . what's that?" said a very groggy general. Slowly, the thick veil of unconsciousness lifted, and the man opened his eyes to be greeted by flashing red lights. The computer repeated its warnings over and over.

"Ah, shit!" Thomas said when he tried to sit up and found himself firmly tied on his back with his arms pinned.

"Ship rotation ceasing; preparing for final countdown," the computer warned.

Eventually the ship ceased its rotation, ending the gravitational effect and allowing Thomas's legs to float upward. He realized Colonel Jackson had saved a gruesome death for him, and his only chance of salvation would be to make it to the control console and abort the thrusters' activation. Once the antimatter pulse engines kicked in, the g-forces would immobilize and eventually kill him. Programmed for ten g's for thirty-five days, the rockets would be relentless, and if that didn't kill him, the vacuum of space certainly would.

Pushing hard off the deck, Thomas flipped over backward and managed to get his legs beneath him.

"T minus sixty seconds; commencing countdown. Abort circuits overridden," the computer warned.

"Arrrgh!" Pushing as hard as he could, Thomas put all his strength into an attempt to break free. Taking deep breaths between efforts, he could feel his shoulder and wrist tendons stretch and tear with an occasional snap, but the restraints would not budge and his thumb joints refused to give.

"Ten, nine, eight . . ." The computer counted out the last seconds while Thomas tried to tear his arms off.

Blam! The tremendous force of the rockets slammed the general down on his face, doubled over with his knees beneath him. His body now weighed an amazing nine hundred and fifty kilograms, and he was barely able to finish rolling onto his back. Breathing was incredibly difficult, and he could only manage short gasps. His arms seemed to weigh a ton, and all he could do was raise them to chest level.

The computer was unfazed by the terrible acceleration and continued its monologue. "Warning! Warning! Depressurization will commence in ten seconds. Abort circuits overridden."

For the first time in Major General Bradford's life he knew real fear, defeat, and failure. This was the most important mission ever to face Earth, and he had failed to carry it through. He was still wondering how it would turn out and what the aliens would make of it, when a piercing headache paralyzed his breathing efforts. His eyes bulged open despite his efforts to keep them closed and his blood began to boil. Fortunately, his brain stroked out shortly before his body exploded leaving a large puddle of bloody goop under his lifeless body.

CHAPTER 1

One Hundred and Two Years Earlier

A SMALL MOON APPEARED TO flicker into existence and begin orbiting the medium-sized water planet that orbited the star, Xi Scorpii. If anyone were alive on the surface of the water planet and watching at the time, this moon would seem to have materialized from a massive, flowing heat wave as it emerged from its intergalactic wormhole. On the contrary, far from being all rock and dust, this peculiar "moon" was the most advanced starship in the known universe.

The occupants of the vast starship had considered it "home" since their planet's core had cooled and subsequently lost its protective magnetic field. The planet's magnetic field had served as a barrier to shield the inhabitants from deadly sun-induced radiation and cosmic storms. To escape this increasingly poisonous radiation, the planet's populace had built a huge starship to serve as their new home. Forced into the role of universal gypsies, these peaceful beings roamed the universe in search of other intelligent life. After searching for thousands of years, they finally found what they were looking for.

The beings received intelligent, albeit disturbing, electromagnetic signals from a planet in a galaxy known—to humans—as the Milky Way. After extensively analyzing the human species, the wanderers concluded humans were incapable of grasping the reality of particle physics without some sort of jump start.

To ascertain if the species would be able to handle the secrets of space travel, the beings chose a small, uninhabited water planet that was so close to Earth that if the universe were one thousand kilometers in diameter, the water planet would be less than a hair's thickness away. The sun for this planet was only ninety-two light years from Earth. So close that the light from each star was clearly visible to the other.

As the starship orbited the uninhabited water planet, they prepared their message; the message that would put to test the very survival and future of the human race.

CHAPTER 2

Launch Inauguration

Premier Abdul Nazir took a deep calming breath, briefly closed his eyes and took a moment for meditation before facing an anxious audience. A hushed silence fell over the vast world stadium like an unfurling carpet as the leader of the World Government strode to the center podium. The entire stadium was packed with crew members, their families, politicians, financiers, and the people who had directly contributed to the construction and design of the starship, *Leapfrog*. Monopolizing the entire planet's video service, virtually all human eyes on the Earth were focused on this incredibly powerful person. He needed no introduction, for every sane person, knowledgeable in current events, knew him.

He felt his wife's reassuring hand on his arm. Samira Abdul, a tall, beautifully aged woman of Indian descent was not only his wife but his best friend and confidant. An intellect herself, they had spent many hours discussing the grim dangers of this project and its importance to the future of humankind.

Abdul Nazir was dressed immaculately in casual but stylish khaki pants and a light blue collarless shirt, with long sleeves covering his muscular arms. Appointed by the World Allied Government for his impressive credentials and confirmed by the peoples' vote, he was without doubt the most powerful man on Earth. He was directly responsible for rallying every industrialized country in the world in support of this massive endeavor. Pooling their resources into the International Space Consortium, each country on the planet that was able funded and technically supported this effort. Universal morale ran high as a result of a common goal, and Abdul, the leader of the movement, was thoroughly enjoying the glory as the most famous man ever to walk the Earth.

Clearing his throat, he began without preamble, "Ladies, gentlemen, and children, it is with great honor that I speak to you at this monumental event." Stepping to the right, away from the podium, Premier Nazir illustrated that he was not relying on hidden notes and prompts for this particularly important speech. He held a PhD in astrophysics and an MD in internal medicine, and he did not have to rely on subordinates to give technical speeches. He was more than qualified, having authored several of the most influential and contemporary books on astrophysics.

His deep, rich baritone voice reached out and touched everyone listening. "As you know, one hundred and two years ago, unknown aliens sent their message, a message that took ninety-two years to reach us. This powerful, deep space radio wave washed over our planet and jammed all of our electronic communication. It was so powerful many communication satellites were instantly fried. We had no doubt the signal was generated by intelligent beings with technology superior to ours. The signal burst lasted ninety seconds and repeated itself every twenty-seven hours for a total of seven times to ensure complete coverage of our rotating planet. The signal's strength, duration, and cycle allowed our scientists to narrow the search pattern to a star in the Scorpios Constellation. After eighteen months, the code was finally broken and the message interpreted."

Abdul forced himself to remain focused on his speech. "The alien message, as you are well aware, shook the Earth to its very core. Another life form existed, their knowledge was by far advanced to ours, and they wanted to share cultures. The message went on to explain that they had chosen the Xi Scorpii solar system and its fifth planet for a rendezvous. Apparently this star is centrally located for other planets exhibiting similar electromagnet intelligence and the fifth planet is uninhabited. Furthermore, this planet is completely covered with water, a major plus for star travelers seeking plentiful sources of hydrogen and oxygen."

Abdul paused for a quick sip of water, and then continued. "The motivating clincher for us was at the end of the message when the host aliens stated that the secrets to particle physics, including wormholes, tachyons, and alternate dimensions for space travel and navigation were stored on removable computers at the site and were to be considered as gifts of friendship and trust. The offer of free secrets that would unlock space travel and enable humans to leapfrog over existing technology collectively reeled in the entire populace of planet Earth. A race started. A race for our very survival.

"Our planet has been consistently plundered and our natural resources have dwindled to a dangerously low level. In addition, governmentally enforced birth control has failed to slow our perilous overpopulation." Raising his voice to its famous baritone pitch, Nazir added, "We need new frontiers; we need to expand, and the sooner the better. Now we are finally ready to begin the most important mission that man has ever attempted."

A loud, standing ovation interrupted him. Even people not physically attending caught themselves standing and applauding. Such was the force of Nazir's charismatic appeal.

All Abdul had to do was raise his hands to cause instant silence from the cheering audience. "Don't applaud me. I have been nothing more than a public bureaucrat administering your wishes. The true appreciation should be directed to the real heroes here. The crew of *Leapfrog!*" His enthusiastic clapping was joined by the whole world.

After several minutes of raucous applauding and cheering, Abdul raised his hands again.

"I know several of you still have questions, so I'm opening the floor to the press."

Hands flew in the air from the International Press box. Abdul pointed to a particularly well dressed, middle aged woman. "Yes."

"Mr. Premier," she began as she perused her notes. "exactly what are the conditions that the aliens limited us to, and are we complying with all of them?"

Abdul was ready for this one. "The aliens' message went on to say that they had built an underwater outpost on a shallow underwater continent of this ocean planet to house various artifacts that might be of interest to other space travelers. Each visitor was respectfully requested not to take all of any one sample and to leave something of cultural interest in return. The owners of this exchange post would visit periodically, approximately once each one hundred Earth years, for replenishment and collection. The aliens also made it clear that they would be the ones to decide if further communications with visitors were to be considered. Also, the aliens made it known that retrieval of these treasures was only to be made by carbon-based, bio-logical life forms; in other words, not robots. This ensured that the seeking species was sufficiently technologically advanced to handle the information. This particular stipulation required us to seek a means for suspended animation."

More hands flew into the air. Abdul pointed to a young man dressed in a toga with a turban on his head. "Yes."

"Mr. Premier." The young man was evidently very ner-vous, as he dropped his small teleprompter on the floor when he stood up. "Sir, why do we have to subject our crew to fro-zen pre-sleep, when there's rumor going about that the test subjects have sustained permanent brain damage?"

Abdul didn't flinch. *Ahh, that didn't take long. Now let's see if I can bullshit my way out of this.* "The humans will travel in a fro-zen state for a good reason. Despite all the advances in space travel, overcoming the acceleration g's required to obtain rea-sonable speeds remains a mystery and is very problematic. In order to obtain a speed close to light and still maintain a mass identity, the ship and the people inside the ship would have to sustain ten g's for thirty-five days. This process will have to be repeated once again to decelerate. This feat is pos-sible only if the passengers are frozen solid and do not require heavy life support systems for the duration of the travel.

"Our scientists tried and failed many times to develop this cryogenic technology, but thanks to the common North Amer-ican wood frog, which can fully recover from a total freeze, we finally discovered how to freeze human tissue without the damaging effect of cell bursting. The major drawback is that human blood has to be removed and replaced with a more suitable antifreeze substitute that just happens to be green . . ."

Laughter interrupted him this time. Holding up his hands for silence, Abdul continued, "Many attempts to dye the substitute blood a more suitable red failed, so the green remains, much to the chagrin of the recipients. To help alleviate severe psychological reactions, the crew has been promised that their blood will be properly stored and then transfused back into their bodies once the thawing process is complete.

"As far as the rumor of any sort of brain damage is concerned, you can rest assured that our scientists have long ago ironed out that wrinkle."

More screams for attention from the press box filled the air. Abdul pointed to an elderly lady with a large, crooked nose. "Yes."

"Mr. Premier," she began carefully. "We've all seen the pictures of this spaceship, but could you please tell us in your own words the challenges this ship has been built around and its cost?

Abdul couldn't help but smile, as this was comfortable territory for a man of his background. "The International Space Consortium took ten years to prepare for the mammoth and tremendously expensive mission and was bankrupted three times in the process. The outcome is a super advanced starship, appropriately named *Leapfrog*, as we intend to leapfrog over existing technology. The colossal ship is roughly the size of a large football stadium, parking lot included, with gigantic antimatter pulse rockets aligned along the bottom. Drag not being a factor in space, the tubular-shaped spacecraft will cruise flat side forward, spinning slightly when not accelerating or decelerating. This spin will allow the astronauts who are in a thawed state the comfort of artificial gravitation. The multilayered hull is also self sealing and is in a constant state of repair.

"Even after developing the cryogenic technology, our scientists still face the problems of speed, distance, and time, which are all horrific barriers in the realm of space travel. The diameter of the known universe exceeds seventy-five billion light years, which makes time and speed major players in the equation of distance, even for the relatively short distance of ninety-two light years. The required technology for speeds above light has not been developed and presents appalling barriers for practical interstellar travel. The new antimatter pulse rockets had previously proven their worth by accelerating several small, unmanned spaceships to the speed of light and beyond, but that was the last anyone saw or heard from them again. The onboard programming to decelerate and return was ignored, and apparently the robots are still beaming about the universe completely unaware that they are now pure energy. Thus, our scientists are blocked at speeds less than light for the foreseeable future, which means that the mission duration will have to be extremely long: approximately one hundred and fifty years each way."

More hands flew into the air. Abdul pointed to a well known Pulitzer Prize winner, a man well into his sixties. "Yes."

"Mr. Prime Minister, is it true that time here on Earth will go by much faster than for those in space travel, and have the psychological factors of this phenomenon been adequately accounted for?"

Abdul paused again for a sip of water. The entire audience, having heard all this before but not from this man, were literally sitting on the edge of their seats, soaking up every word as gospel. Abdul resumed. "The prolonged time required for space travel and the relatively short lifespan of humans make suspended animation unquestionably mandatory. The Twin Paradox presents the last dilemma for future space travelers. Twin Paradox refers to a human in motion aging less than one who is not. How would one cope with coming home to old or deceased family members? Psychological polling among the astronauts pointed out two interesting points. The astronauts did not seem to mind coming back to a future time and catching up on technology, but they vehemently deplored coming back to deceased spouses and children. So, the simple solution for the time being is to freeze them all and take them along. Two hundred and seventy-five souls will be aboard the ship: men, women and children. Extra fuel required for the additional weight will be paid back in full with the increased quality of the volunteers.

"Finally, the mission is ready to depart to the widespread rejoicing of all humankind. Let no one doubt that this is *the* most singular important mission that mankind has ever attempted." Another standing ovation interrupted Premier Nazir. He could not help but wonder, in the midst of all this celebration, how many people really understood the hidden undercurrent agenda that ran strong beneath the veil of "the good for mankind" theme. Secret services, corrupt politicians, and mistrusting military leaders had their own priorities, which directly contradicted the aliens' goal of co-operation and trust. *Oh well,* he thought, *man has a poor memory, and besides, we'll all be dead by the time they return.*

Premier Nazir Abdul decided to end his speech at this highlighted point and stepped forward and bowed deeply to the roaring crowd.

CHAPTER 3

Arrival at Destination

THE REPLENISHMENT TANKER, WHICH THE International Space Consortium had launched two years in advance, was in proper orbit over the designated water planet. The ship, *Leapfrog*, had arrived in relatively good shape; the only surprise was the planet itself.

Unknown to all at the time, the solar system the aliens had picked was not a good choice. Atypically, Star Xi Scorpii skipped its nova stage and prematurely fizzled to a tiny bright dwarf, rendering very little solar heat. The water planet selected was now nothing but a huge ice cube, only a few degrees above Absolute Zero. This ice planet presented major hurdles for the *Leapfrog* crew, who had expected and prepared for a relatively warm water planet. The mission planners had realized and anticipated the atmosphere would be hostile, with near zero percent oxygen, but to be confronted with cryogenic operating temperatures made the endeavor seem practically impossible.

The powerful *Leapfrog* computers evaluated the planet, performed a task analysis, and began the thaw process of those who had been designated essential personnel, automatically excluding all dependents. Secret, side programming allowed the military unit to awaken first, as they had devious projects to complete before their civilian counterparts were awakened.

After selected military personnel had recuperated, Maxwell Finch, Deputy Commanding Officer of Starship *Leapfrog*, was the first crew member to be awakened. Max could only lie still, immobilized until his pile-driving headache subsided. Waiting for the expected headache to abate, he pondered how old he would be compared to his contemporaries, or long-gone contemporaries. Max was a physically fit, slightly overweight, young forty-year-old. He was moderately good looking, bald, and medium height. Along with most humans, he was of mixed blood; very seldom would one see a "pure" black, white, or Asian anymore. The races had started mixing together several centuries before, and most people seemed to be permanently tanned in color.

Looking down, Max could see that his capsule had drained, transfusion lines had disconnected, and his heads-up display had all green lights illuminated. The green lights indicated suitable cabin atmosphere, temperature, and gravity, which meant the *Leapfrog* was properly rotating. Reaching up, Max pressed the green-lighted release button, and the capsule immediately slid open. Noticing the armed guards standing nearby, he gave them no regard beyond a casual "good morning." Max figured they would be on full alert for the duration of the mission and paid them little attention, but could not figure out why they were already awakened and why they were stationed here. When asked, they simply shrugged and said that they were following orders.

With wobbly legs, Max made it to his neighboring crew pod and checked his wife's status. Kim was well along on the thaw phase, with regular breathing and a strong pulse. The computer's countdown gave her another forty-five minutes before she would be released.

Kim happened to be the "wonder brain" of the expedition. The Consortium had wanted to place her in supreme command of the ship, but her often abrasive personality took her out of the "people person" category. Even worse, her dedication to performance, not politics, rubbed too many bureaucrats the wrong way. As a compromise, and to keep her tightly in the command loop yet buffered by her charismatic husband, The Consortium made her the commanding officer of the ship, directly under the authority of Major General Bradford.

After checking on his wife, Max enjoyed his first recycled shower in one hundred and fifty years. Dressed in the standard baggy blue jumpsuit and back at his console station, he had just finished studying the ship's computer log and progress analysis when Kim slipped up behind him and gave him a hug with a peck on the cheek.

With her eyes closed from pain, she said, "I hope you feel better than me. This headache is a killer. I don't care what the cryo-physicians say, something's wrong. Wonder how many brain cells were destroyed during that little nap?" Sliding into her cockpit chair next to his, she silently read the computer messages.

Max slid his chair back, wrapped his arms around her waist and pulled her into his lap. "I can't believe you look so good for being over a hundred and eighty years old." Kim's appearance was about average on the males' lust chart, with a slightly pointed chin, a nose a tad too large and hazel blue eyes so intense most men couldn't hold eye contact with her. Not a striker, but she was definitely not chopped liver. Like her husband, she was slightly overweight with premature worry lines around her mouth and eyes, but when she was in the mood, she had a warm, genuine smile. The loose baggy jumpsuit did nothing for her figure, but her protruding breasts left plenty for the imagination. Max's imagination worked just fine.

Kim purred and kissed him deeply. "Flattery will get you everywhere, including lucky." She batted his groping hands. Not now, big boy. Let's see if we still have a ship first."

"What's with the guards?" she asked as she stood and made her way to her console. "Aren't they still supposed to be in cryo-sleep?"

Max had already come to the conclusion that something was seriously wrong. He gave Kim a few minutes to catch up then leaned his chair back and said, "You're not going to like any of this, especially this." He handed her a red-covered folder with "Ultra Secret" stamped all over it.

Kim quickly scanned through the message and could not help but gasp. "Jesus Christ! I can't believe they want us to do this. What about the artifact collection the Consortium historians so painstakingly put together? Bradford isn't going to go along with this." Turning her head to her console she said, "Computer, display inventory of the artifact hold and status of Major General Bradford."

A soft female voice came back from the speaker, "Major General Bradford is deceased. Inventory list recently edited to reflect additional armament. Artifact cargo holds empty except the seeds bin." The relatively small seeds bin contained an all-inclusive selection of every plant available on Earth. The small storage area was obviously overlooked or considered insignificant by whoever altered their standing orders.

"Empty? Dead?" exclaimed Kim. "Computer, what

happened to General Bradford?"

"Unknown. My memory was violated and edited for deletion."

"Dammit!" Kim responded. "Management had no intention of exchanging culture—just pillage and run. We can't do this, Max. Here's the biggest opportunity for mankind to shine, and we become the chosen ones to screw it up."

Max shook his head and whispered, "We have no choice. Finish reading the order and you'll see. The military contingent is now under autonomous authority and has been directed to kill anyone acting against this order, and, honey, that includes us. Your command position has been rescinded and the military is now running the show with no mention of General Bradford."

As if on cue, Colonel Jeffery Jackson and sidekick Lieutenant Skip Carter walked on to the bridge and the two standing guards snapped to attention. Max wondered if the guards' snappy reaction was only because of Jackson's rank, or because his appearance was a perfect reflection of his personality. Max frowned at the acne-scarred face and chiseled permanent frown beneath cruel, beady eyes.

Carter, although the same size and build as his colonel, was a "poster boy" image of what the armed forces wanted to portray, Max ruminated with wry amusement. Handsome, with long, wavy blond hair, protruding dimpled chin, and light blue eyes, but a fake smile even a child could spot a mile away, he was expected to go far in his career. Max knew this because he was a perfect kiss-ass politician who was adroit in surfing the ever-changing whims of his superiors.

Not saying a word, Jackson marched in front of the seated

pair and glared at them as if he expected them to rise and bow to the new emperor. It didn't happen and he spat out, "I am in charge. You have your orders, and you will obey them or be executed on the spot by my guards."

The guards were visibly not happy to hear that, for they started fidgeting and constantly shifting their weight from one foot to another. "You will be confined to the bridge for the duration of this mission and will conduct business here and no place else. I wanted you left in cryo-sleep, but a glitch in the computer permitted your recovery."

"You killed General Bradford, didn't you?" Kim accused.

With a smug smile, Jackson said, "General Bradford is no longer with us, and if you two don't do as I tell you, you will meet the same fate."

"Listen, asshole," Max said as he stood up.

Fast as a snake striking, Jackson struck Max hard across the face with the barrel of his stun gun, knocking him back in his seat. Blood started seeping from the corner of his mouth.

Max started to rise again but stopped midway after seeing Carter point an electrical stun gun at his forehead. The glaring red "Set to Kill" light was illuminated above the trigger guard. These potent little weapons shot small supercharged batteries with penetrating electrodes up to one hundred yards with pinpoint accuracy. The little batteries packed a walloping, instantaneous million volts with suitable amperage to bring down an elephant. The voltage and amperage combination were not designed to completely fry a brain but were just strong enough to permanently short circuit any nervous system, rendering the victim completely paralyzed during cardiac arrest and suffocation.

"No, you listen, and listen well," Jackson snarled. "You two are nothing but unnecessary baggage at this point, which I can dispose of at any time. You are alive only because of my goodwill and are subject to termination at my discretion. I will not hesitate to execute the both of you should I deem it necessary or advisable. And, I will do it one at a time, slowly, so one can watch the other suffer." This brought a wicked smile to Jackson's face.

"Do you understand what I just said?"

No answer, only a silent stare down.

Jackson pointed the stun gun at Kim. "I said, do you understand what I said?" Kim glared back. Jackson clicked the safety off.

"I understand," Max said through his teeth for both of them.

Jackson kept his gun aimed at Kim for a few seconds, before saying, "I have cordoned off the command center of the bridge and it will be off limits to you and all ship personnel. The area in the far corner is reserved for you and your staff." Jackson re-holstered the sidearm, turned to Carter and, without looking back, the two men marched off the bridge.

After the bridge door slid shut, one of the big guards with "Scoffield" stenciled on combat fatigues said to the couple, "I'm sorry; I didn't know any of this was coming down. Want me to muster up a rebellion or anything like that?"

"No," Max answered knowing the bridge was probably bugged. "That would lead to unnecessary and nonproductive violence. We'll take this to parliamentary justice when we return." Sighing, he added, "I'm sure this mutiny was well thought out, and any attempt to resist at this point would be considered an excuse to exercise lethal force."

Standing behind the bridge door, Jackson removed his earpiece and told Carter, "Hurry and find some reliable guards and have the two on duty replaced immediately."

Kim slumped in her chair, closed her eyes, and groaned, "Do you ever feel like you've just been raped, then forced to say you enjoyed it?" Sitting up and squinting at the computer monitor, she added, "Don't answer that. How about collecting the thawed crew for a briefing and get this show on the road? I'm sure they're going to be as thrilled about the mutiny as we are."

As if absentminded, Kim started typing coded instructions into the computer's programming. *When we return, I'll be damned if those assholes come out of cryo-sleep before we do,* thought Kim. The mutineers had a computer specialist, Lieutenant Carter, but he was not even close to being in the same league as Kim. Kim was not only an expert programming code slinger; she could think in code and was capable of hiding complex executions within subroutines. She could whip up a computer virus in ten minutes that could crash any computer built, regardless of the operating system's protection. So Kim used her computer expertise to alter the order of recovery on their return trip. They might have the advantage now, but she was bound and determined to change that.

CHAPTER 4

"YOU WANT TO DO WHAT?" screamed an enraged Colonel Jackson. This outburst caught the attention of the entire bridge area. Even the constant chatter of the isolated ship's company died. Jackson was fit to to be tied and for good reason. The "water" planet had frozen over solid and was nothing but a gigantic ice ball.

Dr. Jack Mitchell's knees were shaking as he stammered, "Just a small fifty-kiloton sir. Surely the aliens' support base can withstand that."

Jackson looked wide-eyed at his sidekick, Lieutenant Skip Carter. "And, this is our Senior Science Officer?" Carter merely shrugged.

Shaking his head, Jackson returned his attention to Mitchell. "I don't know where you bought your PhD, but you should be able to get your money back." Standing up and towering over Mitchell, he continued. "A moron could come up with a better idea than that. Why would aliens in their right minds protect their cultural exchange gifts with a nuclear explosion-proof building?"

"B-but sir, that would be the quickest way to penetrate two hundred and twenty feet of ice."

Sighing deeply, Jackson addressed Carter. "Freeze him. We can sort this out when we get back to Earth."

"I protest! You have no right——" He was cut off when two burly MPs dragged him from the bridge.

"Next brain in line would be Dr. William Evans," Carter said. "But expect some resistance. He was pretty vocal about our taking over and threatened retaliation upon our return to Earth."

"Yeah, right! Put him on the *special thaw* list." Jackson smirked, well knowing that anyone on the "special" list would accidentally die during their defrosting period. "Bring him over."

Another two guards appeared with a scowling scientist in a lab jacket. Dr. William Evans was just under two meters tall, thin, and fairly good looking, but he wasn't very handsome with the scowl embedded in his face. "What's the meaning of this? What have you done with Dr. Mitchell?"

Colonel Jackson walked over and stood nose to nose with Dr. Evans in an obvious attempt to intimidate the man. From the look on Evan's face, it wasn't working. "I need cooperation. Total complete cooperation. Can I expect that from you?" Jackson hissed.

Returning the stare, but now on tiptoes to ridicule Jackson's intimidation attempt, Evans said, "Fuck you and the horse you rode in on."

"Shoot the queen bitch," Carter said, "then her husband and then randomly shoot everyone in that sector."

"You wouldn't . . . how could you?" stammered Evans as Carter walked over to Kim and drew his gun.

"Okay! Okay, I'll cooperate. Just don't shoot her! Evans screamed as Carter lowered his barrel to Kim's head.

Smiling, Jackson said to Carter, "Hold your fire for now. I think we have the good doctor's attention."

Sitting at the command console, Jackson said, "Here's the problem. Our nuclear generators can melt the ice, but the surrounding air is so frigid that the water refreezes before it can be pumped out. And yes, we tried to thermally wrap the pipes."

Bill started pacing. "If you can't move it in its liquid form, then break it up and haul it out."

"That would take too long." Jackson replied with exasperation. Besides, the jackhammers would freeze up in no time."

"I wasn't thinking about jackhammers. You've got plenty of explosives, right? Use shape charges and work your way down."

For the first time in years, Jackson actually smiled. "I'm putting you in charge of excavation. Report to the shuttle service for the next launch to the ice station with your pressure suit. Keep me informed hourly. And, I need not mention what I'm going to do with Queen Kim if I suspect any delay attempts or sabotage."

Scowl returning, Bill simply nodded and made his way off the bridge.

Eighteen hours later, Bill made the call they all had been waiting for. "I'm going hot for the camera upload. Let me know if it's coming through."

The uploaded visuals appeared on the command center's overhead. "We see several large pillars . . . what . . . five meters high?"

"Yep, at least. These folks must be gigantic! I'm walking in the entrance now and will give you a running commentary. I see two humanlike alien models aligned along the entryway.

Obviously representing the alien's growth, sex, maturity, and aging, the replicas are gigantic. They stand over four meters tall with large, bulbous, bald heads way out of proportion to the rest of their bodies, widely-spaced eyes, high cheek bones, no visible ears, tiny mouths, and small noses."

Bill had the entire ship's attention. All eyes aboard the *Leapfrog* were glued to the video transmission. "Okay, just past these two models, I see a ton of stuff, but haven't a clue as to what it is. I'm sending in teams to bring all we can to the shuttles." There was a brief pause before Bill continued. "Uhh, Colonel Jackson, your troops aren't bringing in our cultural exchanges."

Jackson chuckled. "There will be no exchange. I have no further need of you down there. Return on the next shuttle and report to the cryo-lab."

"Hold on a damn minute—"

Colonel Jackson terminated the transmission.

Turning to Carter, Jackson said, "Have them take everything, I mean everything, plant the nuclear device in the middle of the display, and retrieve all personnel. We're getting out of here as fast as we can."

Carter hesitated. "Uhh, sir, why are we blowing the site? After all, we'll have everything."

Jackson gave Carter one of his dumb shit looks. "Evidence is the number one reason, denial is number two. There's a good possibility that other intelligent life forms are around and can use what we can't find."

"Yes, sir," Carter said simply.

Under constant guard, Max and Kim were forced to stay on the mother ship without access to the communications center. Max called it a mutiny and wanted retribution upon return, but Kim turned to him and said, "Revenge, huh? Like, who's going to be around when we return? Our history was written long ago; we'll be nothing but curious ancient artifacts when we return, with absolutely no recourse. And the political insiders knew it when they set us up; they must have laughed all the way to their graves."

Once the military had finished its pilfering, the scientists hurriedly deciphered as much information as they could and beamed the data back to Earth. Unknown to all onboard, the transmissions were immediately blocked by an unseen force.

The scientists wanted to remain in orbit to analyze the artifacts in more detail and at least learn how to turn on the holographic computers, but then Max sarcastically commented, "And what shall we say to the aliens or other prospective visitors that may come upon us here while we're gloating over our plunder?" That was all it took. They unanimously agreed to leave posthaste.

The crew docked the orbiting replenishment tanker to the *Leapfrog*. After the *Leapfrog* was refueled and provisioned, the tanker was set on autopilot and steered toward the dwarf sun. The small tactical nuclear bomb was detonated at the collection site on the planet to obliterate any traceable evidence and to destroy the radio homing beacon. A visible crater in the ice was all that remained of the aliens' goodwill gesture. Kim looked down on the unconcealed intrusion and thought, *This was NOT a good idea! They, whoever they are, are going to be extremely angry and there'll be hell to pay before this is over.*

At mission completion, the guards escorted the entire civilian crew at gunpoint to their pods and monitored them until all were frozen solid. Only then did the military contingency retreat to their respective pods for their own deep freeze. Once all the humans were frozen, the ship's main drive kicked in and the *Leapfrog* began its acceleration process. However, space debris from an exploding black hole a billion years earlier had other plans for the *Leapfrog*.

The plans arrived in the form of solid, super hardened metallic meteorites traveling just under the speed of light. Without a doubt, the most worrisome aspect of uncharted space travel is the unlikely chance of running into space debris. The designers of *Leapfrog* had that in mind when they developed small robotic probes, or scouts, to precede the huge ship and search for unwanted space material that could harm the mother ship. Radar was the means for detection, but radar waves are also restricted to the speed of light. By the time the scouts discovered the rapidly closing objects, they were engulfed and barely had the time to send warnings back for the massive *Leapfrog* to take adequate evasive actions. Their belated warning did allow, however, for the huge ship's computers to activate emergency lateral thrusters, but they were too little and too late, for the stellar shower had an extraordinary closure rate that overtook the *Leapfrog*. The meteorites were like large particle beam neutrons silently zipping through the hull of the vast starship.

The huge ship's computers had recently finished freezing the humans and depressurizing the living areas for the long trip home. This made the hull penetrations and internal destruction completely without sound in the vacuum.

The projectiles were much too fast to be visible and lent an eerie aura as the cosmic pieces racing through the ship's skin kicked up iced condensation that clung to the ship's innards. Many times faster than any bullet, the pressure-hardened pellets whizzed through the protective titanium shields like bullets through cardboard boxes. Not being discriminatory, the space projectiles took out computers, control panels, three frozen humans and, most importantly, a fusion reactor core.

This premature shutdown automatically sent a signal that secured all pulse thrusters. Fortunately, the gyroscopic stabilizers were not damaged and they immediately activated, which prevented the huge ship from tumbling end over end. Mercifully, the shower was brief and did not completely destroy the ship's integrity. The *Leapfrog* also ceased its ten-g acceleration and started a long coast home at only a portion of the optimum light speed. Programmed for thirty-five days of ten g's, the ship was supposed to approach near light speed for the one hundred and fifty, year journey home. Now all bets were off as to when, or if, the spaceship would ever return to Earth.

The aliens had seen everything. They observed the primitive antimatter fusion reactors that pushed the tiny ship out of Earth's orbit and into the long trek to its rendezvous with destiny. They also witnessed the total disregard that the midgets showed to the unselfish request to share cultures as they plundered and then destroyed the cultural exchange site. Advanced and stealthy spy units embedded in the stolen artifacts transmitted the horrific damage that *Leapfrog* suffered from the meteorite storm. As soon as the radio transmissions from *Leapfrog* were blocked and all human activity slowed for their freeze, the artifacts slowly dissolved in self destruction.

Flickering like a television image, the huge moon-shaped starship slipped out of its visual- and radar-cloak mode. The alien leader of the starship was intently observing the crippled tin can, *Leapfrog*. The mysterious intelligent beings communicated among themselves through telepathy and did not believe in idle chit chat. *Destroy?* thought his first officer

No. Let the human tin can decide its own fate. Retribution is not in our charter. The captain turned his monitor back to the desolate ice planet and activated the second beacon in another area. *Plot a course for the planet that's emitting radio signals. Maybe we'll have better luck there.*

Instantaneously, the huge starship was enveloped in an attached wormhole and disappeared. The stricken *Leapfrog* was left in peace to find its own way home.

CHAPTER 5

EONS PASSED, APPROXIMATELY TEN THOUSAND years, but the deep sleep went on, at least for those still alive. The *Leapfrog* was struck many more times by space debris but was spared any fatal hits.

The frozen humans were thermally shielded from close passing solar systems and remained completely depressurized in a vacuum state. Once every five minutes, a dim, blue spark could be seen glowing from deep inside the capsules. This little electrical impulse kept the neurological systems alive while simultaneously sending flex signals to all frozen muscles.

The *Leapfrog* starship was equipped with multi-stratum nuclear-powered computers. The power source for all computers was 238U, which had a half-life of two and one-half billion years. The first layers of computers were silicon based and wired ten in parallel with a failure step-down feature. As one computer failed, the next one would boot and continue monitoring routine operations. Whenever two failed in a row, the first set of the more advanced plasma computers were "awakened" to guide repair robots. This sequence continued for many cycles with one computer repairing another until the supplies were exhausted. The last set of the plasma computers were on the final set of repairs when the crippled starship finally reached Sol, Earth's solar system.

After five cycles of encrypted radio signals were sent to Earth without being answered, the silicon computers aroused the central, main plasma computer, which then carried out hull repair, repressurization, and finally the initialization of the awakening processes for the long-hibernating humans. Since the encrypted messages were not acknowledged from Earth as expected, all the dependents were kept in their frozen states until further instructions were received by the conscious humans.

"Arrght!" screamed Kim as the first flash of pain seared through her skull. She momentarily opened her eyes only to shut them as fast as she could, for the brilliant white light seemed to blind her. Cringing and wishing for unconsciousness to relieve her, she felt the pain intensify and radiate down her spinal cord to every nerve cell ending. Just as she was about to scream out again, blessed blackness took over and she slid back into a void. The reprieve was short; soon the pain came back with a vengeance and stayed. Slowly, way too slowly, the pain started receding back to her skull. Afraid to move her head for fear of disturbing the headache monster, she slowly opened her eyes one at a time. Again, blinding white light assaulted her, but she forced herself to focus on something, anything. Sluggishly, her vision started to clear and adapt to the glaring white light. There, she could see her HUD heads up display, but all the lights were not green. She had one red light remaining but could not focus clearly enough to read the print underneath.

Memory, where art thou? she thought as she racked her brain for clues about what to do next. Vaguely, she remembered being told many times not to open the pod until all the lights were green. While waiting for the green light to appear, she started an inventory of her body. Legs were still there; she could feel and move them. Arms next; seemed ok, along with all the fingers.

Ten minutes passed before the horrific headache started to ebb. Kim's vision improved to the point she could read the print under the glowing red light: "Transfusion." *Ah shit!* Kim brought up her right hand to verify that the transfusion tubes had indeed been retracted. *What now? Green blood forever?* Finally, her memory came creeping back. *At least four months before my body can replace this shit. No vigorous exercise because the cells can't hold much oxygen. Guess I'll have to live with that. Wonder if the headache will last that long?*

With her right hand, Kim raised the red handle override and pressed the *pod release* button. Quickly, the thick transparent, densely armored doors to her pod slid open. Still not able to focus very clearly, she sat up to swing her feet over the side. *Bad idea, sitting up so fast.* She immediately blacked out and found herself lying down again with the headache worse. The next time she sat up carefully and swung her legs over the side and did a cursory exam of her body. Pea green splotches covered her body, head to toe. *Green? Gangrene?* she thought as she painfully scratched a spot and watched it peel off to expose welting green tissue. *Terrific! No beauty queen material here. Looks like I've got green freezer burn.*

Not trusting her balance, she kept her weight supported on the railing as she edged over to peek at her husband's pod.

The slightest exertion caused her to run short of breath.

"OhmyGod!" Kim screamed as she took in the mummified remains of her long dead husband. His pod still looked moist, but she could not understand why he had shrunk so.

"Murderers!" she screamed when she noticed the finger-sized hole through his chest. Opening his pod, she touched his body and realized how light and dried out it was. Trying to figure out why the pod was still moist, yet his body so dried out, she lifted up his stiff, boardlike shoulders and figured his total weight must be almost ten kilograms. Max was totally dehydrated. Rolling his body over on its side, she saw the impact of the projectile that killed him. The same sized hole was through his pod and the bottom deck. Looking straight up, Kim saw another hole perfectly aligned with her husband's pod.

Meteor strike killed him. His pod remained frozen, but without life, his body just dried up, Kim thought as she slumped to the floor with flowing tears. She curled in a fetal position sobbing while her memory was unmercifully flooded with images of being held hostage on the ship they had commanded and being witness to the ruin of the mission the human race had entrusted to them.

Taking a deep breath, Kim shakily climbed into her jumpsuit and made her way over to the computer control console. "Computer, what's the ETA for synchronized solar orbit parallel to Earth's track?" *Where did all this dust come from? It's absolutely filthy in here.* Kim looked around for something to clean off all the dust.

The same ageless female voice responded, "ETA three hours, fifty-two minutes, and twelve seconds."

"Computer, state the status of military unit," she panted.

"Recovery for the first human expected in four hours, sixteen minutes. Others will be revived within the next eight hours."

"Computer, can you delay their recovery?"

"Delay all thirty-six?"

Kim was having trouble catching her breath. "Computer, yes, I want recovery of all thirty-six military personnel placed on indefinite hold. Wait a minute! You said thirty-six? There's supposed to be forty-five."

"Nine perished; full recovery on six remains questionable with a sixty percent chance of survival. Placing a restraint on their recovery will reduce their chances of full recovery."

Like I give a damn. "Computer, place the entire military unit recovery on indefinite hold."

"Recovery on thirty-six military unit personnel placed on hold status."

The numbers were not adding up for Kim. "Computer, why the high fatality rate?"

"Extended cryo-sleep exceeded computations."

"Computer, what extended sleep? Aren't we on schedule?"

"Negative. Extended cryo-sleep exceeded by ten thousand twenty-one years."

"What?" When Kim did not receive a response, she remembered the protocol of always having to say "computer" first.

"Computer, verify total time in cryo-sleep."

"Total time for you is ten thousand one hundred twenty-one years, thirteen hours, forty-six minutes and forty-one seconds."

"You gotta be shitting me! Uhh, computer, cross-check your calculations."

"Cross-checked; your cryo-sleep period equals ten thousand one hundred twenty-one years, thirteen hours, forty-six minutes and forty-one seconds."

Kim leaned back in her chair, headache long forgotten. "Computer, what happened?"

"Antimatter thrusters secured at 14,722 meters per second after severe damage to the core reactor."

Kim made a quick mental calculation and replied, "Computer, our return still shouldn't have taken ten thousand years."

"We were gravitationally affected by several close solar systems and uncharted black holes that altered our flight significantly. Our digital computers were not programmed for such diversions."

Kim noticed that she was panting again. "Computer, why wasn't my blood transfused?"

"All human blood deemed unsuitable due to extended cryo-sleep."

"Computer, why do I seem out of breath all the time?"

"Artificial blood is unable to carry sufficient oxygen for continual conscious operation."

"Computer, calculate proper oxygen percentage and change cabin mix now."

"Oxygen content increasing to eighty-seven percent."

Kim put her head down and waited for the oxygen to take effect. As much as she wanted simply to sit and do nothing while her headache subsided, she could not keep her mind at peace with all the unknown variables floating around. Keeping her head down, she asked the table in front of her, "Computer, inventory archive storage lockers."

"Lockers empty, no log inputs."

Great! Just fucking great! All this for nothing. No, not all, we've still got some pretty pissed off aliens looking for a fight. Well, if they wanted to kill us, they certainly had a good opportunity while onboard this ship retrieving their toys.

Raising her head a few inches, she asked, "Computer, why doesn't Earth respond to our radio transmissions?"

"Unknown. Unable to receive any signals or the anticipated deciphered code."

"What?" Snapping her head back up, the pain flared back with white hot intensity. "Computer, verify no radio signals at all from Earth."

After a few moments came, "Verified, no signals detected, all known bands."

This was too much, too fast for Kim. "Computer, notify all surviving crew members, when they are able to rendezvous on the bridge ASAP."

"That will take one hour, twenty-two minutes and thirty seconds."

Fucking computers. Kim wobbled to the bridge's first aid station for some heavy duty pain killer and her first recycled shower in ten thousand some odd years. She would read the reports later. Right now, she needed to clear her head for some serious planning.

CHAPTER 6

WHAT A MOTLEY LOOKING CREW. Doctors, scientists, engineers, scholars, and philosophers, but thank God no military people are present. Thirty-two in all, with seven perished during the cryo-sleep, thought Kim as the stragglers wandered about gulping down painkillers by the handfuls. Like mumbling zombies, they each made a beeline for the nearest recliner and plopped down with their heads in their hands. Without exception, they all had a greenish tint to their complexions, and the whites of their eyes looked comically greenish. *No smiles, laughter, or typical joking around with these guys,* buzzed through Kim as she made her way to the supreme command console, which also served as a raised podium. A semicircle of six similar consoles ringed the raised center one as dukes and earls would a king. Smaller, comfortable chairs that could recline were systematically lined out for the audience. Not all had seats; some sat in the aisle or rested against the rear bulkhead.

"Ladies and gentlemen," Kim began as a hush fell over the subdued audience. "I realize all of you are aware of our situation here, and none of us has a clue what's happened to Earth. Just so we're all on the same page, I'll brief you on events up to this point." Kim spent the next twenty minutes reviewing the mission and fielding questions as they arose.

"Doctor Finch." Dr. Carl Manley, a computer research

scientist, stood up and faced Kim.

"Please, Carl, let's drop the formalities. We all know each other very well by now and seem to be stuck on the same small boat," Kim said as she washed down some more Tylenol.

"Fine by me," said the tall and gangly scientist, "but not all of the military unit participated in our little snatch and run. A good friend of mine, Major Gary Hecker, did not participate in the coup. As a matter of fact, the commanding officer of the unit, Colonel Jackson, personally had his name removed from the initial awakening. He's been frozen like the dependents since we left Earth. My point being, this should be sufficient reason alone for his recovery." Carl paused as if something malevolent was hanging on his thoughts. Kim patiently waited for him to continue.

"I have a bad feeling that something terrible has happened down on Earth, and we might need as many defenders as we can get. Look around at us; nothing but scholars and scientists with none of us knowing which end of a gun should be pointed."

There was a little mumbling of disagreement, but no one stood up to counter Carl or volunteer to serve in any defense capacity.

"Carl, do you have any idea as to why this major was side-stepped?"

"No, but I did ask Colonel Jackson about Gary, and he told me to mind my own business and fuck off."

Christine Perkin, the head of *Leapfrog's* medical department, stood up so quickly she had to sit back down. "Umm, sorry, I must have been zoning these last few minutes, but did someone mention Major Gary Hecker?"

Christine was one of Kim's prized department heads. Not only was she drop dead gorgeous and could easily make a fortune as any publisher's cover girl, but she had graduated summa cum laude from Harvard Medical. Right now she looked like the rest of them: no makeup, hair disheveled, and a skin color to match her pale green eyes. Kim forced a smile and answered, "Yes, Christine. That's who we've been talking about."

A bit hastily, Christine said, "I can vouch for him. He's a good man and has a set of twin girls aboard in cryo-sleep."

"I don't mean to pry, Christine, but exactly how well do you know this man?"

Christine shifted her weight to one foot then the other and warily answered, "Very well. We had an intimate relationship before we departed on this ill-fated jaunt. Our individual careers demanded our full attention at the time, and we were to pick up where we left off once things settled down. Gary, Major Hecker that is, for some inexplicable reason remained locked in cryo-sleep during our mission, and every attempt to release him was countered by Colonel Jackson." Christine looked very worried when she sat back down.

Kim turned around to the computer console and said in a loud voice for all to hear, "Computer, what's the status on Major Gary Hecker, and why didn't he participate in the last mission?"

"Major Hecker was denied initial recovery. Unknown reasons."

"Computer, recall Major Hecker's personnel records, just the pertinent information."

The computer did not hesitate. "Major Gary Adams

Hecker, born July 25, 2105, MIT graduate with honors. He served in the United Alliance Army from June 06, 2127 to present as a Delta Special Operations specialist. Many combat awards, no disciplinary record, accelerated promotion, divorced, two children who are onboard."

Kim turned back to the group, "Anyone have an objection to bringing him back?" Many of the greenish faces peering at her looked desperate and forlorn, so Kim was trying to bring them back into the present by having them participate.

When no one objected, Kim faced off with the computer console again. "Computer, recover Major Hecker and have him report to me when he has sufficiently recuperated." The computer's green acknowledgement light flicked once for all to see.

Turning back to the group, Kim continued, "We'll keep the dependents frozen until we discover exactly what happened back on Earth and have some sort of a plan. I want all personnel to report to their respective centers for evaluations. Don't just report a problem; bring viable solutions back with you. I consider life support issues the most critical, so let's get cracking. We'll meet back here when Major Hecker can join us and we're in Earth's orbit. I know it's grim, people, but whatever we are facing, we'd better do it right the first time, because we won't have time to do it again."

Although Kim's audience got to their feet slowly, a purpose and newfound hope showed on their faces, and a few smiles here and there could be seen. Christine dashed out to check up on Gary Hecker and her department.

CHAPTER 7

A BLINDING WHITE LIGHT COUPLED with a splitting migraine assaulted Major Gary Hecker. Gary was a big man, two meters, wide-shouldered, and ninety kilograms of pure muscle. He had a full head of brown hair and blue intense eyes, and he was considered moderately handsome. An old scar that ran across the left side of his face took him out of the "pretty boy" category into the dangerously good-looking slot.

Upon awakening, his first thoughts were *Jesus! I must have taken one in the head. Hurts too much to move. Better play dead and hopefully whoever shot me won't do it again.* Gary lay there until he got the courage to open his eyes again and meanwhile tried to acclimate himself to this strange environment. Opening his eyes, he concentrated on focusing on the little green lights with the tiny lettering below them. All were green but one little one that he could barely focus on, which said, "Transfusion."

Transfusion? What the hell is that? Ahh, now I remember. I'm in the sleep pod. Must have made it to the water planet. Sure seems like I've been out for a long, long time. After opening the pod, Gary eased his way up to a sitting position. Although his vision was still out of focus, he could see well enough to tell that he was the first of the military group to recover. On wobbly legs he crept over to his boss, Colonel Jackson's, pod.

Good! Fucking asshole, still asleep. Cupping his hands over his eyes to block some glare, Gary bent down to Jackson's monitor. "Status—Hold."

Hold? Why? Then the memories came flooding back. Memories of his last discussion with Jackson over the secret orders he had received and the terrible argument that followed. Jackson threatened court martial; Gary threatened exposure, but later wound up consenting to continue with the mission and take up the issue again once they arrived at the water planet. The supreme mission commander, General Bradford, would be the moderator and hopefully rescind the orders. *Hmm, maybe the general caught wind of the orders and had Jackson put on hold.* Creeping over to the next pod, Gary read "Status—Hold." *Good, they got his little kiss-ass crony as well!*

General Bradford's pod was already open, but he was not in sight. Gary did notice that there was a lot of unexplained dust on and in the general's pod. Walking down the row of the military contingency force, Gary noticed that all of them were either on "deceased" or "hold" status. *Not good,* he thought as he made it back to his monitor to read his status: "Recovered." But now he could pick up some small print underneath his status. "Major Hecker, when sufficiently recuperated, read computer log and report to the bridge. Kim Finch." *Kim? Since when was I on first-name basis with her, and where is General Bradford? Ahh, this must be about the disagreement. But why am I the only one they recovered?*

Grabbing a handful of liquefied MREs, meals ready to eat, Gary sat down in front of his pod's monitor and started reading the *Leapfrog's* log. He hastily sucked down the brown-colored crap they called nourishment, and brushed his teeth while calling up the computer's files. As his first order of business, he checked on his twin girls' status, and saw they were still Okay. Next he called up the message log. By the time he finished, instead of having a red face from anger, his face was bright green, giving him a very distinguished alien look. He was halfway out the door before he noticed he was still completely nude. He shut the door and took a deep breath. *Slow down! This is not the time to lose your cool.* But the thoughts did not keep Gary from running to his locker to hastily dress. *Strange. How can I be winded from that little dash?*

The strangest-looking green man jumped out at him when he opened his locker and glanced in the mirror. *"Green? I'm green? What happened? Ahh, that's what the "Transfusion" red light meant.* Opening the first aid kit, he pulled out the skin repair canister and slightly cut the underside of his forearm with his razor-edged K-bar combat knife. Verified, green. He bled pure green without a trace of red. Gary watched it a few seconds before deciding that the cut would clot and stop bleeding by itself. *Terrific! A green scab to boot.*

With that thought in mind, he threw on his blue jump-suit and dashed out of the cubicle directly into the chest of a shocked Dr. Christine Perkin. Kinetic energy favoring Gary, Christine flew backward, landing solidly on her rump. "Ummph! Watch where you're going! And slow down!" an infuriated Christine spat as she scrambled to get up. Seeing who had run her over, she added, "Oh, it's you! Just the person I was looking for."

Gary offered her a hand to help her up and said, "Hi, Christine, baby, it's been a long, long time." He gave her a big hug, and she held him tightly. Pulling back and looking into her jade green, smiling eyes, an old feeling came back to his groin, and he kissed her deeply on the lips.

Parting, but lingering at the light lip touch, he whispered, "We've got a lot of making up to do . . . but right now, I'm wanted on the bridge."

Holding his face in her hands, she could not help but to start to laugh. "Sorry, don't mean to spoil the mood, but I can't remember ever being knocked down and kissed by a handsome, green man before."

Being called green brought Gary back to the present, pressing scenario. Taking a good look at her, he said, "My God, you are still absolutely gorgeous even though you look a little green around the gills yourself."

She laughed and lightly hit him on the arm. "I was on my way to check up on you when you barged through the door and ran me over. You know, you're going the wrong way. The bridge is over there."

"I'm having a little trouble getting oriented." Gary sighed.

"Join the crowd. Come on and I'll walk with you to the bridge." Christine turned and made her way to the bridge and Gary followed, thoroughly enjoying the view.

Kim believed in an open-door policy and had the computer keep the doors open to the bridge. She had just rescinded a previous computer navigational command and had ordered the *Leapfrog* to be dropped to a lower elliptical orbit. Three of her four department heads, Carl Manley, Terry Evert, and Jack Mitchell, were seated in a semicircle observing Earth from the *Leapfrog*'s telescopic cameras. They were all right in the middle of "Oh no, ah shit, and holy shit" when Gary and Christine walked in. The computer automatically blanked the big screen when it sensed Gary as an unauthorized intruder.

"Ah, Christine, good to have you back. Did you manage to reset the bio computers?"

"Certainly did," Christine chirped. "The mainframe should be updated by now." She sat in her seat, joining the other department heads, and waved over at Gary. "Look what ran me down on my way back."

"Sorry to interrupt, but I got here as fast as I could," commented Gary as he walked to the center of the semicircle.

Kim swung around to face him. "Welcome back, Major Hecker. Since we're all in the same crisis and on a very small ship, I suggested that we drop formalities and keep to first names only. So, Gary, I realize you've probably met everyone here, but allow me to indulge. From the right we have Carl Manley, who is our life support department head. Next to Carl is Terry Evert, who is our logistics department head. Next is Christine Perkins, our medical department head whom I believe you're already acquainted with, and last but not least is Jack Mitchell, our engineering department head."

Gary went around and shook hands with all of them, and when he got to Christine, they smiled and stared at each other a little longer than seemed appropriate. Christine broke the awkward silence. "Welcome to headache city; the first aid kit is on the bulkhead behind you. Feel free to pick any flavor of pain pill you wish, but I recommend Tylenol Ultra. I believe these headaches were caused by our extended stay in cryo-sleep and are a result of damaged brain cells." She smiled and added, "Besides, none of us here feels very smart at the moment."

Gary immediately made a beeline for the first aid kit and gulped a handful of pink pills.

Kim waited until Gary was seated in the center of the semicircle before continuing. "Gary, we don't mean to make this into an inquisition for you, but there's a lot at stake here, and we just can't afford to make a mistake. So, to start off, why were you kept in cryo-sleep, thus forbidden to participate in the military coup we experienced?"

Gary's relaxed posture perceptively shifted to a more military composure as he sat up straighter and squared his shoulders. "Colonel Jackson and I had a major dispute over the revised mission plan. Only after Colonel Jackson conceded to mediation with General Bradford, you, and your staff concerning the secret orders did I consent to the cryo-sleep. I had all information officially logged into the ship's computer for future mediation, but I see that all records concerning the matter have been erased. Apparently, Colonel Jackson or one of his cronies tampered with the computer logs."

Kim shook her head. "Yes, someone altered the official ship's logs, but that someone wasn't as bright as he thought. Authorized or not, every entry is transparently transcribed to a secondary recorder. Your protests and a request for hearing were not totally erased."

Kim took her time studying each of her department heads, looking for affirmative head nods. Obviously, they were waiting to hear Hecker's side of the story before deciding his fate.

While she was taking her poll, Gary was wondering whether or not he had just had his minute in court and if the jury was making their decision right in front of him. He doubted they would nail him for the infamous mission, but they might decide to judge him guilty by association.

Kim turned back to Gary. "There, it's settled. We need a new department head for security, and we just voted for you. That is, if it's Okay with you?"

Gary was dumbfounded. "Ah, sure, of course it's all right with me." Catching his balance he added, "But what about the rest of the military personnel, especially Colonel Jackson? He'll be sure to cause us some trouble."

"That brings us to the next order of business. Who, besides Colonel Jackson, were the major conspirators in this mission?"

"I can't speak for everyone, but I do know that Lieutenant Carter and Senior Staff Sergeant Collins were conspirators in the alternate mission."

Kim gazed over at her department staff while they simultaneously raised their hands. Kim turned back to Gary. "Sorry to leave you out of the loop, but we wanted confirmation of information we already had. Christine and Joe thought it would be best for you if we excluded you from the burdensome decision."

"What decision?"

Kim shrugged and turned to the computer console. "Computer, verify voice and bio recognition for maximum security clearance."

"Doctor Kimberly Finch, Commander United Forces, *Leapfrog*."

"Computer, jettison the following personnel toward Sol, Earth's sun: Colonel Jackson, Lieutenant Carter, and Sergeant Collins."

Gary jumped up. "Wait a minute!"

Kim signaled him to sit back down and be quiet.

"Last command involved termination of life. Repeat

command for execution."

"Computer, jettison the following personnel toward Sol, Earth's sun: Colonel Jackson, Lieutenant Carter, and Sergeant Collins."

"Computations complete . . . pods preparation complete . . . three pods jettisoned."

Gary could not stand being silent any longer. "Just like that! You executed three men, just like that?" He was standing with fists clenched by his side.

Carl Manley stood up and was the first to reply. "No, Gary. You've known me for a long time, and you should know it was not 'just like that.'" Their recovery was way past any point of reversal, and our life support supplies are dangerously low. We are not in any position to take prisoners, and that's exactly what those three would be. We unanimously came to a decision prior to your arrival and had the same three men flagged. We used your input for the final say in the matter." Carl reminded Gary of some of his professors. Articulate and confident would be some of the adjectives. All Carl needed was a pipe and a tweed jacket to be the perfect stereotype.

When Carl sat down, Christine stood. "This has not been easy for any of us." Pointing toward Kim, who had her head resting on her hands, she continued, "Kim just had to jettison her husband, who died in a meteor shower. Carl's wife and Joe's son also expired somewhere en route and likewise had to be jettisoned. As Carl said, we are very low on life support supplies and can't support a prison. We can't even thaw out our families. If we do not replenish on Earth soon, we will perish ourselves within four days. I'm sorry it has to be this way, but we don't have many options." Christine sat down again.

Kim turned back to the monitor. "Computer, recover the remainder of the military unit. Include a full debrief in each pod's monitor. Have them individually report online when they are ready for hazardous duty." The green light flashed once.

Kim activated the huge overhead monitor, and a beautiful high altitude image of Earth appeared. Gary followed everyone else by leaning back in the recliner for a better view of the ceiling monitor. Kim addressed her new staff member. "We've got bigger problems here. Earth is no longer the Earth we left, and civilization has taken a huge leap backward."

CHAPTER 8

KIM WALKED OVER TO THE podium and zoomed the ship's cameras down on Earth, focusing on North America. "As you can see, the United States of America is quite a bit smaller. On the West Coast, Baja, California, and everything all the way up to Seattle is gone. The San Andreas Fault was apparently at work. On the East Coast, Florida is nothing but a small stub with the coastline half of what it used to be, and most of the Texas panhandle appears to be submerged." Zooming into Europe, Kim continued, "England is now only a small island; Europe's territory has been reduced proportionally along with the United States. Since the ship's in a solar orbit parallel to Earth's, we haven't seen the night side of Earth. This allows us to study all hemispheres. The cause of the land shrinkage? Probably the combination of an ice melt from Greenland and both poles.

"While we were gone, the Earth's polarity switched, and it appears that the latest global warming will be replaced by a new ice age." Kim zoomed to the North and South Poles to exemplify her point. Small ice patches were scattered about.

Gary could not figure out whether the ice would be receding more or starting to increase, but he held back comments, figuring it did not make a difference anyway.

Kim resumed. "But what really concerns us is what's left

of civilization. Earlier today, while you were recovering, we filmed this little event from one of the tribal factions living in what used to be Georgia, USA."

Kim flicked on the playback and the camera instantly zoomed to what appeared to Gary to be an altitude of approximately five hundred feet with crystal clarity. A circular clearing in the middle of a dense forest was the center focal point. It looked like some kind of a camp with several large tepee-type tents in the middle surrounded by multiple lean-tos. People, dressed alike in drab-colored shrouds, which looked to Gary like animal skins, meandered about on various forms of business. On the outer perimeter of the encampment, several people could be seen bent over neatly arranged garden beds. The camera moved in on one particular person in the garden who was leaning back with his hands on his hips. He was bearded and old, and he was grimacing in pain. He was obviously trying to stretch out some sort of backache pain, but he quickly returned to work, bending over and tilling the soil. Coming into view was a much younger person who appeared, from the lack of facial hair, to be female. She offered the old man a jug of water, and he drank deeply from it. Returning the jug, he leaned over and gave the woman a peck on the forehead like a father would do to a daughter.

Kim narrated. "Here's where it gets gory."

The old man turned his back to the girl and continued tilling. Carefully, she put the jug on the ground and extracted a foot-long dagger from beneath her robes. Swiftly, with fury painted on her face, she lunged and drove the dagger to the hilt in the man's back. He fell to the Earth, rolled on his back, and arched his body in noticeable pain. The girl leapt on top of him and stabbed him again, this time in his chest. The girl, in a frenzy, continued to stab the dead man until his chest was nothing but pulp. Exhausted, she rolled off of him, stripped him to the waist, made a large incision below his rib cage and pulled out a dark-colored organ.

"That's his liver," Christine chimed in.

She put the organ to her face and took a huge bite out of it, then tilted her head back and appeared to be screaming. The camera moved in for a close-up of her bloody face, and her rage and fury could be felt 80,000 km straight up.

"Jesus Christ!" exclaimed Gary as he jumped to his feet. "Cannibals! Look at her! She's completely insane. How can those creatures do that? I mean, how can they be socially organized and still eat the flesh of another member of their group?"

"From what we've seen," Christine chimed in, "it's their way of relieving the elder burdens of their society. This may be some kind of ritual in combination with some other unseen bonding force. In the past, humans have eaten other humans, but only their enemies or perceived enemies. This clearly isn't the case here, and we're stumped, just like you."

The camera backed up and others could be seen converging on the feeding. The girl pointed her bloodied dagger at the people closest to her to protect her prized meal. Collectively, they grabbed the fallen man by his limbs and hauled him off to the nearest large tepee. The girl squatted on the dirt and continued eating, which did not take very long. Finished, she raised her bloodied face again as if to yell at some unseen god.

"Stop the recording!" Gary almost shouted. "There, zoom in. Look at her face; something's wrong. She almost looks like a Neanderthal with her sloped forehead, high, extended brows, and flattened nose." Looking around the room at the faces turned to him, he asked, "Ok, what's going on? Those people aren't humans, or at least as we know them."

Kim pulled the camera back out to the planet view. "Now you know as much as we do. We haven't a clue about what happened, but we have several theories. First, a space exploration team like ours went to some other destination and brought back a virus with them. The virus spread, an epidemic broke out and, *bingo*, we go back to the caves. Second, what we see is the result of a nuclear war or biological warfare, or both. Third possibility? Maybe the aliens that we plundered took revenge."

Terry, from logistics, cleared his throat before speaking, "Or Armageddon took place and we missed the party. What was left was Homo sapiens without souls, with some form of de-evolution taking place." Terry picked up on Gary's skeptical frown and added, "You saw that girl's face: a complete psychopath, and what were the repercussions from her little act of murder and cannibalism? Nothing! That's what. They're all that way and that's why."

Christine stood up and started pacing with her chin in her right hand as she concentrated. "Viral, nuclear, or spiritual Armageddon, it doesn't much matter right now. We need to probe that planet thoroughly before we set foot on it. Any contamination brought back could wipe out the ship."

Kim spoke next. "That takes time, Christine, and time is what we don't have."

Terry jumped in. "We're down to five percent water, which is way past critical. We need immediate replenishment for consumption, oxygen, and hydrogen. We only have enough oxygen and hydrogen for one two-way shuttle mission and four days of life support. Since our burn to get back here involved very little reactive fuel, we've got plenty of that, but no place to go since one of our main reactors took a meteor hit." Carefully looking each individual in the eye for emphasis on what he was about to say, he added, "And that cannot be repaired, nor do we have any spares for replacements."

"I thought the shuttles used antimatter reactors just like the main drives, but smaller?" Gary asked.

"Yes," answered Terry, "but only as main drives to get into orbit and VTOL, vertical takeoffs and landings. The shuttles need the separate oxygen and hydrogen gases for horizontal maneuvering and balancing. The ship's nuclear electrolysis can break the H_2O molecules apart; then we can freeze the gases to their cryogenic states for future use. We have one shuttle being fueled now for a water run on Earth."

"But . . ." Kim said with a grin.

"You need a guinea pig," Gary finished.

"Well, I wouldn't put it like that, but after witnessing the tribal solution to old age social security, I would feel a lot better with a team that knew how to defend themselves."

Christine said, "If you stayed in full space suits, exposure to a virus would be practically nil, and we can decontaminate you when you return."

"Thanks for your concern, Christine, but that won't work," Gary said. "We'll need to establish a secure perimeter and leave a task force there for security, and there's no way we can fight in full space gear, much less spend a few days in one. And assuming it was a virus that turned around civilization, won't the water be contaminated also?" Gary turned to Terry and asked, "How many runs are required to fully restock the ship's water supply?"

That little dose of reality was all it took for Christine to drop her contamination premise. They had to go for it and hope the virus, or whatever, had died out, or they had to catch the disease themselves and manufacture an antibody before they succumbed.

Terry answered Gary's question about the shuttles. "Forty percent of the first load will be required to fuel the other two operational shuttles, but only one other shuttle has been configured as a tanker; the other one is set up for personnel and cargo. Our fourth shuttle took a meteor right through its canopy and is strike damaged. To answer your question, we'll need two shuttles making five runs each to top off our tanks. About six hours round trip plus on-and-off load of one hour each makes one trip per eight hours, times five trips makes approximately forty hours . . ." Terry paused and added with concern, "That's assuming everything works and you have easy access to fresh water."

Gary shook his head. "Things never go as planned, so double the time required to bring the mission into realistic perspective."

Kim said, "Gary, do you have any idea how to pull this water raid off?"

"Ideas are coming and going, and a few are sticking. Move the cameras back to the cannibal village and concentrate on the outer ring of the camp. It resembles an outer defense, but against what?"

Kim manipulated the controls until she had the perimeter in perfect focus.

"Hmm, just as I suspected," Gary said. "Look at those sharpened poles every two feet, and notice the angles. Those guys are ready for something very big that can't maneuver around the large spears. We need to do an infrared scan to try to pick up the threats they're expecting."

"Ah, great!" Joe replied. "Not only are we about 10,000 years late, no civilization to come back to, but we have some unknown, very large predator preying on human cannibals. I mean, just how rosy can this get?"

"Maybe you'd like to help on the shuttle runs, Joe?" Christine snickered.

"I, uh, I've got my plate full as it is. Sorry, I'd love to help otherwise."

Christine rolled her eyes and sat down. "Okay, you win Gary. There's nothing we can really do at this point anyway. We certainly can't stay up here indefinitely, and we don't have anyplace else to go. Besides, we don't have the time for culture growths or immunity development."

Everyone's attention was diverted when Kim's computer monitor beeped. Taking a second to read the short memo, Kim turned back to the group. "I've had the computer radar search and optically scan all satellites within its 2,000 km range. So far, we've got four probable platforms and seventy-six rejects. I initiated the search in hopes that we could find information leading to the demise of our civilization. Geographically, the ship has been exploring for possible underground storage archives. I vaguely remember efforts in our past, but can't seem to recall what it was called or where it was located." Kim paused to look into each individual face. "I know I lost a lot of mental capability. Does anyone else feel the same?"

No one spoke; no one needed to.

"Once we have our life support systems stabilized, I'm calling for an election."

An avalanche of questions followed.

"My tenure was appointed by authorities that are no longer viable; therefore, my position should be filled in a democratic election," Kim added. "Please think it over and pass the information along to those who have recovered. Gary, the military members shall report directly to you for the time being. We can reorganize after we hold our elections. In this election, anyone can run for any position they feel qualified for.

"There, that's been said. Let's get on with staying alive. Gary, what's your plan?"

Gary stood up with his hands clasped behind him. For some strange reason, he thought he could think better that way. "Kim, can you drop the ship into a lower elliptical orbit so we can take a look at the dark side of the world also?"

Kim turned to the computer console again. "Computer, drop us down to a low-altitude elliptical orbit that will not decay over time." A green light blinked once while everyone felt a slight sideward motion. Other small green lights located on the bottom of the monitor started flashing on, indicating individual recovery of the military personnel.

Gary was studying the monitor. "I'd like to find a large, freshwater lake that has an isolated island some distance from land. Assuming they don't have an underwater assault force, we can handle any surface attack the cannibals mount. I don't want the island to be too big; it would thin out our defense. On our vertical approach, we can saturate-fire some nerve-paralyzing rockets with at least an hour hold-over. Once on the ground, we'll initiate a three-part mission. First team will work on setting up the transfer pumps and hoses, second team will set up perimeter defense, and third team will patrol and restrain possible hostiles. I don't think it would be wise to kill anything at this point; just remain physically secure and keep them at a distance. We will keep all defense forces at the site until the water replenishment is complete. No sense in wasting manpower and payload to guard water while returning to the *Leapfrog*, but we will leave two guards onboard this ship to sweep the shuttles as they arrive. Don't want some critter jumping off to make a new home on the ship."

Carl cleared his throat and spoke up. "Ahem, you said all shall remain?"

"Yes."

"Well, ah, exactly who will be piloting the shuttles?"

Gary smiled. "Computers. I see you haven't been inside a shuttle cockpit. You will find no controls, throttles, rudder pedals, or any other manual control devices; only a small monitor with a voice-activated computer. It's way too hard for the human mind to make the rapid calculations and respond with the proper inputs for VTOL and orbital rendezvous. We will program the shuttles for the return trip and then get out of the way. Any problems encountered can be handled through the encrypted data link."

A momentary pause in the conversation was all Christine

needed. "We should avoid personal contact with the people as much as possible. To them, we will be the alien invaders, and heaven help us if one of us gets cut and bleeds green blood. That might prove to be a bonding force to unify them against us." She took a deep breath before continuing, "I can't think of anything more horrifying than being on a planet with nothing but certifiable psychopaths."

CHAPTER 9

LEAPFROG WAS RINGED WITH SIDE thrusters which were identical to the rockets on their four shuttles. The side thrusters maintained balance control and orbital maneuvering power. Fortunately, the low burn trip home left plenty of excess fuel the shuttles could use along with the main ship's side thrusters.

The *Leapfrog* descended to a lower elliptical orbit, which allowed the ship a view of almost the entire planet. This particular orbit looked like it was doing continuous S-shaped turns, which were slightly offset and which repeated the same track every fourteen orbits. The "S" turns were actually straight flight tracks, but thanks to the nodal regression, or bulge, of the Earth, the ground track appeared to be cycling like a wave frequency. Another advantage of this orbit was that it could be synced with the sun so the Earth appeared in sunlight all day.

Everyone on the bridge was glued to the overhead monitor as Kim manipulated the controls for the sightseeing tour. The shapes of the continents were basically the same, but slightly smaller. The big discovery was the remarkable abundance of vegetation. Jungles in the equatorial regions flourished and vast forests covered the upper and lower portions of the planet. Old ice caps were nothing but sparse snow fields. Deserts were rare and meagerly scattered about the inland regions of the continents. Another disturbing find was the total erasure of their past civilization. Not a single trace remained of any human-made structures. They could not even find the pyramids or Great Wall of China even with Kim maximizing the zoom feature.

Finding an ideal island on a freshwater lake was proving harder than anticipated. Part of the problem was the cloud cover, which seemed to be considerably greater than when they were on Earth. Explanations that the crew came up with included the increased temperatures combined with more water surface for evaporation. Many times the ship had to rely on radar for terrain profiling when visual acuity was inadequate.

Although Kim tried to keep the tour mission-related, she could not help but linger and study different encampments scattered about the globe. After moving in and studying several of them, a common theme emerged: murder was rampant. Little skirmishes immediately ramped to the lethal level with no apparent initiation, remorse, or repercussion. A major unexplained concern was the common perimeter defense of all encampments. No one could figure out exactly what they were defending against. The infrared scanning showed normal-sized animals, with the largest identified as animals of the past: elephants, rhinoceros, and hippopotamuses. Nothing appeared large enough to warrant the sharpened pole defense. They were certainly not designed to repel human-sized creatures, for all one had to do was slip between the spears. The mysterious threat was agonizing Gary. The tides of battle were often turned with much less being unknown.

Finally, they found an ideal lake with a ten-acre isolated island that was relatively flat. It was located in the old Victoria region of Australia that had once been tundra, and the site was perfect for water extraction. Huge forests surrounded the lake and overwhelmed the stranded island. Gary made a call to one of his recovered ordinance specialists and had him start to work on several large FAE, fuel air explosive, rocket propelled devices. The devices would be used to clear a landing site on the island for the vertically descending shuttle.

During the same phone connection, Gary transferred over to one of his metalsmiths and told him to cut a large opening in the vast water recovery tank of the shuttle. The cut out piece would be placed back inside and tack welded to prevent shifting in flight. The troops and all the gear they could fit would go inside the pressurized space for the descent. The water shuttle configuration allowed for only four passenger seats and they would need a lot more than that. Once they landed, they would weld the cut out piece back into position for water retrieval.

Kim was impressed with Gary's intuitiveness and impromptu creativity, but could not help but wonder if it was the correct decision to place all their lives in his hands. *Like I have a choice.* While Gary was setting up his mission, she went to the computer. "Computer, calculate time and burn for full shuttle exploratory team to the moon and back. No replenishment. Second computation, calculate geostationary satellites that may be configured for archive purposes and plan shuttle flight trips two ways." The big green light flashed two times and data started flowing across the monitor.

Kim knew that the space consortium had constructed a major portion of the *Leapfrog* on the moon's site. The thinking followed that the huge ship would not be susceptible to the unpredictable weather that they had on Earth. Additionally, the reduced gravity on the moon's surface allowed less structural support during the construction of the heavy pieces. Kim was hoping that someone stationed on the moon's base would have left detailed explanations on one of their mainframe computers.

When Gary finished and broke the video briefing connection, Kim asked, "Once the water transfer is successfully underway, how about scouting around for food? Our dried food supply is plentiful but I doubt very edible."

Gary broke out laughing. "Sure, we'll just grab and nab from the nearest camp and you'll have plenty of food."

Christine jumped up. "No! No, we're not that hungry! What Kim meant was, uh, like go shoot a buffalo or something like that."

Gary just gave her a big grin and Kim started laughing.

Christine, realizing that she was the brunt of the joke, said, "Okay, asshole, I've got your number."

First laughter in 10,000 years, Kim thought. *Ship of laughing fools.*

Joe turned from his console and said, "The shuttle's ready and programmed, pending the cut work the military's doing on the tanker."

"That's my exit cue," Gary said as he made his way to the door. "As soon as we can narrow down the prep time for the tanker configuration, FAE rockets, and nerve gas, I'll let you know."

"Hold on a second." Kim said as she turned to her monitor. "Computer, list shuttle launch windows for programmed destination."

"Next optimum launch sequence 09:33, ship time, which

is ten hours, twenty-two minutes, and six seconds from now, and every twelve hours after that time."

Gary glanced at his bare wrist for time synchronization, sighed, and looked back at the monitor's time. "We should be able to make the next launch window; if not, then the one after for sure. Now, if you'll excuse me, I need to get to my men and start organizing this operation."

"By all means, go to it," Kim replied. "Please physically report back here before you depart. I'm sure we'll have some last-minute information concerning our new Earth and subsequent assignments."

"Ah, excuse me, Gary, but before you run out, may I ask a favor?" Christine said.

"Shoot."

Christine looked a little uncomfortable. "I know this sounds terrible, but if you, um, happen to need to use lethal force on one of those people, please don't shoot them in the head with a projectile weapon. I'd like to do an autopsy and maybe get lucky and find out what happened here."

Gary thought for a second before answering. "Ok, I'll pass that on to my troops. I guess you'll want me to ship the body back on one of the shuttle runs?"

Kim snapped around. "Over my dead body! No one's bringing one of those creatures back on this ship. Period! No telling what virus is living in them or what little creature will pop out of a chest!" Kim was standing now, with a light green tint to her face which turned darker when everyone in the room started laughing.

"What! What's so funny about that?"

"Look in the mirror," Joe said, chuckling.

"Okay, okay, no aliens aboard the ship," Gary conceded as he walked off the bridge.

"Seriously," Christine said to Kim, "you've been watching too many movies."

"Yeah, like this hasn't turned into one science fiction nightmare," Kim retorted.

CHAPTER 10

THE MILITARY FORCE HAD MORE or less marshaled in the shuttle launch hangar, and not one slacker could be observed among them, for they were all hustling.

The hangar bay area was in an industrial mayhem. Metal cutters throwing streams of sparks and ear-piercing screeching, acetylene welding torches flashing like dance floor strobe lights, sergeants trying to talk over surrounding noise only to be overcome by an occasional *brrrr* of someone testing out munitions and guns against a makeshift bullet bunker.

Gary flashed the overhead lights on and off to get their attention and called them all over to the center of the hangar. He then delegated runners to retrieve the personnel in the ordnance shop and other strays who might be doing various and sundry chores.

A large, burly staff sergeant, Jim Scoffield, along with ten other soldiers, walked over to Gary and saluted. "Sir, me and the men here want to let you in on what happened at the ice planet. When we found out that Colonel Jackson kept you in cryo-sleep, we raised hell, but the sonofabitch threatened us with court-martial and slammed a few of us back in cryo-sleep. We figured you'd get your day in court once we returned to Earth, but it looks like you've already taken care of that."

Gary returned their salute, then walked around shaking all of their hands. "Yep, that score's settled once and for all but, just for the record, that wasn't my idea to jettison them into the sun."

"Yeah, we heard. Must be one mean-ass skipper running this ship. Never could tell she was a woman." Scoffield had to move fast to dodge a snap kick from one of his female enlisted women.

"Fucking, sexist pig!" She laughed out loud when Scoffield cautiously ventured back into kicking range.

Scoffield began to give Gary the latest update. "All our electrical weapons are shot. Not one good battery round among them. I guess we kind of exceeded their life usage, but all our projectile weapons seem Okay. We fired a couple, but some of the guidance systems are inoperative. We'll have to lead our targets the old-fashioned way. Lasers seem Okay, but won't know for sure until we put a practice load on the batteries. Nerve gas rockets are ready. I figure six fired equally around our perimeter should do it no matter what the wind's doing. FAE's a little trickier because of its size, but we should have them ready to load and lock in less than two hours. The metalsmiths are tacking the outer shell of the tank to the inside to keep it secure. I wouldn't want that big sheet of iron flying about. The weld crew is also tacking in some tie-down loops inside the tank so we and our equipment won't get too friendly." He winked at the female kicker, but she just rolled her eyes in return.

Scoffield continued, "I was holding off on the ordnance load until I heard from you."

"Overkill, of course," Gary said as he whistled and gave

the "circle the wagon" hand signal. By now everyone had stopped what they were doing to hustle over to Gary's area.

After a minute, all the military personnel had gathered around Gary at full attention. "Please, at ease. As a matter of fact, why don't you just sit down? This may take awhile." Thirty minutes later, Gary was fielding general questions from his troops. When Gary played back the cannibal scene, everyone's attention was totally focused with wide eyes and a lot of "holy shits." Over the next fifteen minutes Gary laid out his *smash, gas, overrun, and defend* plan.

When it came to the nitty-gritty part of the plan, Gary slowly and carefully reiterated each point. "I want everybody armed at all times with nothing less than forty calibers with mercury-tipped loads. If you're on the work party, your side-arm should remain locked and cocked and always at your side. If you're on mission reconnaissance or guard duty I want the lightweight fifty calibers loaded with armor-piercing rounds, and bring twice the ammunition that you can comfortably carry. I would like to totally rely on the laser defense, but if I did that Mr. Murphy would give them reflective shielding. Therefore, we will depend on the tried and proven heavy, fast, and accurate projectile weapons. Make sure that your ID is fully charged because we're putting four laser defense beamers on full power with two nuclear batteries."

"Sir," interrupted a corporal who had "Griffin" stenciled on his uniform and who looked about twenty-two years old. He was holding up his right hand, pointing to the embedded identification. "My tag's dead; been that way since I woke up, and it won't take a charge."

Part of the "awakening" routine briefing went into detail

about how to check personal identification transponders and where to go for replacement batteries. A few comments like "chicken shit" and "wimp" drifted about in the audience. Gary made a mental note to flag him for transfer to ship's company. Cowards were a dime a dozen, and it would be best to protect the rest of his warriors from depending on this weak link. It was common knowledge that the medical department had the ability to repair or replace any component of the bio tag.

"Then you stay on board the ship with one other person to check out the shuttles when they return. No armor piercing rounds for you, just high impact rounds." Addressing the whole group, Gary added, "Make sure your identification tags are working properly at all times. The laser defense system will be on full auto and ranged at two hundred meters. If you are unfortunate enough to lose your right hand, the laser will slice you up like a big pizza." No laughter followed on the attempt at humor. All knew the capabilities of the laser defense system and had a healthy respect for its destructive history. Anything larger than a rat without the proper biological "dog tag" would be first interrogated then instantaneously zapped if the expected response was not received pronto.

"Sir, with all due respect, don't you think this is a little bit of overkill?" a female soldier asked. Gary was thinking he was really getting old, for she looked to be about nineteen.

"I certainly hope so; I really do, but . . ." Gary paused for a moment. ". . . every camp we observed had those long, sharpened poles pointing up. My guess is that they didn't build them for the fun of it."

"Maybe they're all just superstitious, sir," another soldier said.

Gary was thankful that the soldier asking the question looked older than twenty. "I'm hoping for that too. However, I do have input from the ship's quack. If we have to kill some of those slope-head inhabitants, try not to shoot them in the head. I doubt very seriously that they'll be wearing any sort of body armament. The doc wants to slice and dice and try to figure out what happened down there."

Wrapping the briefing up, Gary added, "Okay, in about nine hours we rock and roll. Sleep if you can, work if you must, but everyone will be in full battle dress by launch. Mandatory blood donations will be collected before we depart and will be brought along with us."

Gary heard an undercurrent of rumblings running among his troops. Even the most hardened warrior became timid when confronted with needles. "I know the blood contents are mostly cryo-sleep fluid, but by now our systems have broken it down in various types which may or may not be interchangeable.

"All weapons should be checked, rechecked, locked and loaded when we depart." That brought collective gasps from a few of the troops. Transporting hot weapons was strictly prohibited by regulations. Gary figured regulations were made by desk-bound bureaucrats, not warriors rolling out of a crashed shuttle in hostile territory.

Gary put on his light- and noise-cancelling headpiece and tried to get a short nap in before the shuttle departed, but sleep seemed a little too elusive for him. Apparently, being in a deep sleep for over 10,300 years proved sufficient for the time being. Five hours later, the ship was ready and loaded. All preparations completed with nothing important to do with his troops, Gary returned to the bridge. The same department heads were still at their respective stations. Obviously, sleep eluded them also.

"Morning, Skipper," Gary said to Kim as he slipped into a vacant console chair and flipped on the monitor.

Kim scanned the upper right portion of her monitor and said, "Ah, it is morning, isn't it? What, four hours to go?"

Before Gary could answer, Christine jumped in. "I've been thinking and came to the conclusion that I should come along with you. After all, I have a full staff of three surgeons and nine nurses who are more than capable to carry on without me for awhile."

"Not no, but hell no!" Gary snapped at her, but immediately regretted his harsh tone. "Sorry to jump on you so quickly, but that's not really a good idea. We'll have qualified medics who can be in constant and instant touch with you. All of us will have our helmet cameras and radios, so if the shit hits the fan and a medic needs your advice, you'll be like right over his shoulder. That should suffice until we can bring any wounded back aboard."

"I agree with that," Kim added. "Just don't bring back anything else with you. Maybe during the later stages of this mission when we have a corpse, we can send you down for a field autopsy and bring you right back."

"Uh, still not such a good idea," Gary interjected. "We'll have our laser defense set up and it will see you as hostile since you don't have an implanted dog tag interrogator."

"We've got plenty of blanks," Christine countered, now more determined than ever. "I'll program one and insert it while you're on your first run. I can hitch a ride on the returning tanker when it's offloaded." Giving Gary and Kim her most serious look, she continued, "Listen, for our future's sake, we have to have some idea of what happened down there while we were gone. Otherwise, the same thing could happen to us."

Damn woman. Too bad she's so logical, Gary thought when he lost the stare-down contest.

Kim just sighed and swiveled around to face Gary. "We've decided to probe probable geostationary satellites that may contain archive information. Now that we're down in low orbit, we can see all the objects above us with several being possible candidates. We'll use the passenger configured shuttle for those missions, leaving the two tankers for water replenishment. Once we're completely topped off, we'll send the passenger configured shuttle to the moon and check out the old sites that we know were once there, especially the one used during this ship's construction. On the lunar mission, I'd like at least five armed military guards, and if you're still up for it, I'd like you to lead the expedition. Hopefully, the current mission you're on will be a . . . what do you call it . . . cakewalk?"

Kim flicked up a group of archived photos on the overhead monitor, illustrating an overhead shot of a massive construction site on the moon and large pieces of the *Leapfrog* lying about outside a huge dome. Quickly, Kim flashed through the ancient photos showing a massive construction plant under the dome surrounded by well manicured vegetation. "We relied heavily on building as much of the *Leapfrog* as we could on the moon due to absent weather conditions and light gravity. We found the moon preferable over a zero-g orbit for construction. Too many tools and parts would tend to drift off and become deadly projectiles for other orbital vehicles."

Shifting back to the interior of the dome, Kim went through some detailed pictures of the vegetation and added, "Thanks to the underground frozen lake our ancestors discovered on our moon, we once had a self-sustained habitat fairly well established. I have no idea about its status, but I certainly don't want to run across any of our deranged cousins."

Jack Mitchell, a nerd in Gary's opinion, popped his head up from his console workstation as he picked up the end of the conversation. "There is a possibility that some form of carbon life may still exist there. Those sites were set up to endure the most severe meteor shower. As to the computers, they have the same identical redundancy as this ship, and the plutonium heat generators should still be melting ice. I know; I designed them." If Mitchell was waiting for applause, he definitely had a long wait. Everyone was glaring at him. "Okay, okay, assuming they're still working; I'm sorry I did it so well."

"I'll be more than glad to lead this party," Gary glumly said. "Hey, Jack, want to come along and check on your babies, the heat generators, and computers?"

"That's so thoughtful and considerate of you, Gary. But what do you think would happen to the rest of us if our computers here rolled over and died?"

"My headache's coming back," Kim said as she put her head down on her console. Speaking with her head resting on the top of her hands, she said, "Gary, while you're on Earth, we'll initiate map development and should have some other water recovery sites plotted for your next run. Uh, that is if this one turns south. Speaking of compass headings, keep in mind the polarity on Earth flipped. You will have to recalibrate all magnetic compasses."

"Already done, but if we have trouble with some of them, we'll all switch to true headings to stay on the same page. Umm, I hate to bring it up, but what's the plan if we fail?" Gary asked, very concerned for his twin girls on board in cryo-sleep.

Kim leaned back and audibly exhaled. "That's bad news for us. We'll have to change to a geostationary orbit, have the computers put the rest of us to sleep, and hope some compassionate space traveler comes along." Shaking her head, she added, "Of course we can wait for your party to re-evolve Earth and retrieve us at a later date."

"I'd rather take a space walk without a suit and get it over with," Terry piped in.

"Well, let's not dwell on it. Gary, let's go over plans again and play devil's advocate for any weaknesses," Kim said, trying to take everyone's mind off the possibility of failure.

The team went over every detail again and again until they thought they had all contingencies covered. But perhaps because of their weakened mental prowess, they missed two critical aspects. First, their orbit kept them on the sunlight side of Earth at all times, keeping nocturnal creatures hidden. Second, they assumed that any land threat thrived on land. The infrared detectors could not penetrate water, which now covered over eighty percent of the planet. While they had slept in deep space, Darwin's theory was very busy with other creatures, and man was no longer on top of the food chain.

CHAPTER 11

"THOSE FUCKING ASSHOLES!" SCOFFIELD WAS muttering under his breath as he walked up to Gary. "Sir, ship store's refusing our chit for twenty liters of liquid nitrogen for the laser cooling! They say we can have the liquid oxygen and hydrogen, but not nitrogen because it's needed for life support. Can you imagine using one hundred percent hydrogen or oxygen for cooling? That would make for a helluva firework show, with us right in the middle."

Gary did not say a word. He unbuckled his visual phone and punched Terry's picture. "Hi, Terry. Tell your people to release the liquid nitrogen ASAP." Gary listened for a few seconds while his face turned lawn green. "You got two choices: you can wait for me to come to the bridge and shoot your sorry ass, or you can give me the nitrogen." Two seconds passed. "I'll send them to the gas lab right away. Thanks, Ter—. Can you imagine that? He hung up on me."

"I'll supervise this myself," Scoffield said as he hurried away.

At launch time plus ten minutes, Gary had the entire unit standing at attention in front of the converted shuttle. Everyone was in full battle dress without one inch of skin showing on anyone. *Shit! We even look like alien invaders and bleed green blood*, Gary thought as he finished inspecting his troops.

Gary put himself in the center of the lineup and said in a loud voice that could be heard by all, "This is it. We either complete this mission successfully or we all die. Look around and take a good look at the person next to you. This is the person who just may save your life. Teamwork. We must maintain group integrity or we will perish. We are the last human military force anywhere in this universe, and we will go down in history one way or another. We *will* succeed!"

"*Whoyahs!*" echoed off the walls of the hangar.

"Man up!" Gary shouted as he stepped inside the front portion of the shuttle. Scoffield was one step behind him. Gary waited until the makeshift "All Clear" light illuminated before he pressed the guarded *Initiate Launch Sequence* button. The shuttle's cargo door started down, the hangar's red overhead beacon started flashing, and a loud Klaxon horn blared.

Kim and staff were watching from the bridge's monitor. Christine said, "Kind of gives you the chills, doesn't it? Everything's riding on them, and we sit here helplessly."

Terry blurted, "I want that major arrested when he returns followed by a proper legal hearing. He threatened to shoot an officer of this ship!"

Kim glared at him. "Denied! I heard the whole thing, and you were just being obstinate by holding onto the nitrogen. Now shut up, Terry, or I'll shoot you myself."

Christine almost laughed, but caught herself. Terry looked like a chameleon going from dark green to light green to white as he remembered her harsh treatment of the military mutineers.

The shuttle had no windows, only cameras strategically located on the outside to give a panoramic view on the overhead monitor. Unfortunately, the troops packed in the empty water tank were lacking all standard passenger comforts. They had to sit on their haunches with their legs extended, often interlaced over the soldier facing the opposite direction. Everything and everyone was tied down to keep from floating around as they eased out of the *Leapfrog's* hangar. Although they were each rigged with individual seat belts, rope lanyards with large knots ran across their laps to help keep their torsos semi-lined up.

"Stand by for booster phase," Gary announced over the intercom. Unfortunately, one of the soldiers found zero-g too unsettling and quietly barfed into a small plastic bag. A few seconds later, *Blam!* Everything that was not tied down flew to the rear. A few helmets, night vision lenses, and a puke bag flew to the rear of the tank to find PFC Lewis, the cute little female soldier who had dared to ask her major a question earlier.

Someone's night vision goggles smacked right in the middle of her mouth causing almost instant swelling. The puke bag followed and perfectly centered on her face. Laughter was just starting before she said, "I will shoot the first asshole who laughs." The way she said it, and the fact that she had a loaded gun, quickly dampened the growing mirth.

Thirty minutes later the shuttle was in position for the re-entry and had begun the de-orbit burn when Kim from the bridge on the *Leapfrog* announced, "Bad news. A group of locals just landed on the opposite side of the targeted island. Looks like a large dugout with four men armed with spears and bows, and they're carrying some sort of a net."

Gary keyed the mike. "Roger. Keep us informed. If they stay on the beaches, they should survive the FAE but will get nailed by the nerve gas. How long will we be in blackout on reentry?"

"Negative on the blackout. Ionization will be localized on the bottom of the shuttle, not on top with the antennas."

"Starting to pick up turbulence. Will radio back on the glide. Shuttle out." Gary looked over at Scoffield and asked, "Since when do fishermen fish fully armed?"

Not taking his eyes off the monitor, Scoffield replied, "Fishermen fish fully armed when they're afraid of something that they might catch, or that might catch them."

The monitors switched to instrument flying and graphical illustrations as the shuttle retracted its cameras before being burned off on reentry. Ten minutes of turbulence and the shuttle slipped into Earth's atmosphere. Cameras re-extended and the monitor picked up the descent. Australia came into view and slid under the nose before the bottom cameras took over. Gary checked the computer's timeline and announced over the intercom, "Ten minutes before flare and vertical descent."

Gary was enthralled by the beauty of the landscape. Never before had he seen the sky so clear, water so blue, and vegetation so green. He looked over at Scoffield and witnessed pure fright. "You Okay?"

Scoffield shook his head in the negative. "No, sir, I'm about to die. This thing's too low; it's not gonna flare, and the thrusters won't work." He was keeping a death grip on the armrest with white fingers.

About that time everybody on board could hear the noise reduction caused by the decreased speed, the swooshing sound of their air-to-ground rockets firing, and finally the huge thrusters kicking in and blocking out all other noise. The monitors were completely useless once the VTOL thruster fired up. The FAE bomb completely obscured the cameras with its blast; then the thrusters seemed to stir everything up some more. The computer's radar picked a spot it deemed the most viable and asked the operator to verify. When Gary punched the *Accept/Land* button, six long and spindly landing gears extended and compressed to ground level as the weight was distributed when the thrusters shut down. The shuttle completely settled before the "Open Doors" light flashed on. Gary punched the green light, picked up an intercom, and shouted. "Time to rock and roll. Go! Go! Go!"

This was certainly not a stealthy operation. The FAE not only had leveled all vegetation on the island; it also had shaken the entire valley. Three human throwbacks were instantly incinerated in their tracks while the fourth escaped immediate death because he was squatting behind a massive boulder relieving himself. As soon as the shock wave passed from the FAE, six rockets were equally dispersed along the beaches. Although one of the nerve gas rockets exploded more than one hundred meters from the survivor, he passed out cold before he could manage to run ten meters to the beach. The D-day-like commotion also caught the attention of some other unsavory creatures.

Awakened from the cool depths of the lake, the two-ton creatures started making their way towards the disturbance. Anything that produced such a hefty shock wave must mean

a lot of food just fell down and deserved investigating. Fear
played no role because for centuries the creatures had ruled at
the top of the food chain.

CHAPTER 12

NOBODY HAD TO PUSH ANYONE out for the debarkation. The dust was not close to settling when the troopers were out and running. Their full face masks served a dual function of nerve gas protection and oxygen supplementation. Each helmet had individual channeled audio and video cameras protruding from the sides, and the short antennas sticking up at the rear lent them a truly alien appearance.

Unlike most company commanders who found safe and secure command posts in which to hide and command, Gary mixed with the troops for on-site supervision and also served as a freelance assistant to any group needing an extra hand. Nobody remained in the shuttle except the welding crew that was busy patching the hole cut in the water tank. *Leapfrog's* large overhead monitor was divided into thirty smaller videos, one picture coming from each trooper on the ground. Kim had master control of all videos and audios and could zoom in on any individual.

The reconnaissance team split up into two groups of four each and took opposite directions from the shuttle toward the beach. Once there they would each sweep clockwise until they met up where the opposing team had started, then proceed back to the shuttle. The perimeter defense team also broke into two teams and started setting up the laser tripods

for a four-point defense. The nuclear batteries were to remain
inside the shuttle for maximum protection. The water recovery team likewise split up and went about pulling the hose out and running it down to the beach. It was a two-man job because the reinforced hose was so heavy.

Corporal Tim Matthews had the end of the hose, the floatable pickup filter, and was running as fast as he could toward the beach. PFC Cindy Lewis, the one with the fat lip, had a firm grip on the hose, pulling as hard as she could about fifty feet behind Tim. Matthews and Lewis both had their rifles strapped across their backs to keep their hands free to hold on to the hose. Running across the soft sand in full combat gear and dragging a heavy six-inch hose took its toll and their run turned into a puffing, slow pull. Gary recognized their plight and ran to pick up the hose behind Cindy.

After five minutes of pulling and huffing, Matthews finally made it to his waist-deep goal and was setting out the anchor weights when a monitor controller in the *Leapfrog* shouted, "Look out!" In his excitement the controller went the wrong way on his mike key and transmitted the warning to the entire force. Everyone who could dropped immediately to their knees or belly and started looking out. For what, no one knew, but they were watching out. All except Matthews who was up to his waist in the lake and had no place to drop.

Gary was the first on the ground to see the rapidly moving log that was leaving a bow wake. *Bow wake? Nothing adrift leaves a bow wake!* He immediately dropped the hose and unslung his rifle but had no shot since Matthews and Lewis were in front of the log.

Lewis was on her knees but looking the wrong way. She

saw her major frantically pulling at his rifle, transfixed on something behind her and turned just in time to see Matthews tugged underwater in a large, turbulent pool. "What?" she shouted at the swirling water.

As if in response, the beast rose, and rose, and rose to a towering twelve feet. At first everyone witnessing the event thought it was a huge crocodile, but as it ascended it took on the appearance of a dinosaur. Clutched in the huge jaws was the hapless Matthews screaming and pushing against the teeth that firmly held his legs. *Crunch!* Matthew's torso fell into the lake. The monster raised his head and stuffed Matthew's legs down its throat with two large front arms loaded with claws.

Run! Lewis finally snapped out of her terror shock and took off toward the beach.

"Get down! Get down!" Gary screamed as he aimed his rifle, but had no shot since Lewis was between him and the monster that now dropped low to catch up with Lewis.

Lewis covered five meters in the same time it took the beast to cover fifty-five meters. It ducked, bit her high on the right leg, stood up and crunched, and her body fell back into the water minus her right leg. As soon as the beast swallowed her leg, he regurgitated with a force that blew her severed leg and what was left of Matthews's body for a distance of nearly three meters and onto the sand. As the beast ducked down to sniff his screaming prey, the back of its head suddenly exploded from Gary's fifty caliber high-explosive round. The beast had so much mass, the heavy-hitting round had no recoil effect at all on his body. He dropped straight down, pinning Lewis's remaining left leg with his huge slack jaw.

Gary quickly scanned the water in front of him as he

sprinted in Lewis's direction. Several more logs were making bow waves as they headed for him. Stopping, Gary tugged a hand grenade free from his vest. Pulling the pin with a free finger on the hand holding the rifle, Gary lobbed the grenade in the middle of the mass of logs floating toward him. *Whump!* The grenade exploded with a geyser of water blowing straight up.

Not bothering to duck, Gary continued his dash to Lewis and managed to pull her out from under the creature's head. He was ten feet up on the sandy beach when the first of the support team arrived. "Post guards, armed with fifties, saturate the surrounding water with grenades, and shoot anything that looks like a log," Gary shouted as he tied a web belt around Lewis's bleeding right stump. Lewis's light blue eyes glazed over as she slid into shock.

Two medics squatted next to Gary and said, "We've got her now."

Gary ran over to the pile of vomit, identified Lewis's leg, and examined the severed end, which looked like a guillotine had cut it off. He picked up the leg, boot and all, and ran up to the shuttle. "Empty the insulated packing chest, pre-cool it, and then fill it with liquid nitrogen. We need to cool down this leg right now. We might be able to save it."

"That might work, Gary," Christine answered in his headset. She, along with the entire crew of *Leapfrog*, had been monitoring the activity. "It'll work only because our blood is nothing but some sort of antifreeze solution."

Christine switched back over to the medics' frequency to guide them through the remainder of the amputation salvation.

Thump! Thump! The grenades made a muffled sound as

they exploded in the water. Gary ran back to the beach to reinforce the defense.

"They seemed to have booked after you threw that first grenade, sir." The soldier did not take his eyes off the water while he talked. "We threw in some extra grenades for good measure."

"Okay, but only shoot at a target you can see coming toward us. We may need all the ordnance we have just to stay alive," Gary said as he walked over to the massive predator.

It was a dinosaur all right, but nothing he'd ever seen before in any of his paleontology books. Somewhere between a crocodile, raptor, and Tyrannosaurus Rex, the monster had razor-sharp serrated teeth with a small row coming up behind the front. A new question popped up: Why had the monster thrown up? Something had caused it. *Ah, I got it! We don't taste good. Must be the antifreeze we're using for blood. That just might be our salvation in the short term,* Gary thought.

"Oh, shit!" Kim exclaimed in his ear set, causing Gary to jump and un-sling his rifle again. Gary had temporarily forgotten that the *Leapfrog* was monitoring all their helmet headsets. "Look above the mouth; back some more. Tilt your head a little more to the right. There, let me zoom." There was a brief pause before Kim came back. "This is not good! Look at his head, or what's left of it. There's development of a frontal lobe. This guy can think and also probably communicate with his peers. If he can do all that, he can easily hunt in packs."

"Great! Just great," Gary said. "Just what we need, a smart dinosaur."

Christine came back online. "Lewis has been stabilized

and should survive. Jury's still out on saving her leg, but let everybody know we'll do our best when we get her in surgery . . . Whoa! Turn your head back to the creature's neck and scan the rest of the body." Another pause followed. "Holy shit! Let me zoom in on the skin on the neck area a minute Yep, definitely epithelial tissue for skin that can be used for underwater gas exchange. Probably to support extra large lungs while underwater, which means . . . Uh oh."

Gary hated hearing those two words. "Uh oh, what?"

"Nothing I can confirm from here, but keep an eye out on land also. Those creatures must be amphibians, because there's no way this small patch of skin breathing can support such a large body. Why else would inland defenders keep barriers up? They certainly can't hold their breath that long. Besides, look at the large nostrils."

Christine's breathing had increased to the point she was panting. "Let me have another look at his head, now his eyes . . . Uh-huh, definitely nocturnal, but obviously not hampered by daylight."

Ah, shit! Gary thought as he pivoted 360 degrees looking for more trouble.

"Scan back over the tail section again," Christine said. "And that huge tail must serve as balance on land and pro-pulsion in water. This thing's a marvel! Look at that head, which must support one huge brain. The crocodile scales have been replaced with epithelial tissue, and one claw is slanted like our thumb, so it can grasp. Wow! One thing's for sure: the creature will be the next world's champion. That is, if we don't kill them all before they kill us. If not, we're on one fast track to extinction."

A sudden, premonitory chill ran down Gary's spine. *These things will kill us all!*

There was a pause before Christine continued, "Gary, you'll have to move that water pickup to the other side of the island. We don't need to compound our problems by using contaminated water. This guy must have left a gallon of blood behind."

The conversation and train of thought was suddenly broken up by a perimeter team. "Hey, we got a sleeper here! A real knuckle-dragger for sure, and smells like shit warmed over. We're handcuffing him now and will bring him when we finish our patrol."

BACK ABOARD THE *LEAPFROG*, CHRISTINE looked at Kim and said, "I gotta get down there."

Kim raised her eyebrows. "Are you nuts?"

CHAPTER 13

BY THE TIME THE PERIMETER patrols returned, the nerve gas had dissipated enough for them to remove the full face masks, but they all needed to leave an oxygen tube in their noses for supplemental support. Lewis's bleeding had been stabilized, the water pump was operational, and the defense system was ready to be activated. When they laid his stretcher down in front of the shuttle, the prisoner awakened, took a good look around, uttered something indistinguishable, and promptly fainted.

"Handcuff him sitting up, arms in back and wrapped around that tree stump," Gary ordered. "Post a guard and give him nothing; and even if he can speak our language, stay away from him. God! He smells terrible. Don't they ever bathe?"

The sergeant looked at the water and the huge, dead dinosaur, and said, "Dunno if I want to take a bath here either."

Another soldier who was assigned to the laser defense came running over to Gary. "Sir, the laser's ready; we're real low on nitrogen coolant because of the leg, but what we have should last until nightfall. Want me to turn it on?"

Gary deliberately looked over at the prisoner then back to the soldier.

"Oh," the soldier said. "That wouldn't be very pretty, huh, sir?"

What? Are we all Forrest Gumps? Gary thought.

Gary transmitted his new wish list up to the *Leapfrog* and reiterated his threat to Terry for more liquid nitrogen. Besides a replenishment of liquid nitrogen, he included more RPGS, remote propelled grenades, a few flamethrowers, and extra night vision and infrared devices. Gary had a feeling this was going to be a critical night that would make or break the mission.

Kim chimed him on his headset.

"Gary here."

"I hate to always be the bearer of bad news, but I've got some more. The local humanoids are gathering at the south end of the lake, about five miles from you. They have eight large dugouts and are passing out shields, bows and arrows, and spears. Doesn't look like a welcoming committee to me."

Gary replied, "Swell! Our laser defense will be limited due to coolant problems, and we'll save that for these big crocs, or whatever they are. I have a feeling they're not out of the game yet. However, we may have some problems with restraining many prisoners because of our limited supply of handcuffs . . ."

Kim's return transmission interrupted him. "Negative on the prisoners. We just finished a meeting concerning our interrelationship with these inhabitants and decided nothing good can come out of it at all. Repeat, no prisoners and dispatch all involved in the raid."

"Dispatch? Kill the guys that run away or surrender?" Gary incredulously asked.

"Our resident psychologist believes that a defeated combatant who returns to his tribe will just reinforce their resolve for revenge. On the other hand, if nobody returns, superstition will play more in our favor and delay or forestall another attack. Gary, these creatures are no longer human; they have no conscience and will not have second thoughts about wiping us out."

Gary sighed deeply. "Okay, will comply, but what about 'Bubba' here?"

A long pause. "Interrogate, then activate automatic laser defense," Kim replied sheepishly.

One cold bitch, Gary thought as he signed out.

In the end, the captive was responsible for his own demise. Lance Corporal Johnson had only turned his back for a second, but when he looked back, the primate was on his feet, glaring at him with his hands by his sides, the handcuffs lying on the ground beside him. The prisoner picked up a stick that resembled a baseball bat.

"Halt! Drop the weapon!" Johnson shouted as he started to backtrack. His forty-caliber pistol with the mercury-tipped loads did not waver from the advancing predator's chest. The primate looked at the sentry's puny little stick, then looked at his hefty club and continued to advance in a low crouch. *Blam!* One shot and the surprised Neanderthal flew back one meter with the center of his chest gone and a gaping hole in his back.

Gary was one of the first to arrive at the bloody scene.

A shaking Johnson stuttered, "I . . . I . . . I warned him, s-sir."

"No sweat, Johnson; you did well. You followed my orders to a T." Gary bent down, picked up the still locked handcuffs and went over to the dead primate. *How did he get out of these?* There were some abrasions the handcuffs had left on the prisoner's hands, but nothing to indicate how he had slipped them off.

Christine, who had been monitoring everything through the helmet's camera said, "Aha! Put your gloves on and turn his hands over. . . There, his thumb joint is quite a bit smaller than ours. Also, his thumb is proportionally shorter and more aligned with his other fingers. Looks like no more handcuffs for these guys since that restraint depends on our standard hand and protruding thumbs. Ah . . . is there any way you can cool him down until I can get there?"

Gary was quick to answer, "No way! We'll need all the coolant we can get to keep our lasers operational. But don't despair, Christine. I have a feeling you'll soon have more cadavers than you can handle."

One of the water loaders trotted over to Gary and announced, "Sir, five minutes to go for a full load. You want to load the flight computer?"

"Right, I'll get right on it." Gary ran to the shuttle.

A medic watching over Lewis said, "She'll be okay, sir. She's on her third pint of, uh, blood, if we can call it that. She went into shock, but is now stabilized under morphine."

To Gary she looked awfully pale, but not in pain. "We'll need to raise the armrests and lay her flat. Make sure she's strapped in well because the ascent will be more turbulent than our descent. I want you to escort her back to the *Leapfrog*. You'll sit in the command console with her after I reload the computer."

"Uh, sir? I haven't a clue how to fly one of these."

Gary smiled at him, "Don't worry, son; no one knows. The computers take care of everything. Once you're ready, I'll start the launch sequence via the *Leapfrog* link.

Once the shuttle's door started closing everyone scattered, taking whatever was important with them. When everything seemed secure, Gary gave the "all clear" signal, and the shuttle rose on its spindly gear for a last-minute weight and balance check and then sandblasted the entire island with hot, hurricane-force winds. Up and going, the shuttle shifted on its tail, the main thrusters kicked in, and it was supersonic before reaching seven thousand meters.

The launch was impressive, even more impressive to the creatures just getting in their dugouts. Grunting and waving their weapons, a minor celebration ensued, for they, the mighty warriors of the entire world, had just chased off the demons. Now it was time to see what the demons in the fire bird had left behind.

CHAPTER 14

Sand, sand, and more sand everywhere! The shuttle's thrusters had created a major sandstorm. The sand went to the left, then right, straight up, and back down to converge and clog every crevice on the island. *Shit! Were we always this fucking stupid?* Gary asked himself as he rose and shook off three centimeters of sand. "Okay, people, field strip your weapons and check them out while we have the chance. Next time we'll wrap everything in plastic," he shouted as he sat back down and field stripped and cleaned the sand out of his pistol and rifle.

When everyone appeared about done with their weapons, Gary whistled and gave the "circle the wagons" signal. "We expect an attack from the knuckle-draggers at any time. New ROE (rules of engagement): We don't want any of the creatures making it back to their village, period. The ship's shrink thinks any survivors making it back to their village would decrease our chances of pulling off the mission. We're going to be here a few days, which will increase the odds of the locals putting together another attack, and we don't want them learning from experience. Bottom line: take no prisoners." A collective gasp was audible. "Instead of firing warning shots across their bows, we'll let them fully beachhead before reversing the ambush. We'll save the laser mostly for night defense against the dinosaurs, or whatever they are, so the range will be reduced to twenty meters in case the Mongoloids start to overrun us. We will dig in and conceal as much as possible; keep the lasers down and out of view until they're needed. Keep your full masks close by in case we have to gas ourselves to stop an onslaught. Any questions?" Several questions followed, but Scoffield stepped in and filled in the details.

Afterward, Gary looked about and found the one remaining medic, Sergeant Smithfield, and told him, "Smithfield, I know this isn't your area of expertise, but I need to know whether or not this dinosaur we shot and the floating fish we bombarded with hand grenades are edible. Delegate several men to help you, but do it quickly. Use one of the cutting torches to cook a few small samples."

Smithfield replied, "Aye, sir." But he looked skeptically at the fallen humanoid.

Before Conner had a chance to voice his question, Gary said, "No, don't even go there."

Smithfield smiled and went about his assigned business.

Ten minutes later, Smithfield came back and said, "Both the dinosaur and fish are edible and actually pretty damn good even without salt. I'll start a butchering and cleaning detail and load up as much as we can using the extra body bags we hopefully won't need. But, sir—"

Smithfield was interrupted by a *Leapfrog* bridge page. "Gary here," he answered.

Kim was excited. "They're on the way. There's about fifty of them in eight large dugouts. All of them are armed and painted up for battle. ETA's one hour."

"We'll be ready," Gary replied. "What's the status of

the shuttle?"

"The shuttle will be docking about same time your party starts. We'll keep an eye out for any changes. Good luck, Gary. Kim out."

"Forget the rotisserie for now, and arm up," Gary told Smithfield.

Gary whistled for everyone's attention. "Take your positions; time to rock and roll."

Gary sat next to Scoffield and placed the horizontal situation display between them in case Gary took a round and Scoffield needed the information. Aerial cameras from the *Leapfrog* were providing on-scene overviews. "Yep, there they are, four miles and starting to spread out a little," Gary said as he switched his helmet monitor to "hot," allowing command and control real-time information. He then crawled around the entire perimeter checking on his men, engaging in little chats and encouragements. He not only could see their determination and bravery; he could feel it, and he loved it.

"Three miles now, looks like they've spread out some more, sir," said Scoffield as Gary crawled back to his position. "This is gonna be a turkey shoot; we didn't see any shields at all so I had the boys load up with the mercury rounds. One, two hits max per kill with ten misses each, I figure. These men and women are good, real good, but you and I are the only ones who've seen combat before, so there'll be a lot of nervous, wasted fire. The quack still wants some heads?"

"Not now. The one we have should suffice. Have the troopers take their best shot," Gary said.

That last order was relayed; pure silence ruled. Ruled until the chanting took over. Gary and about half of his company were watching every move the primates made through high-power, glint-resistant binoculars. Fierce. Each and every one of the warriors looked extremely fierce. They were painted in ghoulish, mostly red patterns. They were large; not one less than three meters, with bulging muscles, and they were dressed in loincloths. Another prominent feature was the abundant hair. All had so much hair on their bodies that skin could hardly be seen. Gary also noticed that two men on each canoe, one on the bow and the other on the stern, continuously looked down in the water as if expecting something. Gary had no doubt what that surprise could be.

As soon as the wooden dugouts hit the beach, the warriors were off and running left and right along the beach to encircle the small island. When the leading warriors came across the dead dinosaur in the shallow surf, all of them came to a complete stop. Loud screams and grunting brought the entire landing party to rally around the corpse. The slightly bent-over warrior with the most feathers in his head dressing felt the hole in the monster's head. More grunts followed and then the warriors continued their island encirclement but without their previous enthusiasm. The spears and undivided attention were now exclusively pointed toward the center portion of the island, where Gary and company waited.

"Hold your fire until I'm sure no one can make it back to the boats," Gary whispered on tactical frequency. At last, the humanoids completely surrounded the island, and the chief raised his spear over his head and screamed. They all screamed back and started advancing.

Gary watched through the scope on his rifle until both boat guards came into view. "Scoffield, take the guard on the right at my command. Gary centered the guard on the left in his crosshairs, waited five seconds, keyed his helmet radio and transmitted, "Fire!" then slowly squeezed the big rifle's hair trigger. *Blam!* The warrior Gary had targeted blew up at the same time his companion exploded. Others joined in the firing, making the surreal sound that popcorn does in a movie theater.

Gary swiftly searched for the warrior who had been standing next to his and found him lying belly up in the shallow surf without a head. Obviously, Scoffield did not miss either. In a matter of five seconds, everywhere Gary looked, he could not find a single standing warrior. The noise immediately simmered to an occasional pop or two before fading out altogether.

"Scope them all and make sure they're dead," Gary commanded on the tactical radio. Three more rifle shots followed. "Don't touch anything," he added.

Using his binoculars, Gary could see about fifty stationary logs around two hundred meters from shore, all pointed at the island. Keying the tactical microphone again, he ordered, "Arm the laser defense and set range three-hundred meters." When nothing happened Gary said, "Not enough of them exposed to alert the radar or infrared—" A sudden buzz sounded, and a red beam from the nearest laser station concentrated on one of the primitive warriors lying on the beach. The beam cut a big Z right in the middle of the warrior's torso, and glassed the sand on the other side.

"Must have had a heartbeat," Scoffield remarked.

"Z? Like in Zorro? I think our computer has a morbid personality," Gary added.

"Sir!" one of the soldiers monitoring the laser system called out. "The overheat temperature's already in the red!"

"Shit!" Gary exclaimed. "Turn the system off for now. The batteries must have gone south over time."

The fifty sets of eyes kept their distance. These new two-legged meals were causing them a lot of trouble. Their blood was repulsive and their fire sticks were bafflingly deadly. Clicking like dolphins, they decided to come back at darkness to test the new creatures on their own terms. After all, they ruled here and were not about to settle for second place.

CHAPTER 15

GARY KEYED HIS TACTICAL MIKE. "Gather around the laser batteries for an all-hands debriefing." Soon, all the troops were gathered around thoroughly pumped up on the adrenaline rush of combat. "Congratulations on a job extremely well done. But . . ." Gary paused for effect. "It's not over. We have two distinct, very different enemies here that are by now pretty pissed off. For defense tactics on the dinosaurs, we'll use high explosives alternating with armor-piercing rounds. Armor-piercing is to be used only with the handguns and small automatic rifles. Mercury tip loads in all weapons for the knuckle-draggers. I'm banking on them taking too long to get their shit together, not cooperating, and perhaps fighting among themselves. We denied the slope-heads any benefits of lessons learned and gave them a fear of the unknown. Hopefully, we'll be long gone before they figure out how to mount an effective assault against us. However, we'll need at least four days here to relay all the water and some food up to our ship. Four days is a long time to be under constant siege, but that's what it will take and that's what we'll give." "*Whoyahs*" followed.

Gary continued, "Next shuttle arrival is scheduled at 2100 hours, which closely resembles local time. Sunset will be approximately 1830 hours, which gives us several hours of darkness to contend with. More supplies and especially liquid nitrogen will be onboard, but until then, our lasers will over-heat the batteries if we use them very much. If the batteries do happen to overheat, they will melt-down, causing a China syndrome that none of us will survive. The critical mass will literally explode when it hits the water table, which I imagine is not too deep here on this lake. I'm resetting the max range back to fifty meters, which is roughly our defense perimeter. If the dinosaurs get that close, we might as well take them with us." Nervous laughter followed.

"First priority for now is to get all those bodies out of the water. We don't need them contaminating the water, now or at any time." Gary turned to Scoffield. "Set up par-ties to pick up and bury all these primates, saving no more than two for experimental cadavers. Have the men wear full biohazard or space suits if they physically have to touch any of them." Addressing the complete company, he resumed, "Rest if and when you can; it's going to be a long night with split watch shifts."

Deep underwater in a vast cavern, hundreds of huge crea-tures drifted about gently bumping into each other. A series of alternating sonar clicks and clucks similar to those made by dolphins could be heard echoing off the underwater cavern walls. Hierarchy ruled with the dominant males controlling the group. A series of three loud clucks from a huge male in front brought complete silence to the cavern. At the mo-ment, this large, badass creature held ultimate authority. Any challenge attempted by a younger male or a female was dealt instant and savage destruction by the group. The young kept quiet as ordered.

The creatures had a plan: they were going to try one more time to eat one of the new food things. If the new two-legged creatures had bad blood and meat, they would kill them all at once instead of keeping them alive for a future food source. The newcomers were considered a threat since they had wiped out over three months of their food supply in a very short time.

Unlike other predators, the beasts practiced conservation. They had learned that the nest raiding of the two-legged food animals led to hunger once they wiped out the food's reproductive capacity. Therefore, all the stick-lined nests were forbidden territory. Unless, of course, the pack was starving. Then eat them all; worry later.

The leader finished his clicking and clucking and swam out of the cavern, signifying an end to the meeting. The hungry ones went looking for large fish while the others bedded down in the muddy bottom to rest and wait for darkness and the call to mobilize.

A collective problem confronting the lake-bound creatures was the dwindling supply of big fish. Their ocean-roving cousins had life much easier because of the larger volume of water and the greater fish supply. A captured whale could provide enough food for a pack for several days. Yet the freshwater species had to venture inland for sufficient food. Necessity being the mother of evolution, or hybridization, the lake-bound species had taken a giant leap over their cousins by evolving rear legs, giving them the ability to stand like kangaroos and rest on their tails. Most importantly, a new source of communication was coming within their grasp. Unfortunately for what was left of the human race, the creatures now dominated every freshwater lake and were currently interbreeding with their saltwater cousins.

CHAPTER 16

THE TEMPERATURE FELL AS FAST as the sun. Several fires spouted up and the smell of cooking dinosaur meat and fish filled the air. Edible berries grew around the island along with roots that looked like yams. Soon, the little military contingency was feasting while the ship's company monitored the picnic and drooled. While the food was cooking, Gary had a second team forage the island for more edible food with strict orders to remain armed and stay within ten meters of each other. Gary authorized "hand grenade fishing" as long as the "fishermen" did not linger in the water picking up the concussed fish.

Gary's headset buzzed. "Gary, Christine here. The last shuttle arrived without incident. Lewis is in surgery and it looks like we may be able to save her leg, although with a loss of around ten percent usage. Three millimeters of femur were destroyed, but we were able to graft, splint, and pin. Her track days are over." Changing the subject quickly, she added, "Um, I'm planning on jumping on the next shuttle."

"Any way I can talk you out of it?"

"Nope, there's too much at stake. Besides, I won't be missed much up here; my staff's ticking like a Swiss watch. See you soon. Here's Kim."

"Hi, Gary. Kim here. We're refueling one of the tankers

and will start on the second as soon as the hydrogen electrolysis cranks out the fuel. We're sending down your requested supplies along with Christine. Also, we're testing a third laser battery that may be up to speed, but we won't have that available until the second shuttle.

"The primates on the beach have been pretty docile up to now. They're starting to fight among themselves, and they're disbanding. We figure they won't send out another probe for at least another day. Hopefully, they'll use the same tactics. OK, that's about it. The next shuttle leaves in a half hour and should be there around 2115 hours. Oh, how about sending as much food up as you can? We're starving."

"You got it. Gary out."

Damn, overcast, Gary thought as he checked on each of the four security watch points. *Sure would be nice to have a full moon to augment our night vision equipment.* Gary keyed the headset to the "All" position. "All watches use both IR and light augmentation modes simultaneously." The guards could be seen flipping down both lenses on their helmets.

But nothing could be seen. The beasts used their huge lung capacity to remain submerged, and their body heat remained shielded by six inches of water. After one of them had gotten an eye shot out during the previous encounter, they'd quickly learned to keep concealed as long as possible. Concealment was defined as remaining at a seven-foot depth because one of them had had his spine nicked by a bullet while crawling to a shallower depth. Like large boulders, they lay there completely motionless awaiting the attack command from their leader. These were hunters, the world's new best, and they patiently waited for their call to arms. They would soon put to the test the new two-legged food beings and find out exactly how threatening the unknown weapons were. The only way to do that was to rush them, but first they wanted to taste one and see if it really was as inedible as their dead friend had said before he'd passed on. However, the coming assault would probably be just to kill and not to eat. This concept was new to all of them and starting to excite the younger ones to such a level that they could not remain still. Anticipation of killing just to kill was like a narcotic to the younger beasts. They were feeling a new frenzy, a true killing frenzy.

CHAPTER 17

AT 2101 THE ARRIVING SHUTTLE'S computer announced a VTOL approach would commence at 2123 hours. The same location was targeted, so Gary had the nuclear batteries taken to the outer perimeter and the laser tripods lowered. Gary was feeling pretty vulnerable with the crippled laser lowered and another sandstorm arriving. He keyed his mike. "Do not dismantle your weapons; lie on them to protect them from the sand. If they need dismantling to clear out the sand, don't do it until your neighbor acknowledges that he is ready. We do *not* want everyone taking their weapons apart at the same time. Now let's get in our trenches, but keep an eye out on the water, not the arriving shuttle. Is that clear?"

"*Whoyahs*" followed.

Smitty, PFC William Smith, had to piss really badly. "Hey, Manuel, cover my ass; I gotta take a piss before that shuttle starts down."

Manuel, PFC Jose Manuel, was busy trying to find something to wrap his large fifty caliber rifle in. "No fucking way, man! You stay here and piss yourself, but don't leave this post," he said but only to himself because Smitty was already trotting to the water's edge to relieve himself.

Aha! I'll use my poncho. Wrap it up tight and no sand will leak in, were Manuel's thoughts when he heard Smitty's scream.

Rifle slung over his shoulder, zipper down and fishing for his crank, Smitty reached the bank. Just as he got himself exposed, the water erupted in front of him. Glaring down at him with the meanest eyes he'd ever seen was a huge mongrel dinosaur with the biggest teeth imaginable. His scream and urination began simultaneously.

Lowering itself on massive rear legs, the dinosaur sprang and was on Smitty mid-scream. As fast as a snake strikes, the beast leaned forward and snatched up the petrified Smitty while he was still screaming and peeing. The scream suddenly turned into a squeak as the massive jaws tightened around Smitty's chest. Smitty heard the most horrifying sound in his life as the teeth crunched into his chest cavity.

"What the fuck?" Manuel exclaimed to no one. The monster had the kicking Smitty in his mouth and was staring down at Manuel. "Shit!" he yelled while pulling his rifle out of the poncho. The animal could have had Manuel easily but did not make a move in his direction. When Manuel looked up again, the dinosaur was gone, along with Smitty.

Manuel keyed his mike to "All" and screamed, "Holy shit! It just ate Smitty! Smitty's gone! Fucker took him."

Gary sprinted over to Manuel and Smitty's post while keying his mike to "All" and transmitting, "Keep all weapons at the ready! I repeat, do not store your weapon! Prepare for attack!" Gary dove into the trench with Manuel and rolled over on his belly with his rifle on his shoulder pointing at the lake.

Manuel was almost in shock and started stuttering incoherently.

Without taking his eyes off the water, Gary said, "Calm down Manuel. Take some deep breaths, and tell me what happened."

"Big, huge, just like the one you shot, grabbed Smitty and ran off with him," Manuel finally managed.

———

The young beast had Smitty in his jaws and squeezed until all movement ceased. Swimming out to the middle of the lake, the creature had to stop and gag. Blood from his prey had flowed back into his throat making him involuntarily regurgitate. The large, vicious leader swam by, snatched Smitty by the legs and bit them off. He swallowed both legs without chewing but did not have to wait long for the legs to come flying back out. "Kill! Do not eat," he clicked underwater.

On signal, all seventy-six monsters stood. To the defenders, it looked like a huge wall suddenly popped out of the lake, just a few feet in the water.

Sweet Jesus! This is where we die, Gary thought as he placed his crosshairs on the one directly in front of him. Just as Gary squeezed the trigger, *Boom!* The shuttle's thrusters kicked in, blowing all cloud cover away and revealing the awesome glory of powerful pulse rockets.

It saved the humans. The creatures had reared back on their tails and were starting to roll forward on their hindquarters when the sky opened up. All the creatures stopped to stare at the apparition with their concentration totally broken. It was the break the humans needed. Approximately twenty-five fifty calibers opened up with their lethal high-explosive loads. The defenders kept firing until the visibility dropped to near zero from the blowing sand, only then momentarily stopping while the soldiers flipped on the radar imaging filters on their scopes. The creatures quickly recuperated and continued their attack; however, the initiative was lost, along with their vision. Clucking the retreat signal, the remaining creatures literally vanished into the lake.

The beasts were further confused by their enemy's ability to see when they could not. The creatures did not know what had hit them or what had happened. The sun exploded, the wind sandblasted them, and half of them died right on the spot. For the first time in their lives, they experienced fear. All who could swim hurried back to the underwater cavern, their vicious leader conspicuously absent. They would have to develop new tactics, and a new leader had to take charge. A pack bonding tightly tied them into a common goal: *the two-legged killers must die.*

CHAPTER 18

CHRISTINE HAD JUST FINISHED UNSTRAPPING when the shuttle door opened and sand poured in. She was fully suited in combat gear identical to what the troopers wore and she half expected a huge mouth to reach in and snap her right out of her seat. She had been monitoring the tactical frequency when Smitty was attacked and all hell broke loose. Although she had been sitting at the control console, she could not find the *Abort*, *Go-around*, or *Wave-off* button for the life of her. She was unaware passengers did not have the authority to alter a mission, and with all the confusion at the landing site, no one remembered to divert the shuttle during the battle. The firefight seemed intense, and the last thing she wanted was to land right in the middle of it.

However, she was a little reluctant to start pushing buttons she did not understand for fear of repercussions. After all, what if the computer became confused and said something like, "auto-pilot disconnected, manual override activated." Like she would really know what to do then.

With the sand still blowing around, visibility was reduced to one arm's length; however, the guns continued firing based upon the individual scope's built-in radar returns or infrared imaging. As the huge doors slowly opened, the sandstorm followed, covering everything inside and filling every nook and cranny.

Although the sandstorm began to subside, Christine thought it would be a good idea to stay seated, as least until the guns stopped firing. Finally the gunfire ended, and the transmissions over the headsets diminished to panicky voices seeking some kind of reassurance that their comrades were still alive. Now she could see the open doorway and made her way out, stumbling over the medical chest that contained the necessary autopsy equipment.

As quickly as the sandstorm began, it ended, the settling dust making the scene appear as if a fog bank had rolled in. Cordite hung in the air along with a pungent smell of blood and fear. Floodlights lay scattered on the ground, all of them overturned by the blast and some pointing straight up. Soldiers who were scurrying about carrying heavy ammunition pouches to the perimeter defenses looked like alien creatures with their full face mask helmets. Christine could catch glimpses of Gary as he dashed back and forth making sure all perimeter defenses remained intact and operational. Once the floodlights were shining back toward the threat area, Gary made his way over to Christine, who had managed to drag her hefty medical trunk from the shuttle.

"You came right in time," Gary panted as he strode right past her and clambered into the cargo hold.

"Ahem, I could use a little help here," Christine chided.

Without looking back, Gary answered, "If we can't get this laser defense up really soon, we will all be bits and pieces, and the shuttle needs water before it can go anywhere."

The revelation blew away Christine's early escape options. Dropping all pretense of requiring chivalry, Christine added, "Let me give you a hand." She followed Gary into the cargo bay and helped him drag out the heavy nuclear generator. Once clear of the shuttle, Gary opened the console and initialized the unit's diagnostics.

While Gary was preoccupied with the generator, Christine took a good look around her. The scene appeared chaotic on the surface, but below the bustle was structured military order and charged adrenaline. Each soldier had a duty and wasted no effort or time in idle chatting or loafing. The water crew had the water transfer pumps running before Gary and Christine could drag the generator from the cargo hold.

"Ah, shit!" exclaimed Gary as he typed in new instructions on the small console.

"Tell me you didn't say 'ah shit,'" Christine said as she leaned over his shoulder to take a peek.

"Terry's people didn't do such a great job refurbishing the power units. This one, although considerably stronger than the others, is way below specs. It can only generate a discharge once every five seconds. Normally, or I should say when new, the discharge rate is five times per second. I guess that's what ten thousand years does to you."

Christine sat next to Gary and said, "What do you expect from something that's over ten thousand years old? And that's not the only thing that's gone south around here. I need to talk to you, Gary."

"I have a feeling I know what's coming, but can it wait a few minutes while I try to get this unit set up for parallel operation?"

Christine shrugged. "OK, swing by the tent morgue

when you can. I've got to take a close look at the Neander-thal head you saved for me. I, uh, would really like to wait until daylight before I venture over to the dinosaurs, or what-ever they are."

"That . . ." Gary hesitated, "would be the best idea any-one's had tonight."

———

Christine was so engrossed in the autopsy, she did not even hear Gary when he approached the tent and said, "Knock, knock," then entered. Walking up behind her, he started off by asking, "Well?"

"Aieee!" screamed Christine as she spun around and dropped her electric skull saw. "Oh, it's you. You scared the living hell out of me." She picked up the saw, tested it, and put it back on the assist table.

"Sorry. I guess this is *not* the place to slip up on someone, but I did say 'knock, knock.'"

"No, it's me. I always seem to get too involved and forget my surroundings." Looking forlorn, Christine added, "I only wish I could forget this place, wake up from this nightmare, and pretend none of it ever happened."

Motioning with her head toward a couple of boxes in the corner, Christine slipped off her latex gloves and said, "Have a seat. You're not going to like what I have to tell you."

"It's not my girls, is it?" Gary asked apprehensively.

"No, well, no more than everyone else." Christine sighed and continued, "We've been doing random MRIs on ourselves and have found some very disturbing damage. Without exception, we all have lost around five to ten percent of our brain mass. This must be from the extended cryo-sleep, for who would ever have thought that we'd be frozen for ten thousand years? The area most affected centers in the upper part of the cerebral cortex, which seems to have a damaging effect on our ability to draw causal relationships and project the outcome of simple events. Case in point, our failure to foresee possible nocturnal threats or to foresee the shortcomings of infrared scanning of land masses only. God only knows what else has slipped past us."

"I had a feeling you were going to say something along those lines. Ever since I've come out of the cyro-sleep, I've been feeling like I'm in a mental fog bank and not firing on all eight cylinders. Assuming I had eight to start with." Gary leaned back and put his hands behind his head. "So, what's the prognosis, doc? Are we going to get any of it back?"

Christine sat up straight with moist eyes. "Nope, it's gone forever, but the human brain is phenomenal. Another portion of the brain that's not used much and not damaged will pick up the slack. It will take some time, but in the meantime we may have some severe challenges, and quite frankly, I don't think we're up for it."

Gary laughed and said, "Then you haven't been in the military, doc. There're times when I'm sure no one's got an IQ over eighty-five, myself included. As far as being up for it, what's our choice? Why bother to go back to cryo-sleep? We'll probably all be zombies the next time we wake up. Besides, no one will rescue us because we burned our alien bridge a long, long time ago. Who knows, though? Maybe these evolving crocs will come and bring us down for hors d'oeuvres. By that time we'll be like sheep, so who cares?"

Christine's façade of scientific composure instantly dissolved as she erupted in sobs. Bowing her head and putting her hands to her face to help hide her emotions, she started convulsing from a complete meltdown.

Gary moved over to her box, sat down beside her, and put an arm around her shoulders. "I'm sorry. I didn't mean to sound so fatalistic. I can be such a jerk sometimes."

Between sobs Christine managed to get in, "No, no, it's not you or what you said. It's just the reality of our situation finally sank in, and it seems so hopeless. L-look at us! Misplaced ten thousand years, homeless, mentally handicapped, with limited resources." She relapsed into hysterical sobbing.

Gary held her tighter and said, "It's not all lost. Yeah, we took some hits, but not bad enough to take us out of the game. Just ask all these dead bodies around us. If we can stick together, we'll make it, but it won't be a walk in the park, and as far as being homeless, home is where you make it; we just haven't decided where yet, not if. We also need to find our enemy's weaknesses, capitalize on them, and reestablish our dominance."

Looking up at him and chuckling between softening sobs, Christine said, "Just like that, huh?"

"Yeah, just like that!" Gary answered snapping his fingers.

Offered a handkerchief, Christine tried to daintily blow her nose, but it came out more like a moose call. Smiling and wiping away the tears, she looked into Gary's light blue eyes and felt something stirring deep within her. Bitter memories of her last failed romance came flooding back, bringing along the horrible arguments she had had with her lover. He absolutely refused to can his career as a professional athlete and tag along on her space adventure. Christine also had refused to decline the offer to be part of the adventure. Their relationship ended in loud shouting matches and slamming doors. Hardly a fond farewell. She had just started dating Gary and was beginning to feel strongly about him when the firestorm of *Leapfrog's* responsibilities swamped her. They had mutually agreed to postpone their relationship until things settled down. That had never happened.

Snapping out of her trance, Christine stood, pecked Gary on the cheek and said, "Okay, enough of my childish display; let's get to work on Bubba here and see what's cooking inside his head." Turning, she briskly strode to the makeshift autopsy table and picked up her skull saw. Swiftly, she finished cutting the last two inches of the skull. With a *pop*, she pulled off the top of the Neanderthal's skull.

"Oh, man, look at that!" Christine exclaimed.

Gary was beside her but standing slightly behind the table. "Err, what's so exciting about that?" All brains and guts looked alike to Gary.

"Look at the texture. It's almost all smooth, hardly any wrinkles. Look at the super small frontal lobes. This guy went through some serious de-evolution." Christine looked over and saw Gary's frown of misunderstanding. "The wrinkles in the human brain drastically increase the surface area of our brain. It's kind of like supercharging our brain and keeping it in a relatively small space. This guy lost most of his wrinkles, which would dumb him down considerably, plus the loss of all this frontal lobe area drops him down another peg. Gary, this guy dropped several pegs on the food chain when he lost all this."

"Then we can't expect too many surprises from these people?"

Christine was beaming. "No, this guy is lucky to still be able to use primitive tools, much less conceive a decent defense against us."

Christine was a master at work with her scalpel. Skillfully, she opened up the cadaver and examined each organ with the detachment only a surgeon could exhibit. Gary, on the other hand, was not holding up as well and beginning to feel a little woozy when Christine said, "Hmm."

"Hmm, what?"

Christine seemed surprised by the interruption. "Look at the relatively high location of the larynx in the neck. Look at his vocal tract; it has more of a curve than a right angle. Anatomically, he's closer to a chimpanzee than a human. He can probably eat and breathe at the same time but there goes his voice. He must communicate with grunts and growls and hand gestures. Vocally, he's like a mute. Summarizing what she had been observing, she added, "He has fewer sweat glands; hairier, smaller, realigned thumbs; small eye openings, white part of the eye much smaller; thinner lips; retracted chin; smaller sloping forehead; larger canine teeth. The reduction of sweat glands is significant because of the adverse affect on his cooling system. His brain would rapidly overheat in any type of endurance situation. Eyesight would be less effective than ours, but his sense of smell much more sensitive. Look at the huge olfactory bulb of the brain." She picked up the brain and pointed to a small area on the bottom portion as if Gary was knowledgeable enough to tell the difference.

Scoffield stuck his head in the tent. "Sir, we need you for a minute out here."

Gary, more than relieved to leave the autopsy, made his way over to the tent's exit flap. Stopping at the threshold, he turned to Christine and said, "Thanks for the good news. Let me know if something else of significance comes up."

Before Gary could complete his hasty escape, Christine said, "I'll need to take a look at one of those creatures as soon as possible. This guy still needs some attention, but those damn dinosaur monsters are the real mystery."

Scoffield, who was standing behind Gary, said, "Not a good idea ma'am. They seem to think they own the night, and they're back circling the island just outside of rifle range. Besides, we've got another shuttle en route, and we need to get this one out of here before it arrives." Needlessly, he added, "You remember all the confusion when you landed?"

Pallor seemed to wash over Christine's features, coupled with a case of hand tremors. "Ah, is this a good spot? Or should I move somewhere else?"

Gary answered, "I'll get you before the rocket blasts start another sandstorm."

"Umm, do you mind if I stick pretty close to you? I mean until, at least, let's say sunrise?" All of a sudden her little tent seemed extremely vulnerable and unprotected.

Gary and Scoffield exchanged glances and mutual smiles. "Tag along, if you'd like, but I can't guarantee your safety," Gary said. "For that matter, I don't think there's a safe place anywhere around here. This will have to be our last night at this location, or at least within five hundred miles of here. I have a feeling the inhabitants are picking up more than we're giving them credit for, and I'm fairly certain another attack is imminent. Probably not tonight since we stung them so hard on their last raid, but by tomorrow night we need to be long gone." Christine and Scoffield enthusiastically nodded their consent.

As Gary and Scoffield roamed the perimeter defenses, giving kudos and encouragements, Christine tuned into the *Leapfrog* and relayed her findings and Gary's recommendation of changing sites.

Kim answered back on the tactical common frequency for all to hear. "Understood, and agreed. We have another site 950 kilometers southeast of your location that fits our parameters. Additionally, the area we suggest is landlocked with a sheer cliff backing it, eliminating the need for rear defense." Everyone could hear Kim's deep sigh as she added, "Well, at least until we discover that these beasts can also fly." Audible groans could be heard from the extraction site.

Kim continued, "After two more runs, we're almost at our replenishment goal and should be able to complete replenishment in another thirty hours. Hopefully, we'll be in and out of our new location before any threat can organize an attack."

Kim switched back to a secure channel before continuing. "After this next run, we're sending down the personnel transport shuttle to move our operations to the new site. Keep the personnel shuttle until we finish with the tankers, and we'll recover both on the same orbit cycle.

"On another matter," Kim went on, "we're planning a lunar exploration and would like a small security contingency to accompany the mission. Still interested, Gary?"

Gary replied, "Understood and will comply, but what

threat can there be with a ten thousand-year-old lunar base? Anything that was once alive will be long gone."

Kim was quick to answer. "Don't be too sure of that. The huge ice lake was warmed by gigantic radioactive rods whose half-life was around one-half billion years. The domed garden houses had self-sealing transparent ceilings and were to receive sunlight twenty-four hours straight. A gravity-fed perpetual irrigation system continually cycled the thawed water, and the plants replenished oxygen and filtered out the carbon dioxide. All the plants that were originally chosen could provide nourishment. However remote the possibility of life, I'd like an armed force to accompany the exploratory team. Hold on a sec . . . Okay, just got word that the next water shuttle was entering Earth's atmosphere, so I'll get back with you once things settle down there. Good luck, *Leapfrog*. Out."

"Ten minutes to get this shuttle airborne," Gary transmitted to the ground crew. Someone answered back that they could have the shuttle ready in six minutes. Gary unslung his rifle, slid the silencer extension up, locked it into position, and went over to the highest perimeter posts.

Intuitively, Scoffield pulled out his multipurpose binoculars as he followed the major to the post. Gary assumed the standard rifle prone position while Scoffield scanned the surrounding lake's surface. "I spot seven IR contacts at seven hundred meters, one contact at six-fifty with a three-knot closure. Looks like he's testing us." Scoffield spoke in a quiet voice.

Christine was standing behind the two men wondering what they were up to. Gary turned to her and said, "You should button down your combat suit and put some gloves on before that shuttle gets here."

Christine thought he was crazy, wanting to close off the hot, baggy uniform and wear gloves.

Gary went back to his scope and turned his helmet mike on for all to hear. Everyone had already had enough surprises and Gary did not want to set off a panic. "I'm going to fire a silenced round at the closest amphibious rascal to get the surface guys to back off some for our shuttle recovery. After I fire, I want at least ten concussion grenades lobbed at various close water positions. No telling what's lurking off the beach. You've got three minutes heads-up before I fire."

Exactly three minutes later, Gary radioed, "I've got a radar lock on the one at six-fifty, drifting now to six-forty, switching to gyro-stabilization, selecting auto-fire." After an eternity of five seconds, the gun's fire-control computer satisfied its solution for range ballistic and platform motion.

Pfttt! went the big fifty caliber silenced rifle. About a second later, a small, misty red explosion was seen off in the water. The rifle's action smoothly slid another case-less round in the chamber while the stabilized scope kept a steady radar bead on the vaporizing head. *Whump, whump* went the concussion grenades in the shallow water. A smaller than normal beast close to an exploding grenade staggered to its feet and wobbled back and forth, obviously in a dazed state. A soldier called, "I've got it!" *Boom!* An un-silenced rifle barked, and half of the beast's head turned into a red mist. Everyone was in a state of heightened anxiety as the water not far from shore swirled around, followed by some subdued splashes.

"Two-minute countdown for liftoff," someone transmitted

on the tactical channel. Gary jumped to his feet, grabbed a startled Christine by her hand, and said, "Time for low profile." They scurried off to the nearest foxhole and jumped in.

Gary pulled Christine close and said, "You'll need your full face mask; stay as low as you can, and don't wander off too far from me."

Yeah, like that's going to happen, Christine thought as she scooted closer to Gary.

Christine, who figured she had just about witnessed every conceivable surprise, was soul shocked when the shuttle's booster rocket fired. *Blam!* The Earth itself seemed to come apart while she was bounced six inches straight up. The following sand blast was horrific, stinging exposed flesh to a point where she swore the bones were exposed. Visibility dropped so low, Christine could not see anything except the insides of her face mask. Intense heat followed, along with a noise so loud she could feel the reverberations deep within her chest. *Thank God for the sonic headsets.*

The only good thing about the shuttle's departure was the peace and quiet that followed. Still not seeing very well, Christine stood up only to be tripped by Gary. "Don't stand! The next shuttle's right behind this one, and the landings are worse than the takeoffs."

"Holy shit! This gets worse? How can it? I guess my tent's long gone," Christine shouted as she cuddled up to Gary while fumbling to get her suit fully closed and her gloves on.

All Gary said was "Landing's take longer. Your tent and gear were stowed."

Much to Christine's chagrin, Gary was right. The noise, heat, and blast seemed to last forever. Christine made a mental note never to volunteer for anything again and to make first reservations on the next departure.

CHAPTER 19

THOROUGHLY HUMBLED BY THE SHUTTLES' blasts, Christine decided to spend the next hour and a half before daylight in the foxhole. She was tired of all the life-threatening surprises and wanted some time to do some thinking, which seemed like a good idea since they all seemed to have suffered a minor lobotomy.

First on her mind was what happened to the humanity they had once known. *Are these Neanderthals a new breed of humans, or are they the result of some kind of devolution? Tissue samplings from the autopsied Neanderthal should be arriving soon at the* Leapfrog *laboratory. DNA or RNA analysis will decide which way these slopeheads are going. Whichever way, what could have possibly happened to accelerate the process? Is a viral outbreak, viral engineering, biological warfare, or another* Leapfrog *ship that we don't know about bringing back alien goodies, responsible for the outbreak? Or,* she shuddered, *is this payback for the alien's site robbery? Would the aliens have been so vicious as to completely wipe the human race from the universal picture?* Would she, if she were in the aliens' shoes? *Better walk away from that thought.*

Next, what's with the crocodile dinosaurs? What should we call them? Hmm, crodines, or crocodillas sounds good. What happened to them and why didn't whatever happened to them, happen to the other animals on the planet? Selected breeding? Someone been tinkering around with Mother Nature's DNA codes? Is another related viral outbreak responsible for this accelerated evolution? How many other animals, plants, fish, insects, or bacteria have been infected or altered that we don't know about yet?

These and many other thoughts kept rattling through Christine's head. Finally, exhaustion took over and Christine fell into a restless, dream-filled sleep only to be awakened by the gentle contact of Gary's hand on her cheek.

"Hi there, Sleeping Beauty. Sun's coming up. Want to check out these creatures?" Gary said as he sat down next to her. "Next shuttle will be here early this afternoon for our transfer to another site. However, as much as I enjoy your company, I think it's best for you to shuttle back to the *Leapfrog*. No telling what we'll encounter on the next site, and you'd just be a liability if the bad stuff hits the fan." Gary sighed and added, "Again."

Christine smiled. "No argument from me. The sooner I'm out of here the better. Hmm, I smell something cooking, and I'm famished."

Taking Christine by the hand, Gary led her to the campfire for a gourmet meal consisting of grilled dinosaur meat, some kind of stewed roots, and coffee.

Once the sun broke the horizon, Gary, along with four soldiers with rifles, took Christine to the nearest beast, which was only fifty feet from the perimeter.

"Oh, my God!" a stunned Christine exclaimed. "These are even bigger than I thought. Your headset camera didn't do them justice." Remembering her own headset and camera, Christine flipped the "On" switch to "hot" so her images could be uploaded to the *Leapfrog*. "You getting this, *Leapfrog*?"

she asked.

"*Leapfrog*'s medical is online, and we're getting it all right. Doctor Perkin, make sure you get all the measurements before you start cutting."

Christine sighed and put her laser scalpel back in the medical bag; then she took out the measuring instrument, started at the tail, and worked forward. After about fifteen minutes, Gary gave up on her and went about checking into the camp's routine. He called a replacement over and gave the other guards explicit instructions to stay alert for subtle shifts in water currents. Anything with that big a mass must push a lot of water around when it swims. *If in doubt, use grenades*, was the plan of the day.

Gary was outside the shuttle checking the downloaded photo reconnaissance pictures of the proposed new site when he heard Christine scream. Grabbing his rifle, he made a dash over to her location while ordering the remaining perimeter guards to keep their posts and continue their lookouts.

As he scrambled over the last dune, Gary saw all four guards at shoulder arms, pointing at various bearings on the lake. He would have heard the rifles firing because all rifles had their silencers lowered on the barrels.

Christine was standing over the beast's head with what looked like a small white pillow in her hands. Her hands were visibly shaking and she stuttered, "Th- . . . th . . . this brain is huge!"

"What? Did it bite you?" Gary held his rifle waist level as he walked around her.

Christine finally regained her composure, rolled her eyes, and sarcastically said, "No! Brains don't bite."

Gary looked over at the other five guards and asked, "What?"

They all shrugged and the tallest said, "Dunno. She screamed and scared the bejesus out of us."

Gary turned back to Christine. "You screamed bloody murder because it has a big brain?"

Christine, feeling a little embarrassment for inadvertently being so melodramatic, defensively replied, "Look at this! This would make anyone familiar with pathology scream. It's absolutely huge, way out of proportion to the size of its host body." Taking a step closer to Gary, she held up the brain for his observation. "Look at the gigantic frontal lobes and the beginning of wrinkles. When this thing gets a super-charge boost from the wrinkling, I wouldn't be surprised if it picks up telepathy for communication. Where else is all that capacity going? Also, I wouldn't be too surprised to see them using their claws as hands. The fifth claw appendix is offset, allowing the creature to grasp, which means tool usage."

Obviously receiving vocal inputs from *Leapfrog,* she muttered something in return and rushed over to her medical bag to rummage out a scale. As she continued to talk excitedly to her counterparts on the *Leapfrog,* Gary strode over to the guards.

"Don't worry; she scared the shit out of the whole camp. More the reason to get the hell out of here pronto before these walking teeth creatures wise up." They all nodded vigorously.

Christine left the brain on the scale and walked over to Gary and the guards. "Bad news, I'm afraid. These creatures must have evolved extremely fast, and their brain mass is equivalent to three point seven percent of their estimated body mass." Not getting the expected response from the men, she added, "We run about two percent."

That did it. All six men instantly deflated with sagging shoulders. Gary responded, "Terrific, just terrific," then turned to a young corporal and said, "Pass the word around. Leave nothing behind, absolutely nothing. Police the area thoroughly and pick up everything that has any semblance of technology. We need to leave this area completely sterile. Anything they find and recover may take them one step closer to our technology."

"Aye, sir." The sergeant scurried off to pass the word.

Christine walked back to the fallen beast and started to collect her instruments. Calling over her shoulder, she said, "I'm about through with this one, since the body shot pulverized his internal organs."

"Well, we've got plenty to choose from," Gary replied while looking at all the dead beasts littering the beach. "Let's check out this big one over to the right that's completely out of the water. Looks like most of its head is gone, so the body should be okay." Gary started walking over to the fallen beast, followed by five crestfallen soldiers.

"This one's perfect," commented Christine as she extracted her laser scalpel. "Uh, is this a safe spot?"

This time Gary got the chance to roll his eyes. "No! I don't think anywhere on this godforsaken planet can be considered safe."

Gary walked to the water's edge. "Lob three grenades, here, here, and here, and make the range thirty meters from shore." He pointed out bearings starting to the right, working left.

As the grenades were being thrown, Gary and the others

went shoulder arms in anticipation. *Whump! Whump! Whump!* The grenades threw ten-meter geysers of water in the air, but no attacks or rapid swirling water currents followed.

"I guess that means they're learning," Gary despondently said.

Bzzzz, Christine's powerful laser scalpel made short work of opening the beast's chest cavity. The accompanying smell did not resemble the campfire's aroma of sizzling steaks. The smell was more like burning hair.

Christine, not wanting to stay in her location any longer than possible, hastily examined each organ and tossed them into an opened body bag. She stopped at the creature's heart and carefully studied, measured, and weighed the organ. She engaged in some technical communication with her team on the *Leapfrog,* placed the heart on the beast's flat shoulder, and deftly sliced it in two pieces. Picking up the pieces, she spoke in a loud voice for all to hear, "Four-chambered heart, so they are warm-blooded."

Looking at Gary, she continued, "This is not good news for us. It means they may be able to thrive in cooler temperatures, unlike their predecessors who could only cope in tropical environments. Doesn't look like it can yet make it in a freezing climate, but this little fuzz growing between the scaly flesh means he's working on it. And look at this," she went on while cutting along the neck with her scalpel. "These lungs are enormous. They have about five times the alveolar sacs we have, and I'm betting the hemoglobin is loaded with bicarbonate ions." Seeing the puzzled look on Gary's face, she added, "Bicarbonate ions accumulate the oxygen, thus allowing a timed or regulated release of oxygen molecules."

Gary nodded as if he understood what she had said, hoping she would not quiz him. "So what's the bottom line? How long can they hold their breath?"

Christine thought carefully before answering, "Hard to tell without further studies, but I think it would be safe to say two hours active, eight to ten inactive."

"Whew," Gary muttered. "We're really outclassed here, aren't we?"

"Yes, by far, and I suspect the gap is still widening with each generation."

As she was cleaning her tools, Christine said, "The reproductive system is still a mystery. Live birth or not? I suspect that they're still in the egg-laying phase, which would not encumber the parent with maturing young in their bodies."

Gary interrupted, "I thought all mammals, and they would fall into that group because of the four-chambered heart, had live birth."

"No, the duckbill platypus and the spiny anteater are mammals that lay eggs rather than give live birth; all mammals must be able to feed their young. Anyway, these two samples must be males." Closing up her medical bay, Christine concluded her summarization of the field autopsy. "We are way over our heads on this one, and it will take some time to catch up. All I really know is that we're going to definitely have to think outside the box from now on."

Kim, who had been monitoring the conversation, jumped in. "*Leapfrog* here. I agree. Who knows how many other animals are affected in one way or another. By the way, the lab has isolated a strange virus found in the last tissue sample sent up, and we expect to develop some form of immunization within a few days. I think that should be sufficient even with a short germination period. The virus unquestionably has designer engineering signatures, which points to DNA sabotage. I just pray that the aliens who sent us out on our ill-fated adventure didn't bring their revenge to Earth. Responsibility for the demise of the human race is more than any of us could bear."

Gary flipped his headset's *transmit* button on. "Isn't ten thousand years a little too long for a virus to be passed on?"

Christine answered through her headset also so all could hear. "Not necessarily. If designed properly, a virus could be passed on from one generation to the next. Each time the egg was fertilized, the virus could put a little zap into its DNA or RNA coding—which I'm beginning to think is what happened here on Earth. There is some opposing link between the new crocodiles and Neanderthals that is in play. We just don't know what or how at this point. I highly suspect foul play that somehow included an innocent bystander, the crocodile. Our knowledge of DNA transcribing and alterations was peaking when we departed, but we were still in the dark when it came to the trigger mechanism for evolutionary jumps. History is packed with recorded instances where one particular species would be dormant for eons, then out of the blue they take a giant leap forward."

Kim came back online. "Just got another report from the lab. It appears the new form of humans, which look like Neanderthals, has definitely descended from our genetic code. This makes it similar to the link between Neanderthal and Homo erectus. If this is the case, then a disastrous intervention occurred in the human evolutionary cycle that would

cause such a rapid reversal. Also, those new dinosaur creatures are positively descendants of our old crocodiles. That's
a couple of big pieces of our puzzle that just fell into place.
Now all we need to do is figure out what to do about it."

Meanwhile, across the lake and out of sight of the invading
islanders, a medium-sized crocodile swam up on a deserted
beach with a prize in her mouth. The torso of a hapless Smitty
was dropped on the sand. The creature could focus better out
of water and wanted to study her specimen in detail. With a
razor-sharp claw nail, she cut open his chest cavity and pulled
all the organs out. Even inside his body, he retained his foul
chemical smell, but hidden in that odor was the sweet smell
of blood. Her prize did have some edible blood in it after all.
He had just enough blood to tantalize, but not quite enough
to digest. Flipping the body over, a shiny object fell out of
what appeared to be some sort of material that all the other
two-legged food sources wore. Curiosity now controlling, she
shredded the remaining material in search of other goodies.

Some sort of rope wrapped around the torso seemed interesting. It had a pouch with a hard object inside. The pouch
was a little more difficult to cut, but once sliced through, a
strange object fell out that had a small hole at the end. Thinking it too complicated to investigate further at the moment,
she went back to her shiny object. Picking it up, she examined
it while probing, and a white light jumped out at her enough
to jump two meters straight in the air.

Curiosity overwhelmed the desire to flee, and she picked

up the strange light source and probed it again until the light went back off. On, off, on, off, the creature was thrilled with its find and started calling her friends so they could witness the magic light. Making sure she got everyone's attention, she started clucking then resorted to howling.

Across the lake, everyone in the shuttle camp could hear the familiar clucking, then an eerie howl. Shortly afterward a loud boom sounded, the unmistakable sound of a firearm.

Scoffield and Gary were going over the reconnaissance photos when the howling began, paused, and was followed by a gunshot. They were looking at each other when Scoffield said, "Should we go get it?"

Gary thought for a minute. "No way. One of those crocs must have the gun, and all it needs to do is jump in the water. We don't even have a boat, much less a submarine to retrieve it. Let's just hope the doc's wrong about her brain assessment."

About fifteen meters away, sitting on her medical trunk, Christine turned white. *This is the beginning of the end for us. We just leapfrogged the crocodiles.*

CHAPTER 20

GARY CALLED UP THE *LEAPFROG* and gave Kim the bad news. There was a pause before Kim replied, "What else did Smitty have on him?"

"Standard issue protective clothing, a helmet, a knife, a flashlight, and a sidearm with lots of ammunition," Gary answered.

"I'm conferring with my staff; please hold on a sec." Kim came back after five excruciating minutes. "We're going to nuke the lake as soon as you're clear, and we're talking megatons here. We decided we can't allow that technology to fall into the hands of an enemy who is potentially more intelligent than we are. We're putting the bomb together as we speak, and it should be ready by the time you leave. We figure it's only a hop, skip, and a jump before they're into manufacturing duplicates. In the future, we'll need to take more care in selecting our landing sites."

Outside the box! Gary reminded himself. "Roger on that. You decide when we will be clear of blast effect for the launch. When's the next shuttle due?"

"Within the hour," Kim replied. "The next shuttle will be our only personnel carrier and will remain with you on the second site until water replenishment is complete. Uh, Gary, please don't lose it."

Before Gary could think of something cute to say, Kim continued, "Eventually, we're going to need to know more about these new crocs, and the only way to do it is to penetrate their habitat. We need to know their social hierarchy, superstitions, religions, and if there's a structure established for education. That's not on today's or tomorrow's plate, but for planning purposes you might rattle that one around. I really hate to dump it on your lap, but we'll need to know all this if we're to survive."

"Robots," was all Gary could think to say.

"Robots? Ah, of course. I'll have the structural lab start to work on some submersible remote-controlled vehicles. Have any particular specs off the top of your head?"

Gary thought for a few seconds. "Yeah, relay to engineering that we'll need them small, quiet, good camera resolution, and with light enhancement, a complex, full spectrum audio recorder, a couple of small pickup arms, stowage device and, most importantly, a very powerful self-destruction device. Also, right away we'll be needing some sort of underwater remote patrols and some underwater mines integrated with nets. We barely made it through the last rush attempt. The only thing that saved our bacon was the shuttle's landing that got them distracted."

"That should keep engineering busy—" Kim stopped mid-sentence. "Hold on a sec. . . Shit! Now we've got a raving lunatic scientist trying to annihilate the entire Earth. I have to run. Will talk to you soon. And your shuttle's leaving the docks now; send up the tanker soon. *Leapfrog* out."

Gary and Christine looked at each other wondering what exactly all that meant.

"We're ready," Scoffield transmitted over the headset to Gary. "Send over the doc and her gear, and we'll send her on her way."

Christine had been monitoring the frequency also and sauntered over to Gary. "I'm having second thoughts about abandoning the team," she said in a quiet voice. *What am I doing?* she thought.

For the last few hours, Christine had been contemplating the status of her life, its direction and future. The meaning of her life, her goals, and a new feeling had overwhelming contradictions. Her entire life had been centered around her profession and its future, secure, safe, and satisfying—at least until now. Now, mixed emotions were interfering with her projected role. Life to Christine was now much more tenuous and filled with uncertainty. Second chances, lost opportunities were a thing of the past. Christine was a new woman. The frontier spirit had her hooked, and she did not want to sit idly by on an orbiting spaceship observing the action. She wanted a piece of it, and she was very much in love. The new Christine was *not* going to be passive and let another opportunity pass by.

Gary placed his hands on his hips and glowered down at her. "No! Absolutely, positively, no! You will be useless to us. Furthermore, you may get in our way and be accidentally shot. That, I can do without."

Christine, not taking kindly to being called "useless," stood her ground and countered, "Useless? Who the hell are you to call me useless? I am a fully trained physician specializing in trauma care. I have all the medical support equipment right here . . ." Turning around, she pointed at the medical chest being loaded into the shuttle. ". . . to function as a complete emergency medical care unit. You need me more than you think. Besides, if push comes to shove, the military fully qualified me with small arms. I won't be your best shooter, but I can empty clips in the right direction."

Without hesitation, Christine stepped forward, grabbed Gary by his collar, and pulled his head down to hers. Helmet to helmet, visors up, nose to nose, Christine continued in a low, confidential voice, "Listen, buster, this is your first and last shot here. I'm taking a big risk in opening up to you, but I feel we don't have a whole lot of time left to go through another courtship. Bottom line, I've fallen in love with you and will do anything to be with you. If you don't feel anything for me, just say so and I'll fade to smoke and leave you alone. So, what's it going to be? Am I staying, or am I gone?"

Gary was flabbergasted. Never had he been approached so daringly and suddenly. Shocking, but nevertheless exciting, the mutual feeling burst to the surface and overwhelmed him. "Please . . . don't go. Y-yes, I love you too. I just don't want anything bad to happen to you, that's all."

Christine let her breath go, but continued to hold his collar in a firm grip, still helmet to helmet, nose to nose, eye to eye. Kim, from *Leapfrog* control, broke in. "Ah, nice soap opera, kids, but do you realize you've been 'hot mike' on all frequencies?" Cheering and hoots could be heard in the *Leapfrog*'s background radio reception.

Simultaneously looking left and right with their helmets still together, Christine and Gary saw everyone was smiling and had stopped what they were doing to observe the budding romance. Helmets still together and now looking at each other, Gary whispered, "Shit."

"Shit," Christine replied as Gary bent down and kissed her softly on waiting lips.

The *"whoyahs"* shattered the silence.

CHAPTER 21

WITHOUT A WORD BEING SAID, Christine's medical trunk was removed from the shuttle and placed in a deep foxhole in preparation for the upcoming blast. Before the cargo door was closed, Gary stepped in and removed the spare rifle, ammunition pouch, and sidearm belt. Walking back to Christine, he said, "You sure?"

"Damn right, I'm sure." Christine professionally field checked the weapons and loaded the clips in the rifle and pistol. "Point toward the hole you're planning to hunker down in; I'll be nearby and meet you there when you finish your rounds."

Gary pointed to the hole they were in before and said, "The same one will do just fine. While you're waiting for me, make sure you're checked out on the rifle scope's features. It has infrared, light augmentation, and radar imaging. Radar imaging is the most useful when the sand kicks up. I'll be along in about five minutes."

While Christine walked over to the foxhole, she could not help but noticing that something had changed. The men of the detachment were looking at her differently. They were still smiling, but they were not giving her the once-over as they had before. It was as if Gary's and her little unintended proclamation of love had changed everything. They were considered now as a couple and not open targets for potential mating; it was almost as if they had just been married, barring official sanctions.

The five-minute warning was announced and those not already in their holes scurried for safety. Gary jumped in the hole, gave Christine a quick peck on the cheek and lowered her face mask. Checking her over, he noticed her suit was completely closed, and her gloves were on.

This blast was as intense as the last, but to Christine it was only an inconvenience as she cuddled up next to her man. Gary kept constant vigil, expecting the crocs to make a rush, but the launch and recovery were uneventful. Little did they know that the majority of the crocs were on the other side of the lake.

The creatures were arguing and fighting over the new possession that had the power of life and death. Confusion reigned over how such a small device could inflict so much damage. Consensus was that it must be the magic noise that was responsible.

The finder had long ago been pushed aside as her mate and other males took over her prized possession. Unnoticed, she sauntered over to the edge of the beach where the forest began and in earnest dug up her primary prize, the small shiny light maker. Looking over her large tapered shoulders to make sure she had remained unnoticed, she darted into the thick wood and started her long journey to the faraway lake that was home to her parents. She decided that the best course of action was to show the magic light maker to her father, for he was much wiser than the big brute who owned her and subsequently claimed mating rights.

Setting a pace that she could maintain for at least a day, she inadvertently crossed a pack of the two-legged food source. They were still screaming and running about in panic when she cleared the top of a hill at forty kilometers per hour. She noticed a boom and bright glow behind her as another fire bird landed.

———

Kim motioned to the armed guards to follow her as she walked through the entrance of the structural lab. Five technicians were closing the hatch to what looked like a miniature shuttle with small stubby wings, but minus thrusters. Dr. Jack Mitchell looked up and waved her over.

Dr. Mitchell was tall and lean, and he had a permanently hollow-looking face. Kim always imagined him as a perpetually starving refugee. The staff who worked for him called him "Dr. Death" behind his back.

"Over here, Commander. As you can see, we're finishing up and will have her in the docking bay shortly." Not waiting for Kim to reply, he continued, "Yield set at eighty megatons. That's a large, deep lake, and in order to build up to targeted 50,000 PSI with thirty percent vaporization, we had to bump the power up some."

"I thought we agreed on 20,000 PSI. Why the overkill and subsequent excess fallout?" Kim fired back with irritation in her voice.

With a smirk, Mitchell replied, "We figured there might

be underwater caverns that could dampen out the pressure."

"Is that right? Who is included in your 'we'?" Kim looked at the associates while they silently shook their heads in the negative. "So this was your decision alone, and you more than doubled the tonnage without consulting my staff?"

Mitchell glowered at his associates, then answered, "I did the most prudent thing considering the ferocity of these beasts."

Kim put her hands on her hips and sighed. "No, that was not prudent; it was malicious. This is still Earth, our home, that we must return to. Your calculations are off. Any freshman physicist is aware that the compressibility of water is minimal, and with your calculations of thirty percent vaporization, your pressure increase is even higher."

Kim waited for a response, but all she could get from Mitchell was a greener face. "Okay, you're fired." Turning to the guards, she said, "Remove this man, revoke his clearance, and have administration start monitoring his location." On the *Leapfrog* all personnel positions were monitored by small electrical devices embedded in their identification cards. Anyone roaming about without the proper identification or in a restricted area where he or she did not have sufficient clearance was flagged by the hallway computer monitors. Bells and whistles followed.

"As the guards stepped forward, Mitchell shouted, "I demand a hearing. You have no right to remove me. I am the director and department head of this division."

"You just had your hearing, and I have all the authority I need. Now report to administration for your new assignment before I change my mind and have you placed in the brig where you belong." Kim's eyes burned laser beams through Mitchell as he turned and followed the guards.

When the door slid shut behind Mitchell, Kim asked the remaining group, "Is there any way to tune this down and still make delivery schedule?"

"No, ma'am," a prematurely bald scientist, with the name Evans stenciled on his white coat, replied.

Obviously he was well respected, for the others waited for him to continue. "No way can we power down this baby without taking it apart and starting all over again. Ahem, we all tried to talk Dr. Mitchell out of this, but he insisted he was following specs. I decided to go to you directly to try to stop it."

"Bill Evans, is it?" He nodded as Kim stepped forward and shook his hand. "Thanks for sending me the heads-up. I don't know what Mitchell had in mind, but he has no right to increase the power like this just for the hell of it."

"I think something snapped in him when he saw the video of the soldier being bitten in two," said another scientist to Bill's left.

Kim stood looking down on the deadly projectile and asked, "Besides the fallout, what's the downside of using this much power?"

Bill answered, "Our unshielded shuttle on Earth should be over one thousand kilometers away at least to avoid EMP, electronic magnetic pulse, damage. I recommend they be at least that upwind distance and safely on the ground."

Kim interrupted, "Isn't EMP damage most intense at higher altitude detonations? This one will be right on the deck to wipe out that lake and any crocs that may have stolen our technology."

Bill shrugged. "Granted, but I'm talking worst case scenario here. All of our circuits are old, and the circuitry insulation is brittle and falls apart with minor flexing. If this bad boy decides to pop prematurely and makes a high air-burst, the onboard shuttle's computers will get cooked. I don't think we have anyone qualified to manually fly the shuttles when the computer rolls over and dies."

"Damn! Why do things continually get bad instead of better?" Kim sputtered.

Bill just smiled. "Uh, remember we're not spring chick-ens anymore ourselves. We spend most of our time spraying insulation goop all over our circuits just to keep them from shorting out and starting fires. Commander, electrically this ship's a mess and in dire need of complete rejuvenation."

Kim crossed her arms and leaned on the nuclear projec-tile. "Okay, let's have it. Where are we going with this?"

"Ma'am, we need to get this decrepit bucket of bolts into a permanent orbit, grab our families, and bail. Every time the side thrusters kick in to change orbits, sparks fly, fires start, and we all panic in this shop. Granted, we got a reprieve on oxidation damage due to our vacuum state while we were in cryo-sleep, but time still took its toll."

Bill sighed and leaned on the monster nuclear bomb next to Kim. "Timeline? One more orbit adjustment, and we've got a month max before we lose it. Everything we touch breaks; everything we fix breaks again, and so does the part next to it; the cycle continually gets worse. It's like a tar baby and we're up to our elbows and knees as we speak."

"You are simply a ray of sunshine, Bill," said Kim, cringing.

"I know, I know, you didn't mean to be doom and gloom negative," Kim said, relenting a little. "And I actually appreciate your candor, but we're doing everything we can to find out what happened before we send our dependents down there to become crocodile chum."

Another scientist sauntered over to the killer bomb and leaned against it as if in defiance of the horrible carnage it would soon create.

Tom Haggard, who had been quiet up to this point, jumped in. "Other than the fallout downsides include possible earthquake antagonism, prompt ionizing radiation, minor weather alterations, and loss of innocent life. Jury's still out on that one though. We've talked about this before when Dr. Mitchell was playing 'Dr. Death,' and while we don't think the big blast is a very good idea, it's better to let it go as it is now, instead of waiting for our technology to escape."

Kim straightened and asked, "Is that the consensus?" All reluctantly nodded in the affirmative.

"Okay, then, finish launch preparation. Bill, you are now in charge of this division, and I'll need an update on the underwater robotic probes as soon as you can spec it out. Thanks again, all of you, for doing a splendid job of keeping this can together."

She shook hands with the men, then turned around and walked out of the technical shop.

As the door slid shut, Bill openly observed, "Yeah, and she's a fox, too."

CHAPTER 22

"Eighty megatons! Holy shit, somebody must be mighty pissed off at this lake," Gary replied to Kim's transmission.

The last shuttle arrived without incident or interruptions from the lake's host. The water crew had finished topping off the personnel shuttle's smaller water tank, and the perimeter defenses were being stowed. Under a protective guard, a team of soldiers ran a metal detector over the entire campsite looking for misplaced objects. Nothing but bodily waste was to be left behind even though the ground would soon be glass.

"It's a mistake, and it's my ultimate responsibility, but in order to drop the power, we'll have to wait another eighteen hours, and we don't feel that's prudent, given what we lost and the crocs' possible intelligence level," Kim replied.

"Well, as long as we're upwind, on the ground, and at least nine hundred kilometers away we should be okay, but please let us establish a landing before you send the mother of all bombs down. I'd hate to have to be in the middle of a diversion when she blows."

"Well, I don't mean to rush you, but our launch window just slipped by and she's on her way now—"

Kim was interrupted by Gary's transmission. "What! She's already been launched?" The news stopped and dropped the jaws of all within hearing range.

"Sorry. I should have told you, but we're back in geostationary orbit, and the projectile won't be entering the atmosphere for another five hours. That should give you sufficient time, and if all else fails, we can alter the reentry point and self destruct her." Kim started wondering why they were calling the horrendous bomb "her" when a man was responsible for overbuilding the thermonuclear horror.

Gary flipped the transmit button on his helmet to "All" and shouted, "Time's up! Wrap up what you're doing and get aboard. That goes for everyone, sweepers too because there'll be nothing left to sweep in a few hours. We've got an eighty-megaton blast heading this way, and we need to be gone ASAP." Gary sent runners out to scout for stragglers. He was amazed by how fast they could run when properly motivated.

One of the younger troops settling in next to Christine asked, "Doc, is eighty megatons big?"

Christine watched his face go white as she said, "Bigger than any bomb ever dropped, bigger than the combined total of all the bombs ever dropped, and big enough to completely vaporize this lake."

Sheepishly he asked, "Is that very smart?"

Christine looked over at him and smilingly said, "Absolutely not, but it's about par so far." Seeing his puzzled look, she added, "None of us are very smart anymore, and we need to get used to it."

Nodding, he replied, "Yeah, I can relate to that."

From a safe distance, dozens of eyes watched the firebird blow sand and fly straight up. Once the noise abated, they made their way to the aliens' camp to look for more forgotten treasures. After accidentally killing one of themselves with the noise maker, they figured it wasn't the noise that killed but the missing head of the expended, hollow, chewable shell left behind. Now all they had to do was figure out how it happened, make others, or get more.

Still clutching the light stick, the female ran across a two-legged food source nest. Hunger was setting in and she began stalking. She picked a large male to harvest and plotted her attack, sneaking from one large bush to another until she reached the clearing.

Silently, she lay behind the bushes waiting for the opportunity to strike. She did not have to wait long, for her food turned his back to her and started walking away. Rushing, she approached the raised sticks and leaped right over them. Landing inside the perimeter, she snatched the startled, frightened male in her jaws and continued right through the camp and over the top of the raised sticks on the other side.

The prey stopped struggling when she closed her jaws down until the crunching sound began. Careful not to bite the prey in two and lose part of it, she ran back into the bushes before she severed the prey's head and legs. Picking up the amputated limbs, she stuffed them in her mouth, after checking to see that she did not also swallow her prize. Stretching her neck to assist in swallowing the food, she continued on the journey to her old home.

She had just set her pace when she heard a thunderclap, but there were no clouds in the twilight skies. Fearing that perhaps her mate was behind her and in pursuit with the noise toy, she accelerated, running through the forest at about fifty-five kilometers per hour and barreling through the thickets like a raging elephant. Meanwhile the departing shuttle passed overhead unseen, easily slipping through the speed of sound for a destination lake much farther away than her home. One more ridge to go and she would be back in her old stomping grounds. The shuttle had a much longer trip but would arrive at the same time.

CHAPTER 23

USING THE JOYSTICK ON THE side of his console, Gary guided the descending shuttle for an observation lap around the lake. Although Gary "piloted" the shuttle, he did not really control it. In reality, the joystick was nothing more than a modest request to the computer for flight deviations. Once the request went outside the autopilot's parameters, the onboard computers took over and returned to the programmable flight plan.

Each seat in the shuttle also contained individual monitors that permitted the occupant to zoom and focus on different points of interest. Infrared filters were available and in use by most of the soldiers. Gary, however, was more interested in the pre-selected landing zone. Obviously a river basin for seasonal rains, the delta was flat with low growth and one hundred and eighty degrees exposure to the lake. In Gary's mind, this reduced viable threats from the crocs by half. The shuttle defense crew had ample infrared and night enhancement aids, but their underwater defenses were limited.

Leapfrog was restricted in its meteorological capabilities and depended mostly on bird's eye viewing, but someone somewhere on the shuttle, had promised no rain for at least seventy-two hours. The shuttle crew did not need a monsoon storm to surprise and wash them away. Satisfied that the pre-selected area was adequate and not teeming with some kind of monster jamboree, Gary centered his crosshairs on the optimum spot and selected "Land." The shuttle's computer resumed control and configured itself for final approach.

While on "Final," Gary briefed the landing plan. First, a skeletal perimeter defense was to be established; second, the inflatable boats would be used to create a two-layered net-type minefield in the water, although the volunteers for the mine-field duty were less than thrilled to set out on the lake in small rubber boats. Once the preliminary defenses were set up, the restricted laser towers would be raised and the water crew would start to work. All, of course, was to take place while a thermo-nuclear holocaust took place at their point of departure.

Literally flying over the ridge, the female made a beeline for the lake's beach. Once submerged, she lay still while calling her clan for an emergency meeting. The sun was fully set when all two hundred and seventy-eight members of her family came to her. Now standing ten meters from the water's edge, she watched as her clan came to shore and formed a semicircle around her, chattering and complaining about the roust.

Finally, the tribal chief, her father, arrived and stood in front of her. Excitedly, she explained her light magic and the firebird creatures. She held the light stick high over her head for all to see and, as expected, her father demanded a dem-onstration. While she fumbled for the unfamiliar switch to turn it on, the pack grew restless, some even returning to the deeper water.

Then the sky lit up brilliantly white, temporarily but painfully blinding all the semi-nocturnal creatures. Stunned, they looked around trying to get their vision back when the Earth started shaking, making the lake's frothing water appear to be boiling. Not knowing which way to run, the creatures stood frozen in place until the shock wave, albeit buffered by two large ridges, reached them and tumbled them end over end. Some broke their necks, some snapped their tails while tumbling, ensuring a slow death by starvation, and others broke arms and legs. The other ninety percent of the beasts were pissed and simultaneously tried to tear this female sorcerer apart. She did not stand a chance of fending them off, and they ripped her to shreds before she could regain her footing.

The flashlight tumbled on the beach and was carefully avoided. The deceased female's father declared the beach forbidden territory, and anyone seen on the beach, much less tinkering with the light magic, was to be killed at once. As they retreated back to the safety of the depths, some of the juvenile beasts started making their own plans.

CHAPTER 24

BILL EVANS RELUCTANTLY WALKED THROUGH the open door to the bridge and apprehensively looked around until he spotted Kim seated in front of her console. He walked past more than a dozen people, a few of them looking up with a smile or nod. Kim was obviously in deep thought while giving the ship's computer verbal programming.

Bill waited patiently for a few minutes until Kim finished her programming. *Amazing!* he thought as he inadvertently eavesdropped. *She's verbally programming without any aids. Wow! I didn't know anyone who could do that, at least reliably.*

Kim had paused for thought when Bill said, "Ahem, sorry to bother you."

Kim swiveled in her chair with a beaming smile. "Oh, it's you. I've been hoping you could make it here, but I really didn't expect you so soon. I hope you have some good news." She slumped and added, "I guess you saw our 'bad boy' do its thing. What a shock wave. It must have extended over a hundred kilometers. Have a seat." She pointed to one of five chairs surrounding her console.

Bill settled in and said, "It was a bad boy, all right. It's going to take months for the atmosphere to rid itself of all the debris it kicked up, but that's not why I came. Actually, I do have some good news: thanks to our master welder and metalsmith, we have the fourth shuttle up and ready, but . . ." Bill paused, ". . . it won't be able to handle Earth's reentry burn because we lost the upper forward thermal heat shields."

Kim sat up straight. "Even so, that is great news; now we can start looking at satellites for possible explanations about what happened on Earth." Furrowing her brow in concentration, she added, "Will the ship be spaceworthy enough to handle a long mission, like a lunar roundtrip?"

"No problem there. As a matter of fact we can make a few permanent modifications to increase the ship's endurance." As if taking the cue from Kim, he too wrinkled his brows in thought. "We can beef up the fuel, oxygen, and other life support accommodations, but we'll lose seating capacity; I'd say by half. To be on the conservative side, say, a maximum of seventeen." Anticipating Kim's next question Bill said, "As far as a timeline, I'd say no more than forty-eight hours if we work twelve-hour shifts twenty-four hours a day straight through."

"Absolutely marvelous! I'll set that shuttle up as a lunar scout party, with one tanker in a low elliptical orbit for home base reconnaissance and the other a personnel carrier for satellite exploration."

Bill queried, "And the fourth, the tanker?"

"Rescue, of course. Something's bound to go wrong."

Bill echoed, "of course," and turned to walk away.

"Bill," Kim said softly.

"Yes—"

Kim stopped him by raising her hand. "Please don't say 'ma'am.' It makes me feel so old." Smiling, she added, "Naturally, I don't consider being over ten thousand years old,

old." Kim waved him over to sit back down.

Bill was feeling giddy. *Maybe she likes nerds?*

Swinging around in her swivel chair, Kim crossed her legs and said, "It's been so hectic around here just trying to stay alive that I've overlooked one of my most important duties. Getting to know my crew. Bill, we've got a few minutes. Why don't you tell me about yourself."

Breathe, breathe deep, and don't stutter.

———

On the far horizon, the darkening sky flashed white like a huge lightning bolt emanating upward from the Earth. A few seconds later, the ground started rumbling as if an earthquake approached its zenith, then changed its mind and retired back to the inner Earth. Some soldiers scrambled for safety in fear of an upcoming blast, while others stood their ground staring at the horizon. Gary, however, took off for the shuttle to check for possible EMP damage. Relieved that the computers and communications systems were still functional, Gary announced on the tactical radio that all was well and not to expect any blast effect since the atmosphere's compressibility absorbed and dampened wind damage. He also gave them a heads-up that the next water shuttle was due within thirty minutes and, above all else, that they should keep an eye out for the crocs.

CHAPTER 25

THE MINOR EARTHQUAKE DID MORE than just shake the ground. Several crocodile creatures were still on the edge of sleep when the Earth's shudder shook them awake. Rising to the surface for curiosity's sake, they found a most unusual visitor on the river's delta: a tent with two-legged food beings running about. The crocs were about three hundred meters away and approaching cautiously when two of the most forward clan members literally blew up and sank to the bottom of the lake in a flowing trail of blood. Hastily submerging, the remaining crocs followed the descending bodies until they reached the bottom at a depth of thirty meters. Although the visibility was greatly reduced by all the blood and silt that was kicked up, it was clear to all that something very big and bad had taken a huge bite out of their heads. The eldest croc chirped out an urgent call for a clan meeting and took off for the underwater cavern. The younger crocs lingered a little longer trying to put the puzzle together.

A baffling question continued to haunt them: how could those two-legged beings strike from so far out? The wounds from their fallen clan members did not look like bite marks that they had seen before. Surrendering to the repeated gathering calls, the younger ones, however hungry, made their way to the underwater cavern. The temptation to eat their fallen clan was nonexistent, for the younger members never ate other crocs, no matter how hungry they were.

Gary had his telescopic, night-enhanced visor down on his helmet and witnessed the two crocs exploding. The two soldiers stood up from their prone positions and slid the silencer sleeves down on their smoking fifty calibers. "Nice shooting. That should keep them off our backs for a few minutes," Gary commented as he scanned the surrounding water.

Scoffield, who was also checking out the surrounding water, said, "Sir, we have the claymores laid out, but we need to know whether or not you want to go mechanical or enable the electronic identification."

Gary thought for a minute before answering. "Go mechanical. We don't want these crocs running off with one of us again." Looking over at the parked shuttle, he added, "Button up the shuttle; we have another tanker due in ten minutes."

As Scoffield walked off to carry out his orders, Gary flipped his headset microphone to "All" and transmitted: "We have the two incoming water shuttles, the first in ten minutes out; the second to follow after the first one departs. When we refill the second and send it on its way, we're out of here pronto on the personnel shuttle."

"*Whoyahs*" could be heard among the perimeter guards. "Dig in and keep a good eye out for mischievous crocs. It's dark and they're nocturnal." A collective sigh floated across camp.

CHAPTER 26

IT WAS DECIDED. THEY WOULD attack these newcomers, take them apart, and see how they managed to destroy heads so easily and from so far away.

Silently they slid through the dark waters, clucking occasionally to keep their formation tight. Approximately five hundred meters from shore, they were about to separate and start their flanking maneuver when the sky lit up again. Cautiously, they all rose to the surface to see what could possibly be the cause of all the light.

Descending from the sky was a huge sun roaring its way down to Earth. Fascinated, all the crocs held their positions.

Christine had just finished collecting her water, soil and atmosphere samples when Gary rushed up to her and blurted, "We need to dig in right now, honey. The shuttle's approaching its flare for VTOL and the rockets will kick in at any minute."

Christine took off after him, thinking she liked the sound of the word "honey." It had been a long time since someone had called her that, and it made her feel warm and fuzzy. At least until the overhead rocket motors kicked in.

CHAPTER 27

AWED AND STUNNED, THE ELDER crocodile and his entire clan watched the falling sun gently touch the ground. The bright light, along with the loud roar, ceased while the sandstorm quietly died out. The two-legged beings could be seen scrambling about as the mouth of the now-depleted sun gaped open to reveal its secrets.

Not a sun at all, but some kind of huge fire-breathing egg capable of flying and making light and lots of noise. For the first time in his life, the elder wanted a material possession, not another mate, not eggs and subsequent offspring, but a tantalizing and unfamiliar object. What bragging rights he would gain over his rivals. As he daydreamed of future glory and adulation, a huge splash erupted just centimeters from his head. Swiftly submerging, he heard and felt the thud as his neighbor lost the top of her head. He followed her sinking corpse and examined the massive wound. Not a bite at all. Something had struck her hard and whatever it was had barely missed him.

Anger rising from the loss of his favorite mate, the elder clucked the order to continue the attack.

"Major Hecker," Scoffield transmitted over his headset. "We got one, but I think we missed on the second. Looks like they've all submerged again. I estimate fifty to sixty crocs in all."

Sixty! Shit! Another assault underway. These crocs don't waste any time, Gary thought as he keyed his mike. "High alert! All personnel not directly involved in water recovery, go to your battle stations. Imminent attack expected."

Gary expected Christine to cuddle or cower next to him, and only stick her head up out of morbid curiosity, but was pleasantly surprised. She had her fifty field rifle stripped and cleaned, and she was reassembling the old but proven weapon.

Slapping a clip in the magazine and chambering a round, she looked up and saw him staring at her. "What? I told you I can carry my weight when it comes to weapons. As a matter of fact, I didn't see you cleaning the sand out of yours," she taunted.

"Yes ma'am," Gary countered as he started the field cleaning process.

CHAPTER 28

THE ELDER HAD JUST DUMPED some of his air ballast and sunk ten meters to the bottom of the lake to continue his trek inland along the bottom of the lake when he saw the light then felt the pressure from the blast of the egg thing. Cautiously rising for a quick peek, the elder popped up in time to see the egg rising on a tower of flames and noise. Immediately he submerged but was savagely knocked down two meters as an explosive round blew a large water hole from his subsiding ripples. Dizzy, disoriented, the elder sank back to the bottom and waited for the ache in his head to die down. Rousing himself out of his slump, he continued forward again but much faster. No telling if the one remaining egg would fly away or not before he had the chance to capture it.

Scoffield radioed, "We have twenty to thirty large infrared contacts circling our flank behind us on land. Looks like they're getting smarter."

How could they? pondered Gary. *We nuked the last site.* He radioed back to all, "Roger that. When the sea mines start going off, lob in as many grenades as you can before they surface."

Anxiety was at its peak when the elder became entangled in the invisible netting. Struggling to free himself, the elder was half blown out of the water by an exploding concussion mine. He died before he knew what hit him, but his death was not in vain. A gaping hole had been made in the two-legged trap. Angrily clucking and clicking, the others charged inland; some to become trapped in the same webbing, while others snaked through the holes in the nets.

CHAPTER 29

THE SAND WAS STARTING TO subside from the departing shuttle's blast when all hell broke loose. *Thump!* The first underwater mine went off, followed by others, and water geysers flared along the coastal waters. Gary fired off three flares to assist the night vision equipment as the first croc hit the beach in a full run. The gigantic croc was almost on top of a defending soldier when, *Bzzzt!* The laser defense beamed a killer red shaft of light straight through the tough scaled hide and carved a Z in its body. The flares temporarily blinded and startled other creatures, causing them to stop in their tracks or misdirect their rush. That was all the shooters on the other end of the fifty calibers needed. *Thud! Thud! Thud!* The creatures started coming apart with pieces flying left and right. The blood misted and slowly settled, causing a bloody fog to float over the beach.

The claymores started going off after the underwater mines but were much less effective. The upgraded armor piercing claymores were designed to shred the light, protective armor of a human soldier but merely seemed to bowl the crocs over only to have them rebound and continue their terrifying charge with blood-painted sides. Many of the defending soldiers were horrified and forgot to follow the lead guidance their scopes were providing. Instead they shot directly at the creatures, lagging them by a good half meter.

Christine surprised everyone, herself the most. Instead of merely emptying her clips blindly, she was methodical and religiously followed the directions her scope provided. After selecting each target and switching the gun control to "Auto," she reverently guided her gun to match the steering receptacle. *Blam!* Not even bothering to take the time to see what damage her round had done, she picked up the next threat and repeated her actions. On and on she went until her scope flashed pure red. Without raising her head, she released the empty clip, and slapped in a fresh one. Off she went again with hardly a hesitation. Gary, in a prone position next to her, found that he was having trouble keeping up with her and wished he had not called her "useless."

The laser's fire-control system computer was learning also. Instead of wasting its energy in the overkill Z cuts, it found that the victim's heart would stop faster if it decapitated the opponent. This required a third of the energy, which promoted the fire rate three times. *Zzzt, zzzt,* the heads really started rolling, just in time because the claymores and sea mines were depleted.

Fearlessly, the crocs charged despite their comrades falling in death. At the surge of the attack, one particularly hideous creature with a shredded left side made it to the perimeter, leaned forward, opened its mouth, and encompassed a soldier whole, but before it could bite down, *Zzzt,* his head was severed. The soldier, fully trapped in the creature's mouth, could not stop screaming. Another creature, which was directly in line behind the beheaded croc, paused to listen to the scream before he too had his head cut off.

168

The attack ended as quickly as it began. There were no retreats, no sneaking cowards, and no sheltered generals skulking back to where they had come from. They were all dead or dying. All that was left of the attackers was a handful of young creatures lurking and observing out of range.

Gary, followed closely by Christine, ran to a screaming dinosaur/croc head. It was the most bizarre experience Christine had ever experienced: a severed dinosaur head screaming with its mouth closed. Christine bent over and through her headset saw the soldier screaming in the creature's severed throat.

Scoffield saved the day when he came running up with a crowbar. Knocking teeth out until they could pry for leverage and also keep from cutting off fingers on the sharp teeth, they finally pried the screaming soldier out of the croc's mouth. Christine air-injected him with a quick-acting sedative and briefly examined him for cuts. Amazingly, the soldier only needed twelve stitches.

Scoffield had completed his perimeter patrol and came back to check up on the soldier. Smiling, he said to Christine, "Corporal 'Dickie' Dickson's new nickname is gonna be 'Deep Throat.' Fitting, huh?"

The other five soldiers got a good laugh but laughed even harder when a female soldier said, "See, I told you those damn things wouldn't swallow.

Christine blushed green.

With the perimeter defense remaining on station, Gary ordered the laser defense dismantled and stowed and the few remaining claymores be deactivated and collected. He had decided the lake was far too dangerous for water mine retrieval efforts, so he ordered the remaining mines be remotely detonated. Two crews performed the metal sweep, making sure that they did not leave any technology behind. Satisfied the grounds were sterile, Gary called them all onboard for a last-minute role call, then stepped inside and activated the launch sequence. Not one eye strayed off the monitors; as if they were expecting a massive croc rush before the rockets had a chance to kick in. The shuttle departed without incident and without leaving anything of technological value behind.

What was left behind was an entire pack of evolved dead crocodiles and memories. The young crocs would remember this day until they died and would be sure to pass the slaughter events on for years to come. Other eyes also witnessed the bloodbath. These were the devolved humanoids, and they were impressed indeed. So much so that from then on they considered the firebird creatures to be gods.

CHAPTER 30

RELIEVED THAT ALL FOUR SHUTTLES were safely tucked away in their docking stations, apparently in operational condition, Kim slumped to a lower level on her console recliner. She really needed some well deserved sleep, but stress induced insomnia relentlessly drove her on. Carl Manley, from Computer and Life Support, had just given her an update: the oxygen and water levels were currently in the green and would remain so for at least a week. She could concentrate on phases two and three: discovering what went wrong on Earth and finding a safe home site for *Leapfrog's* inhabitants.

It was amazing to Kim how fast the military unit disappeared when the shuttle door opened in the recovery bay. They seemed to evaporate right before the cameras' lenses, Christine and Gary included. Kim figured Christine and Gary had sneaked into Christine's private stateroom since Gary's shipboard accommodations were separated from the troops by only a thin curtain. She decided the mission debrief could wait a few more hours after all.

Meanwhile, Kim planned and launched two other shuttle missions: the first was the lower orbit reconnaissance for possible home site locations, which utilized one of the tankers. Now that they had some idea of what to expect on Earth, they could hopefully come up with a secure site that would support a large landing party. Fortunately, Colonel Jackson and company had overlooked one of the smaller archive storage bays and left them with a sample supply of various seeds from Earth that was originally intended to be a token of cultural exchange with the aliens. Reflecting back on the disastrous mission made Kim sick to her stomach, but she did get some relief knowing the guilty parties would soon be approaching the outer limits of the sun's solar flares.

The second shuttle mission involved the search for dead satellites that might offer a clue to what had happened on Earth. The repaired shuttle with reentry restrictions was designated for that mission. It had been retrofitted with radiation-sensing arms in case any of the satellites' nuclear batteries had failed and eroded. Also, all of the passenger seats were removed to accommodate any recoverable objects.

Kim decided to hold off on the lunar launch until she had a full complement of military advisors available. Deep down, she had a really bad feeling about the moon's old support base. She realized it was practically impossible for any life form to still be alive in that hostile environment, but here they were, ten thousand years later, up and about. If Gary didn't show up in eight hours, she would personally go to Christine's stateroom and roust him. Inwardly, she envied Christine, for, God knew *she* could certainly use a good man about now. She fell asleep dreaming about Bill.

Surprise, surprise, it was Gary who rousted Kim out of a deep, needed sleep. Unable to fight off fatigue any longer and with insomnia fading, Kim had fallen asleep in her console chair.

"Ah hah," Gary said directly over Kim, startling her to

an upright position. "I knew it! Here we were out busting our butts, and you're sleeping."

"Wha —! What? Oh, I must have fallen asleep." Kim looked at the console clock and was stunned to see she had been asleep for nearly ten hours. "Wow! I guess I needed that." A smiling Christine was seated in one of the chairs surrounding her console. "Well, Christine, I see you're happy today."

"All in the line of duty, ma'am." Christine laughed as she said, "Don't forget to get your immunization shot. My staff feels pretty certain that they've isolated the guilty pox virus strain and the immunization will be ninety-nine percent effective. We sent a nurse to the bridge for you and your staff, but she didn't want to wake you."

Kim's eyebrows furrowed when she asked, "Any idea of the strain's origin? Certainly the people on Earth could have developed and produced an immunization before it infected the entire planet."

"*Au contraire*," Christine replied. A suspicious DNA-RNA protein belonging to none other than the crocodile family was found latent in the guilty virus. Bioterrorism seems to have been at work; the bug was armed to be passed down from one generation to another."

"Crocodile?" Gary sputtered as he jumped into the conversation. "Why crocodiles, and why couldn't an immunization be developed?"

Christine sat up and leaned forward before replying. "That's the big piece of the puzzle. We do know that the crocodile species has the most advanced and durable immune system of all known creatures. That's the main reason they've outlived all of the dinosaurs. The crocodile was directly responsible for the discovery of a cure for AIDS, a plague that harassed Earth's inhabitants centuries ago. During the experimentation phase, the HIV virus literally blew up when introduced to the crocodile's bloodstream. My staff is now speculating that some bioterrorists created a virus from the crocodiles that proved fatal to humans, and I have a few theories of my own also."

Kim patiently waited for Christine to continue, but the suspense was too much for Gary. "Okay, you've had your fun, now out with it."

Christine frowned and said, "This is everything but funny, but here's what I think may have happened: our orbital reconnaissance readings indicate a very high radioactive concentration in the Middle East, particularly in a country once known as Saudi Arabia. The area's still so hot it's dangerous for human life. I suspect a nuclear war broke out after this virus was released."

Kim replied, "Granted, that would terminate life in that area, but what would cause humans to devolve and the crocodiles to all of a sudden take huge evolutionary leaps?"

"Radioisotopes," was Christine's answer. "Here we have a group of bioterrorists ginning up some potent DNA-RNA viral infected death gene, releasing it into the populace, then getting nuked as their just reward. However, their little stockpile of genetic soup gets a shot of radioisotopes that alters the genetic code and then gets shot into the ionosphere for distribution. Presto, we have Armageddon."

Gary was pretty impressed, but Kim replied to Christine, "That's a pretty weak scientific supposition, but it's a start. We'll never know for sure until we find some historical artifacts, and that's where we are now.

"Back to duty . . ." Kim turned to Gary, "we've got another mission for you; that is, if you're up for it?"

Christine jumped in, "It's the lunar base. Isn't it?"

Kim slowly turned to Christine. "I was speaking to Major Hecker about a possibly dangerous mission. You are not to be included. Your presence here is much more valuable than playing 'Annie Oakley' with ferocious dinosaurs."

The 'Annie Oakley' part got Christine on her feet. "'Annie Oakley'? Lousy comparison there, Kim! And exactly how many dinosaurs did little 'Annie Oakley' shoot? To insinuate that I've been wasting my time playing with guns is an insult. No one, yourself included, has done more productive research than I have. I have literally carried the entire endeavor up to now, and here you are telling me my time would be more valuable sitting in a lab, studying tissue?"

The sudden outburst took Kim by surprise. "I didn't mean to insinuate that you've been nonproductive; I'm saying this next mission could be much more dangerous, and you're way too valuable to be used as cannon fodder."

This response only made Christine madder. "Shit! Now I'm cannon fodder?"

Kim started to interrupt, but Christine flew across the space to get directly into Kim's face. "No! You hold it right there!" Christine shouted. "Gary, who was the most valuable asset on your landing team?"

Gary had hoped he would be spared and was trying to make himself as small as he could, but now he was trapped. "Uh, well, since you outshot all of us . . . I'd say with your science and medical background, you are probably our most important asset."

Christine snorted and nodded at Kim as if to admonish her.

"Thanks a lot, Gary," Kim sighed. Turning to Christine, she added, "You're turning into quite a frontier woman, but don't you think you'll be a tad over your head on the moon?"

Christine was quick to answer, "No more so than anyone else on the Earth's landing party." Gary had to secretly agree with her on that one.

Kim knew when she was defeated, so she gave up hopes of bottling Christine aboard the *Leapfrog* for safekeeping. "Okay, you can go, but I'm letting you know here and now that it's against my better judgment."

"Thanks, Mom," Christine murmured as she returned to her seat.

"And I'm *not* your mother. I'm only five years older than you and, if I may say so, a lot wiser too."

"But of course," Christine taunted, smiling since she got her way, again, and the last word.

Getting down to business, Kim continued, "We had our engineering department retrofit one of the shuttles for the extended-range lunar mission. We have room on board for ten people, life support, and moderate defense weapons."

Gary could not help but jump in at this point. "Defense? Against what? It's been over ten thousand years since anyone's been up there. Nothing could sustain life that long without major assistance."

"I wouldn't be too sure about that." Kim leaned forward and said, "I don't know if you can remember, but years before the *Leapfrog* began construction, a vast amount of ice crystals was discovered in the Oppenheimer Crater. So much, in fact, that once melted it would yield a small lake. The space consortium decided to build their construction site on the center of the crater with the thawed water surrounding the site. To melt the ice crystals, they encircled the site with nuclear reactor heat rods that had a million or so years' half-life. The evaporation recovery and atmosphere development were taken care of by enclosing the entire crater with a transparent, self-sealing dome. Plants from Earth's rainforest were imported, and with the aid of vast nuclear electrolysis, oxygen was generated, and the dome eventually pressurized. It was this oxygen generation that provided the pressure to inflate the huge dome. Some of the hydrogen byproduct was burned for heat and steam generation, but the majority of the gas was released into space.

"The plants naturally took over the oxygen production and likewise consumed the carbon dioxide that the animals created. A nice touch was the built-in sprinkler system for irrigation. As the heated water built up steam pressure, a mechanically operated valve would open, allowing the steam to condense and flow through overhead pipes. Some big questions here are: what is the current atmospheric composition, if any? And did whatever happened on Earth happen there also?

"Theoretically, this ecological system was to exist without the support of computers. The builders were reluctant to depend solely on electronic devices and favored mechanical means. Not that I blame them, but it would be a major mistake to rule out the chance that there's still some form of life remaining. Unless, of course a meteor of significant size just happened to target the site."

Christine was looking puzzled when Kim asked, "Something bothering you, Christine?"

"Yes, it is. How can a site like this maintain a consistent core temperature? I mean, the temperature fluctuations must be severe from day to night."

"You're half right. The site is located in the southern hemisphere of the moon, which is not exposed to the direct rays. Plus, the deep crater walls shadow the site by ninety percent, and you can't rule out the heating production caused by the greenhouse effect."

Gary bolted upright and exclaimed, "Hold on a minute! Won't this 'greenhouse effect' also produce a flammable gas like methane?"

"Right on!" Kim said as if congratulating a meriting student. "The computer estimated that the site will probably consist of sixty percent oxygen, twenty percent carbon dioxide, fifteen percent methane and five percent hydrogen. The light hydrogen gas cannot escape the dome's atmosphere like it can on Earth, so we can expect it to be concentrated in the higher parts of the dome."

"Pardon my rudimentary chemistry, but isn't that an explosive mix waiting for a spark? And wouldn't it just blow the top of the dome right off the site?" Gary probed.

Kim turned to her console and pulled up an expanded view of the moon's surface. She laser pointed to an obscure crater on the south side of the moon. "See that crater there? If you look real close, you can faintly see the dome, and it doesn't look partial. We can't get a better view because half of the crater's on the edge of the far side, and the tidal effect from the Earth's gravity keeps the moon facing one way all the time. So, as far as we can see, the dome's still there.

"Back to your question, yes, I'm sure there've been many flash fires from the methane and hydrogen buildup, but the computer projects no total loss of life or atmosphere." Kim raised her brows, sensing something else was on Gary's mind. She was right.

"Then . . ." Gary began slowly, ". . . we should not depend on any weapons that can produce a spark and trigger an air explosion?"

Christine put her hand up to her head as if struck by a headache. Kim slumped lower in her chair and responded, "No, a spark-producing weapon is not prudent. Additionally, a full space suit will not provide adequate protection against a sudden pressure increase. The flash ultrahigh temperature would be resisted, but the suits are built for vacuum pressure, not explosive overpressure."

Gary leaned back and put his hands behind his head. "Speaking of being prudent, if we find hostiles in the site, wouldn't it be wise to perhaps retreat, torch it, then explore it thoroughly after destruction?"

"I'll leave that call entirely up to you and your definition of hostile, but remember: after the dome explodes, it just may fall back down on itself, rendering searches impossible."

Gary stood up as he asked, "When will the shuttle be ready?"

"Within twelve hours, we should have it fueled and supplied. The flight plan looks pretty good with a total of fifty-two hours ETE, estimated time en route, round trip, and a thirty percent reserve. The flight is programmed for twenty-six hours each way. Any faster than that would burn too much fuel in both the acceleration and braking." Kim frowned and added, "Ah, this may be a long trip, because the shuttle will be zero g until it reaches the moon surface; once there you'll be around twenty percent g."

Christine sprang up and said, "We can handle that. I've got some things I need to do before we leave, so I'll excuse myself and start getting ready."

Gary said, "Same here. We'll meet for final instructions before we sail."

As they were walking away, Kim softly said, "God bless."

CHAPTER 31

BLAM! THE SHUTTLE'S ROCKETS KICKED in pinning all the crew in their seats. Christine tried to raise her head, but the efforts were futile. *How many times,* she wondered, *could the shuttle possibly hold together through these cyclic-g forces?* Glancing over at Gary, she saw that he too was testing the four-g acceleration; however, he managed to raise his arms and lift his helmeted head a few inches. As the g's began holding, they let go and everyone lurched forward. The green "Safe" light illuminated and, in unison, everyone twisted and lifted his or her helmet off.

The zero-g was initially unsettling to Christine. She always felt as if she were on an elevator that had lost all its cables and brakes. After a few minutes, her stomach settled down, and she unbuckled and did a few loops around.

However, a few of the troops didn't share her enthusiasm. One particularly green soldier barfed before he could find his barf bag. The partially digested breakfast literally blew across the cabin shotgunning everyone in his line of fire. This certainly did not help the borderline troops doing their best to control the impulse. The sight and smell of the regurgitated mess was all it took to start a chain reaction. Fortunately, the rest managed to get their bags before blowing their breakfasts.

Christine just closed her eyes and grimaced as little pieces of vomit floated about, sticking to whatever they touched. While waiting for the filtering system to do its thing, she put her helmet back on, leaned back, and dialed up one of her favorite movies on her overhead console. Gary set up cleaning details, admonished the ones not using the bags, and thoroughly reviewed the proper use of the zero-g toilet. It was going to be a long, long flight.

While en route, Gary went over the old schematics of the lunar site in detail. No one knew or could guess what modifications had been made since the schematics were published; thus, he stressed the importance of improvising and staying fluid. Christine was impressed that Gary actively sought out independent thoughts from his troops. Corporal Freddie Nelson, in particular, was enjoying the opportunity to stage his talking abilities when Scoffield, the communications expert, told him, "Nelson, shut the fuck up!"

During the meeting, Gary decided not to even attempt to enter via the main airlock but go directly to the rescue tunnel with a cutting torch and a large pressure tent. Since the batteries in the stunner guns were all dead, they loaded their projectile sidearms with mercury-tipped rounds. All armor-piercing and high-explosive ammunitions were to be left behind. Christine fielded several questions about what to expect as a threat, but all she could say was to be prepared to find Neanderthal type people but not to expect to find crocs. She believed the crocodiles needed much more water than the heat rods could produce. There was a small possibility that surviving animal life had not been affected by whatever had happened on Earth and, again, she stressed that it was only a remote possibility any life form existed at all. None of the troops bought the line, but at least they were courteous.

Finally, the braking thrusters kicked in, slowing them down to a stabilized low lunar orbit, offering excellent views of the Oppenheimer Crater. Directly in the center lay the smooth shape of a gigantic superdome that stretched across two hundred and seventy-five kilometers. Surprisingly, the entire dome's surface appeared unscathed by the chaos surrounding the site. There must have been some source of positive pressure left to be able to support the massive weight of the flexible dome.

Gary instructed the computer to drop the shuttle out of orbit and make a low-altitude pass over the dome. Besides tons of dust covering it, the structure seemed sound. The designers of the enormous site had intentionally located the command and control close, within two kilometers, to one of the emergency evacuation exits, and Gary had no trouble picking out the landing pad designated for that access. Fortunately, it was clear of visible debris. He marked a spot in the center and selected "Land."

Just when everyone aboard thought they were going to die, the landing thrusters kicked in. Gently, the shuttle settled down in the moon dust directly in the center of the aged landing pad. Prodded by Gary, everyone psychologically geared down by checking and rechecking their personal space suits and their neighbors'. Once satisfied, Gary delivered the debarking orders. "Stand by for depressurization." *Whoosh*, the air vented. "Opening door now; everyone exit slowly. There're no threats out in this vacuum." The door slid open, letting buckets of lunar dust creep down and cover everything. Then the dust slowly cleared, revealing a stark, colorless, and hostile landscape.

The slanted sun rays cast a long shadow across the crater's surface. The shuttle's computer informed the landing party that the sun was in setting mode and visible light would be available for twenty-nine hours. Each lunar day equaled twenty-seven Earth days, lengthening the sunset or sunrise process. Gary figured they would be gone long before the sun finished its business anyway.

The space suits' computerized temperature control units immediately hummed on as the door fully opened. Christine noticed that her HUD, heads-up display, was recording a minus one hundred and twenty-two degrees Celsius, the atmospheric pressure was zero, the gaseous content was also reading zero, and the gravity index was showing seventeen percent. *Nice place for a holiday. If you're a dead grasshopper, that is,* she mused to herself.

Warily, the landing party debarked from the safety of the shuttle. The pressure containment crew was the first to head over to the stone wall where the old schematics illustrated an emergency escape airlock. In no time, the crew found the exit and with a little muscle pried the outer door partially open. CPO, Chief Petty Officer, Frank Tomilson, was in charge of torching the inner door but came up to Gary before wheeling his equipment over. "Sir, I think it's best if I'm the only one in the cutting area. If there is a high concentration of flammable gas in the dome, I don't think you want everyone standing around just for the hell of it."

"You're absolutely right," Gary replied. "We'll close the outer door behind you, and when you get the inner door removed, give us a pressure check, and we'll join you. However, I don't want you going inside the dome until the rest of us have a chance to catch up."

"You don't have to worry about that, sir. That's the last place I want to be right now." Tomilson saluted and returned to his heavy duty torching equipment.

The outer pressure door was difficult to pry the rest of the way open even with the combined efforts of three men. Apparently, the zero humidity and lack of atmosphere preserved the inner mechanisms, but the inner door was completely fused to the metal bulkhead. As soon as Tomilson lit the torch, the other two assistants instantly vanished.

Gary and the others stood by the shuttle with their life support umbilical cords attached for continual recharging. On the intercom system, communications were broadcast to everyone. The system had a design that permitted selected channels and some degree of privacy but, in general, private conversations were frowned upon.

Christine, along with many of the others, stood facing the dome. Speaking to no one in particular, she mused, "I wonder if anything's alive in there, and if there is life, what is it?"

Scoffield was the first to answer. "I have a real bad feeling about this. Somewhere, deep in my gut, is a very bad feeling. I mean, they built this thing to last an eternity, and in human life years, it's been an eternity."

Gary confidently added, "There won't be anything alive in there; and don't worry, last time I looked crocodiles weren't included in the lunar inhabitants."

A smattering of nervous laughter followed. Actually, he did not buy his words either.

The creatures' sensitive internal sensors picked up the unusual vibrations and sent them scampering into the overgrown vegetation. There, they would patiently wait to trap their next dinner.

CHAPTER 32

TOMILSON DOUBLED CHECKED TO MAKE sure the dome's outer lock was securely shut. The last thing he wanted was to be blown out a couple of kilometers by the escaping dome air. Assuming, of course, there was an atmosphere still inside the relic.

The laser torch cut through the weakened and corroded metal door like a red-hot knife through butter. Almost as soon as the beam touched the metal, the molten metal blew back and over his shielded arm. *Positive pressure! No explosion? Is this good? Must be, because I'm still alive.* These and many other thoughts ran through Tomilson's head as he continued to cut a large hole in the pressure door. Within five minutes, he stood back and pulled on the cord that he had attached to the door's wheel-like handle. Slowly, the door tilted and fell at his feet, kicking up a dust storm.

Tomilson radioed the "All Clear" message and moved his equipment aside in the narrow passageway so others could get by it without rubbing against the still glowing hatch. He never considered himself to be overly brave, and prudently decided to wait outside the fallen door, just in case. He figured the laser torch he held in his hand could make short work of any dinosaur, should one happen to stick his nose in there. Swearing he could hear noises inside the dome, he started hyperventilating.

For psychological relief, Tomilson fired the laser beam through the empty door just to discourage potential and imagined threats. To his surprise, the beam only extended a meter before fading out. *You dumb shit!* he thought as he remembered that the cutting torch was limited to one meter to keep collateral damage on the other side of the cut to a minimum. Plus, there was no telling if the atmosphere was explosive.

After what seemed to be a lifetime to Tomilson, the outer pressure door opened, and Major Hecker stepped in. "Nice job, Tomilson. We brought a couple of suit replenishment kits, so why don't you recharge yours while we reconnoiter the entrance area?" Gary then called the rest of the landing party to the dome.

Gary was the first person to go through the door in over ten thousand years, and the area inside looked appropriately abandoned. It was a poorly lit, steamy jungle of riotous vegetation. Gary could not identify anything showing the influence of man. Overhead lighting was long gone, along with walkways or trails. Huge, densely packed trees reached toward the upward sloping dome with brown and dying limbs. The ground was covered in a swampy soup mix at least ten centimeters thick. A strange static-like noise penetrated his pressure helmet that sounded like the hiss of an out-of-tune receiver. Sidearms at the ready, they formed a semicircle, facing outward to guard the open door.

Christine was in the center studying the atmosphere content: her instruments registered forty-four percent oxygen, seven percent methane, forty percent carbon dioxide, and nine percent nitrogen. Radiation levels were reading over four hundred mRem per hour and were a major cause of consternation for her. The level was equivalent to one barium enema per hour, way over the recommended maximum annual dosage for humans.

Atmospheric pressure was steady at 1005 millibars, which was only slightly lower than Earth's standard of 1013 millibars. Temperature was warm at twenty-three degrees Celsius. Broadcasting to "All," she transmitted her recordings and added, "The greenhouse effect, with all this methane breaking down into carbon dioxide, must be responsible for the heat. Better keep our suits sealed up; we've got a lot of methane, which will probably be pretty obnoxious. It's my guess that the upper part of the dome's something like one hundred percent hydro —"

She was abruptly cut off by someone screaming, "What the fuck's that?"

Radio reception through the headset being unidirectional, everyone but the speaker started turning in circles. Gary transmitted, "Who said that, and what did you see?"

Still unidentified, the frightened voice came back, "Some sort of huge, fast, black bug. Must have been the size of a shoebox!"

Adding to the confusion, another unidentified caller yelled, "There! Over there! Another one! Shit, it's a gigantic fucking cockroach!"

Gary went over to the only two space suits pointing guns and said, "Radio discipline! You're confusing everyone by not identifying yourselves. Who saw what, where?"

"Roberts, sir. They were enormous cockroaches. I lived in Florida; I know what cockroaches look like, and it was one hundred percent, pure cockroach. Except it was as big as a shoebox."

"Okay, everybody, listen up!" Gary transmitted. "Nobody, that means nobody, shoots at any bugs. Cockroaches don't hurt people; they just eat rotten plants and other bugs. If you saw two in this short time frame, you can bet there're at least several million of them, and we don't have that much ammunition and, furthermore, there's enough hydrogen and methane in here to blow this dome right off."

Hmmm, Christine thought as she scrambled through her backpack looking for something large enough to contain one of the "cockroaches."

"This is *Leapfrog*. We confirm from the helmet video that the variety you see is a greatly enlarged version of the Madagascar Hissing Cockroach, or *Gromphadorhina Portentosa*. They are wingless, basically harmless, and hiss a lot when they mate or get upset. Some people even had them as pets. That's probably how they got smuggled in to start with. And, Christine . . ." Kim paused.

"Christine here."

"Don't even think about bringing one of those bugs, or any other animal or plant life, back here. That goes for all of you.

"On another subject, we're about to lose our data link with you. We don't have any satellites to bounce our radio waves, so we're restricted to line of sight communication. We anticipate communications outages of up to twenty hours, which is unacceptable. If we don't hear anything from you within eight hours of your expected launch, we will commence the sequence for a rescue shuttle. That should give you enough time to scout the area, return, and have the shuttle in position for a status report. If, for some reason, you get detained, you may have to wait a couple of days, but you should have enough life support supplies onboard to survive. Uh oh . . . we're starting to lose our link as I speak. Good luck, *Leapfrog*, out." Kim ended the transmission.

Christine looked up at Gary, who was smiling at her through his faceplate, and asked him, "How do you turn off these helmet cameras? And, uh, one little question here— what eats these cockroaches? I mean, that's the way ecology goes, or was supposed to go."

Everyone's attention was focused on Gary's answer. "Not necessarily so. Previous studies showed that the cockroach would be the dominant animal on Earth should a nuclear holocaust occur. Obviously, that didn't happen, but being totally isolated, these critters just picked up the evolutionary ball and ran with it."

Military etiquette prevented any of the soldiers from speaking out, but Gary could see in their faces that they weren't buying that line one little bit. He did not want to admit it, even to himself, but there probably was something that lived off the cockroaches.

Gary mustered the troops for a final mission brief, leaving the details and personnel assignments to Scoffield. With all eyes scanning the foliage in front of them, Gary emphasized, "Don't, under any circumstances, shoot straight up. That's where the hydrogen would accumulate. Hydrogen on Earth is so light, it escapes to space; here, it has nowhere to go but overhead. Obviously, the atmosphere down here doesn't have enough methane to support combustion, as Tomilson proved with his 'Darth Vader' laser sword."

Tomilson's face went pale with embarrassment, for he had forgotten everyone had access to his helmet camera. The laughter that followed helped relieve some of the tension that had been building.

As Scoffield and Gary assigned platoon duties, Christine did a quick check on the centralized life support monitor that kept track of everyone's suit status. She could not help but gasp out, "Oh no! We've got some serious problems here, guys." That brought a screeching halt to the energetic chatter. "Our batteries are not holding their charges. Not one battery can hold over six hours. After that, our oxygen recycler shuts down along with the lights and radios."

"Damn!" Gary muttered. Thinking out loud, he continued, "Okay, we've got two kilometers to the command center, and I figure no greater than about one-half kilometer per hour cutting through this foliage. We'll cycle the lead to minimize exhaustion. Going back should be a lot easier since we'll use the trail we blazed getting there. That eats up four hours to get there, one to reconnoiter the site, and half an hour to make it back here with a half-hour reserve. It's a pretty tight schedule, so we'll have to really hump it."

Complete silence followed. Obviously, no one was eager to run out of oxygen, much less stomp around in a mushy swamp filled with giant cockroaches. A few unenthusiastic *"whoyahs"* chimed out as the men prepared for their adventuresome trek.

While the soldiers were organizing themselves, Christine knelt down and pushed her machete down into the muck as hard as she could to test the depth of the soil. She pushed the blade down eight to ten centimeters before she felt positive resistance from the bedrock. When she put her full weight on the blade, it continued to slide down. "Roots!" she broadcast to all. "The lunar surface rock layer is being broken down in the same fashion as on Earth. This is truly amazing." The researcher side of Christine was taking over, and she was beaming like a child at Christmas.

However, her enthusiasm was not shared by a forlorn looking corporal by the name of Freddie Nelson. He was delegated to remain behind to guard the gate in case any Neanderthals or wayward mutant crocodiles should come across their exit.

Freddie was still mentally kicking himself for asking so many dumb questions during the brief as he watched the expedition disappear into the thick brush. Once everyone was out of sight, Freddie turned off his helmet video and lay down. He found that the soupy ground made a perfect water bed, and his space suit instantly adjusted the temperature, making him feel warm and cozy. Freddie figured crocs and Neanderthals were safely left behind on Earth, and the cockroaches could never chew their way inside his reinforced suit. Besides, he did not resemble or taste like a rotten leaf. As Freddie drifted off to sleep, he convinced himself Scoffield was punishing him for trying to dominate the initial briefing by asking so many dumb questions. He would show them. Let them stomp around, sweat, and burn their oxygen. He needed a nap badly because sleep had evaded him during the long, cramped trek in weightlessness. And the snoring, when the others slept, was like a symphony of badly tuned instruments without a conductor.

Obviously, he was more affected by the cryogenic lobot-

omy than he realized. This was the last time he would nap
on the job.

And one of the many creatures watching would make sure of that.

CHAPTER 33

"GIANT COCKROACHES! GOD KNOWS WHAT they're going to find next," Kim said to a small group sitting around her console. Bill Evans had come to the bridge to give Kim an update on the underwater surveillance robots and to report that the satellite recovery shuttle was ready for launch. Carl Manley and Terry Evert were glued to the monitor watching reruns of the giant cockroaches scurrying about.

"How do you kill cockroaches the size of a shoebox?" Carl wondered out loud.

"Nuke 'em!" Terry replied.

Kim sighed and said to Terry, "Stay away from Dr. Mitchell. Heaven help us if the two of you ever get together."

Kim turned to Bill and said, "That's great news about the bots and shuttle. I suppose you want to command the shuttle's search?"

Bill beamed when he said, "Yes, please. I've already programmed a flight plan based on this hemisphere and all promising large, orbiting debris. Some of the most promising satellites appear to have decayed orbits and risk reentry within a decade or two, so I'll check those out first."

Kim shook her head. "No, Bill. Just stick to our list and grab the closest first and hope to hit the jackpot before we're forced out of space. We don't have that much time to scour all the possibilities, as you so painfully pointed out to me last week."

Bill slumped farther down in his chair. "But of course we will." He sighed and continued, "Sometimes, we lose the big picture down in the lab. We get so wrapped up in our projects that we can't see the forest because the trees are in the way. It shouldn't take me more than a few minutes to reprogram, and we'll be on our way within the hour."

Kim's smile seemed to brighten the entire bridge. "Join the crowd, Bill. We continue to drop the 'big picture' every time we turn around."

Bill stood and started making his way to the exit when Kim called out, "Good luck, Bill, and by the way, please don't bring back any souvenirs."

Bill turned and saw that Kim was still smiling. Their eyes stayed locked a little longer than either had planned. Finally, Bill returned the smile and left Kim wondering what was happening. *Didn't my husband just die? Why aren't I mourning? What's wrong with me?* She shook her head as if to clear out some cobwebs. *Duh, girl. I've been a widow now for over ten thousand years. I should start accepting that fact.*

CHAPTER 34

CHRISTINE KEPT HER DISTANCE. FOUR men wielding machetes at the same time and proximate location were a disaster waiting to happen. The initial pace was excruciatingly slow with only one lead cutting the trail, but it finally picked up when Gary assigned four trailblazers to the point. The lead cut a swath large enough for one person to edge through. Two machetes on each side broadened the path and the fourth in trail of the other three cleaned up and cut the vines that would trip or snag on their suits. The alternating four kept constant vigil for threats, but the only living things they came across were cockroaches; however, the bugs scurried away every time the crew approached them. The men rotated shifts every fifteen minutes and did not stop until Gary's navigator indicated they were at their destination.

"This is it?" Christine queried as Gary signaled for a halt. Nothing visibly remained of the old command center. Evidence of its existence was completely erased and buried under centuries of rubble, mush, and thick vegetation. Christine found an opening in the forest's canopy and peered up. Nothing, nothing at all, remained of the huge aerators that had once magnificently draped over the entire dome. The overhead ducting system had obviously corroded out and collapsed long ago, leaving the still active reactors buried deep within the ice lake. The resultant moisture was the boil off from below that was not being piped up.

"Take ten, but keep within sight," an exhausted Gary transmitted. He found a huge fallen tree and plopped on the trunk. Christine wandered over and sat next to him.

"I've been sporadically keeping track of our life support batteries; now that we've stopped I'll run a complete diagnostic. Hmm, seems like our gatekeeper turned his monitoring system off. I'll page him." Christine paused as she waited for Freddie to answer.

"Sorry sack of shit's probably sleeping," Scoffield inserted. "He's been written up two times before for that very same reason. Got his ass busted back in rank each time too. Want me to send a runner back there?"

Gary answered, "No, we won't be here very long. After our break, we'll make a cursory metal detector sweep of the area, then press back. I'm afraid any clues as to what happened are long gone."

"I'll up the ante and send out an emergency page. No one can sleep through one of those," Christine said.

Freddie was having a horrible nightmare. He was stuck in a barrel going down some vicious white water rapids. Just as he launched over a bottomless waterfall, a horrific scream woke him. "Wha — what . . .?" he said to himself as he fumbled to turn off the screeching.

Odd. When he tried to turn off the pager alarm, he could not move either his arms or his legs; they were locked together so tightly he could not even bend or budge them. The control panels were located on both his chest and right arm, but no matter how hard he tried, his arms would not budge.

There went the rolling sensation again, but this time it wasn't a dream. He was lying face down in the murky slop and something extremely powerful picked him up and rolled him over several more times. Mud caked his faceplate completely, obscuring his vision, but after what seemed like an eternity, he was dropped face down in a semi-clear puddle of water that thinned out the mud on his faceplate.

The obtrusive pager finally ceased screeching, to be replaced with some sort of crunching and squeaking sound. Freddie was still lying face down in the puddle but could slightly turn his head inside his helmet to check out the noise. "Oh, my God!" Freddie screamed to himself since his monitor was turned off. His helmet was no longer round. The sides had been caved in and were still slowly moving inward and finally stopped when they reached his temples.

A brief reprieve made Freddie hope that whatever had tied him up had left and would not return. Then a hydraulic vice locked around his shoulders and jerked him in an upright position.

Freddie could see out now, but whatever was holding him up was behind him. Turning his head was hindered by his partially collapsed helmet, but if he leaned forward, then twisted his neck, he could see at almost a ninety-degree angle. Nothing to the left. He turned to his right, and he picked up two moving large sticks. *Sticks! Ah shit! Those sticks got joints and are moving. Those aren't sticks. They're legs!* Freddie felt something warm run down the inside of his left leg as he involuntarily soiled himself. *Huge insect legs!*

Freddie had just finished a long, loud scream when he was violently whipped around and faced the monster face to face.

Big, black, bulbous eyes the size of saucers glared back at him. Below the eyes, a huge set of pincers opened and wrapped around his shoulder again. *A giant ant?* Freddie could see brown goop running down his faceplate and knew enough about bugs and biology to know the goop was supposed to have been injected into his body to digest him from the inside out. Petrified, Freddie could not even get out a scream. *This is not an ant; it's a huge spider, and I'm wrapped up in its web!* Freddie screamed louder, but there was no one to hear him.

The monster spider tucked its prey under its belly, flexed its long spindly legs, and burst into the air, flying over the treetops. The spider immediately coiled its legs and sprang again. This continued four or five times before the spider scurried inside a dark, webbed den. Freddie's suit noticed the light change and automatically illuminated the two remaining unbroken small headlamps on the sides of Freddie's helmet. Startled, the spider leaped backward with all eight eyes glowing from the reflected light like bright lanterns. Freddie got a good look at his executioner and promptly fainted.

The spider, a member of the wolf spider family, was gargantuan. The body had evolved to the size of a Labrador, its eight legs were over ten feet long, and it was covered in bristly, brown, sensory hair. Four large posterior eyes studied its prey for a few moments before deciding the light was no threat and time for feeding was overdue.

Excruciating pain in his right thigh snapped Freddie out of his comatose state. Looking down, he could see that his entire body was tightly wrapped in thick webbing. The nightmarish spider had his leg in its pincers and had penetrated his space suit with a sharp and powerful grip. The pain intensified unbearably when the poisonous digestive fluids entered his blood system. It was as though he had been injected with a huge dose of sulfuric acid. The burn shot up and down his leg and swiftly reached his waist. His testicles felt like they had burned off. His toes swelled until he thought they would explode.

The spider gave its prey a few moments to become nice and juicy before it straddled the victim around the middle, tore a small hole through webbing, space suit, and skin and started sucking out Freddie's dissolving guts and blood. Freddie tried to scream again, but his lungs collapsed before the scream reached his throat.

The spider finished its meal, picked up the bound carcass and dropped it out of the web nest. Although the meal was foul and barely digestible, it was easy prey and there were many others that had crawled out of the same side hole. They would also escape through the same tunnel like the bugs she lived on. The spider set off in haste with hopes of preventing the new and easy prey from escaping.

CHAPTER 35

"SOMETHING'S WRONG!" CHRISTINE EXCLAIMED RIGHT before all hell broke loose. She was paging Freddie for the third
time when the pandemonium erupted.

Blam! Blam! "Kill the motherfucker! Kill it *now*! Get it off
me!" someone screamed. The commotion startled Christine
backward off the tree trunk, and into the mushy sod.

Gary sprang to his feet and stood on the fallen tree, trying
to find the source of the commotion. He did not have to look
far. Directly behind him a huge spider had one of his men
pinned down and was rapidly rolling him over and over while
it spun a web around the man's feet, working up toward his
knees. Three other men had formed a semicircle around the
monster and were systematically firing their handguns while
being careful not to hit their comrade.

Scoffield had just emptied his clip and was reloading
when he realized the mercury-tipped rounds were not penetrating the spider's exoskeleton. They were definitely leaving
some good dents, but as far as he could tell, none of the rounds
were getting through the insect's natural armor. "These ain't
working! Cease-fire!" Scoffield shouted.

Gary had just taken position beside one of the shooters
and was about to fire when he heard Scoffield. Holstering
his sidearm, Gary unslung his machete, stepped forward, and

took a hefty swing at one of the spider's legs. *Snip!* He hit right at the joint, and the lower portion of the leg fell off, followed by a stream of clear fluid. The fluid initially blew out like a severed hydraulic line but slowed to a trickle. In a blur, the spider turned to Gary and pounced on him, decking Gary flat on his back. Huge pincers opened and started closing in on his head when Gary brought his arms up and shoved his machete directly between them. Unknown to Gary at the time, it was a lucky thrust. The most vulnerable area on a spider was its mouth.

Immediately the spider reared up on its two hind legs and let out a shrill that penetrated the suits' noise-reduction systems. Capitalizing on the opportunity, the three soldiers rushed the spider with machetes swinging. Confused, the spider turned on each attacker, trying to fight back, but each time a machete swung, the spider became lower to the ground. Finally, when the spider had nothing but wiggling stumps, the soldiers attacked the main body and continued swinging until the spider stopped moving.

Panting, with his suit completely drenched in spider goop, Gary transmitted, "Well, I guess we have a good idea about what happened to Corporal Freddie Nelson."

Scoffield replied, "Beam me up, Scotty. This place sucks."

Christine finally got her breath back and walked around the pieces of the huge spider. "I bet there's a lot more like this one around. Look how large the abdominal section is. It's like a beach ball. Must be enlarged by the web sacs."

"Uh, excuse me, please, but could someone help me get this spider web off of me? I can't seem to cut it." Petty officer Peterson was still on the ground trying to cut the web bindings off his legs. Even with three helpers, the webbing was impossible to cut. Each strand seemed have some kind of self-healing power. Every time they thought they were getting somewhere and one fiber started to yield, it started growing back again.

"Shit!" Gary exclaimed. "This is like flexible steel cable. I've never seen anything like it before. There's no beginning or end to the loops. It's like all the strands are permanently fused together. Heat! We'll need to torch it off. Christine, bring over your laser cutter."

"Uh, one little problem with that." She paused for effect, which was immediate and intense. "The laser cutter isn't portable. It weighs a ton, and it's not part of a medic's survival kit. The shuttle's kit has one on board though. It's not that far and shouldn't take too long since we've already blazed the trail."

Gary stood up and looked at the nonexistent command center. All he could see was overgrown vegetation without a hint of civilization. "Let's review the facts. It's getting darker. I think these particular spiders are nocturnal hunters; there are bound to be more of them; there's nothing here at all to collect, much less to learn from. The corrosive atmosphere and constant vapor saturation has turned everything man-made to dirt. Mission accomplished with negative results. Let's get out of here."

A few *"Whoyahs"* could be heard.

Scoffield and two others scurried about rigging up a makeshift stretcher for Peterson, while Gary walked around with the metal detector. He stopped a few times, knelt down to investigate whatever gave a reading, shrugged, and continued searching. Christine was performing a crude necropsy on the giant spider, gasping every now and then at each new discovery.

When Scoffield had the stretcher ready and Peterson strapped in, he transmitted, "Okay, sir, we're ready to transport."

Gary stopped scanning, stowed his detector, and turned his suit's helmet lights on high while he looked around at the darkened, forbidding treetops. Deep within the branches and otherwise hidden from sight came back the reflection of dozens of eyes, each of them shining as brightly as LCD lanterns. "Oh, damn!" Gary muttered as he scanned the treetops.

They were being watched, and the watchers were being watched. Bright lights at various heights beamed back at them. Some of them moved back when they were spotlighted, but never completely out of view. Others stood their ground and continued to glare back.

"Oh, my God!" Christine stuttered as she peered about. "There're dozens of them. Hopefully, they're just curious and not part of a pack hunt."

Scoffield could not resist. "Pack hunt! Spiders aren't supposed to hunt in packs. They're solitary creatures that only socialize to mate. This is getting to be too much: crocodile dinosaurs on Earth, cannibal cavemen, and monster man-eating spiders on the moon. What else can there be?"

Gary picked up the despair in Scoffield's voice and was sure he was expressing the feelings of the other men also. "Okay, Scoffield, let's book. I'll take point; you take the rear, and make sure you keep an eye out behind us. We'll rotate positions halfway and relieve the stretcher carriers the rest of the way."

Christine fell in behind Gary and un-holstered her fire-arm. "If they get close, shoot them in the eyes. That was about the only soft, vulnerable spot I found on their exoskel-eton during my necropsy."

They had just gotten underway at a fast trot when Gary held up his hand in the halt signal. He fell to his knees to get a closer look at something on the higher and dryer ground.

Once stopped, Christine saw it as well. "Oh no!" she said.

"'Oh no' what? Is it time for us to start screaming again?" Scoffield called out as he came up from the rear. The stretcher bearers bowed their heads, willing the bad news away. Peterson closed his eyes and said a silent prayer.

"Footprints, barefoot, and right on top of the ones we made coming in here. We got some Neanderthals here after all, and they've been stalking us along with the spiders."

CHAPTER 36

"WE'LL NEED TO FIND AN area south of the permafrost and north of the tropics," Kim said to Tom Haggard, Terry Evert, and Carl Manley. They had been reviewing possible home-sites on Earth but were not coming up with any viable locations. "The computer's calculated guess is that these newly evolved crocodiles are homoeothermic, that is, warm blooded, but only able to cope with moderately cool temperatures. It suggested a site where Saskatoon, Canada, used to be. Temperate zone resembles the North Carolina area we were familiar with. This zone is too cold for the larger reptiles but warm enough to support a lengthy agricultural growth period."

Tom Haggard kept studying the overhead reconnaissance console and manipulating the controls for zoom. "There's a fairly small lake in the basin that should be too small to support any of the large crocodiles even if they did live this far north. And up here . . ." Tom used the laser pointer to highlight a semi-flat area, ". . . is a perfect site for a secured encampment. If we cleared out the perimeter, a surprise attack would be very difficult from either the crocs or Neanderthals."

Carl Manley had been quiet since they sat down for the brain session and seemed lost in thought when Kim asked him, "Carl, you've been awfully quiet and withdrawn. Have any thoughts you'd like to share?"

"Well, yes. Our situation is extremely perilous, we all realize that, and I don't want to sound all doom and gloom, but here's how I see it: We need to reestablish our human culture and that seems to be outside our realistic grasp." Carl held up his hands in a supplication posture. "See. Told you so. Just like I threw cold water on your party, but seriously, how are we going to reestablish an industrial base, develop mineral production, provide protection in a hostile environment, and manage to feed ourselves? The task just overwhelms me."

Kim clicked the large overhead monitor off to capture everyone's undivided attention, leaned back, and sighed deeply. "Carl, looking at the big picture would overwhelm any one of us. The only way to cope with our situation is to divide the problems into smaller tasks. First, our safety—we need to find out what happened to the humans on Earth to keep the same thing from happening to us. Second—we need to get off this ship pronto, because it's coming apart at the seams. Third—the rest will fall into place. Further micromanagement would be futile because our situation is way too dynamic to accurately predict. So here we are just trying to go with the flow, hoping the flow doesn't take us over a waterfall."

Carl seemed visibly more relaxed and said, "Thanks, coach. I needed that. Sometimes I get wrapped around the axle and start spinning my wheels."

Kim gave him one of her starburst smiles and continued to address the rest of the staff. "Okay, let's focus on the computer's recommendation. A warmer climate would make our basic survival easier, but—" Kim's sentence was abruptly interrupted.

"*Leapfrog* base, Shuttle Two."

Kim keyed her microphone. "Go ahead, Shuttle Two."

Bill Evans was on the other end and the excitement in his voice was apparent. "I think we've got the baby! Found it in an elliptical orbit along with a zillion other pieces of trash. It's the only one with a beacon antenna, albeit defunct, that we've seen, so it must have been launched with the intent of recovery or interrogation. It has an MIT logo on it and has archive symbols on all quadrants. Looks like its nuclear battery pack was cleanly smacked off by a meteorite eons ago; reads nil on the Geiger counters, which will allow us to immediately dig into it without decontamination. We were almost full when we ran across it, so we picked it up and made a beeline back here to analyze it. We're in recovery orbit now and should be docking on *Leapfrog* within the hour. Over."

"Shuttle Two, stay in your suits and follow decontamination procedures. We're not taking any chances with this and will work in partial vacuum in case there's a booby trap or any contagious viral strains still alive. I'll have your spaces decompressed and set up by the time you arrive. *Leapfrog* out."

Kim clicked the overhead monitor back on, and the returning shuttle filled the screen. "I don't know about the rest of you, but I've got to see this for myself. Meeting adjourned." She literally jumped out of her chair and dashed off the bridge, leaving the remaining men in her dust.

By the time the satellite was wheeled in, Kim was fully clad in her deep space suit and had the workshop partially vacuumed and the tools set up. Bill walked over to her and said, "Nice. I see you've set up everything, so let's start taking this baby apart. Looks like it was designed for easy access, so it shouldn't take very long at all."

Sonar microphones were strategically placed throughout the room to pick up any noises that might have been missed by the vacuum state of the area. The stray meteor, or whatever hit the satellite, could not have done a more perfect job of removing the nuclear-powered battery.

Kim was studying the hole where the battery used to be. A few strands of some new sort of fiber optic wiring were strung about, but they could not possibly represent the entire wiring schematic. She said, half to herself, "This wiring is state of the art. It seems to be compartmentalized to support the transfer of neuron memory blocks."

Bill had the inspection cover removed and was reading the instructions printed on the inside. "Hmm, this is more advanced than we originally thought. Odd voltage and frequency requirements, but we should have no trouble jury-rigging an alternate power source." As soon as he said that, an assistant appeared with power clips.

"Okay, that should do it. Let's power it up and see if it'll still work after ten thousand years." Bill did not notice the others taking a step backward.

The vacuum microphones picked up a slight hum before a rotating hologram symbol zipped into life right above the satellite. After a few seconds of nothing but a holographic light show, Bill picked up the cover and continued to read the instructions.

A flabbergasted Kim remarked, "You mean you didn't finish reading the instructions before you powered it up?" More people stepped backward.

Defensively, Bill answered, "You would think something

this advanced wouldn't need instructions. I had the word *intuitive* in mind."

"Do you realize that there's a direct, but distinctly reversed correlation between intuitiveness and intelligence?" Kim fired back.

The satellite's onboard computer obviously gave up waiting for instructions and started making a whirring noise. In unison, everyone stepped back even farther. The hologram stopped spinning and an elderly man with a white beard flickered into view. He was standing behind a podium and looked stern.

"Greetings, space traveler. My name is Professor Lyon Travis of the Massachusetts Institute of Technology. I have been tasked to assemble, program, and coordinate the launch of an archive satellite, which you have apparently discovered. The purpose of this satellite is to serve as a warning and an explanation of what caused the end of the human race, at least as we know it.

"The intended audience would be either the crew of the Leapfrog *or* Explorer. *Both of these starships were lost in space and were never heard from again. If you do represent one of these starships, welcome back. Unfortunately, there's not much left to welcome you back to."*

"Let me go back to the beginning. Shortly before we launched the Leapfrog *on its deep space misadventure, a truly remarkable invention came about. I dare not compare it with a perpetual motion machine, but it came close. Tonaka Kimioto, the inventor, developed a small, portable, nuclear fusion electrolysis process that rendered the internal combustion engines obsolete overnight. The machine could crack water molecules into hydrogen and oxygen and use the resultant gases to drive a small, but very powerful, steam engine. The exhaust, pure water vapor, would then be condensed and recycled in a continual loop. A five percent loss*

was the average. Supplied with proper filters, this machine could also process salt water. Larger machines were built for the express purpose of desalination. Coastal farming began to thrive with the availability of unlimited irrigation.

"As far as control went, consumers did not own the radioactive rods; they leased them from various power companies. Each rod had a small, permanent GPS locator that was constantly monitored by a central computer. Encased in titanium, these rods proved indestructible in even the most severe crash tests. All airplanes were eventually converted to the secondary thrusters that were similarly used in the Leapfrog and Explorer but were much more powerful.

"Once released from oil-dependent slavery, the world economy boomed. More and more revenue was committed to education, health, and research than had ever been dreamed of in previous generations.

"The future finally appeared positive and stable for all of mankind until some evil men developed the "God Syndrome" and decided to alter human DNA.

"Unfortunately, not all countries benefited from the water electrolysis invention. The need for crude oil fell overnight, which sank the entire economy of the Middle Eastern states into a severe depression. Freed from the chains of oil dependency, the industrial world virtually isolated the once prosperous oil-rich nations. Many politicians jumped on the bandwagon, telling bankrupt sheiks, "Eat your oil; we don't want it anymore."

"Although considered manageable, the Middle East became a cesspool of terrorism. The bitterness and hatred eventually led to the demise of the human race. The Arab oil barons, facing certain poverty, decided to tilt the scale permanently in their favor. They secretly spent billions of euros developing the "mother of all plagues," the primary purpose being to wipe out the entire population, excluding themselves, of course. Instead of *the expected nuclear holocaust, they gave us the DNA holocaust.*

"The Arabs wisely chose the crocodile DNA to develop a virus so lethal and so fast-spreading that immunization attempts would prove futile . . ."

Kim, not realizing that her helmet microphone was still set on "Hot-" exclaimed, "Oh, my God!"

This was followed by anonymous exclamations of "Holy shit!" and "You gotta be shitting me!"

The airwave interruptions did nothing to deter or distract the droning professor.

". . . arrest the spread of the new virus. The crocodile was chosen because it had the most resistant immune system of all the animals.

"The virus, once in the human system, was specifically designed to alter the genome structure and revert pseudo genes to a past state. In this case, the designer virus was to reverse human evolution. Pre-immuniza-tion was critical, and the Arab states attempted to mass immunize their populace in complete secrecy. To the surprise of the rest of the world, they were successful, and once immunized, they strategically released the virus to efficiently infect the entire industrialized world. A monstrous killer plague overwhelmed the Earth. Those who weren't mercifully killed outright had their reproductive systems permanently altered. All of this happened before an immunization could be developed and cultured.

"The Arabs were patient and content to go back to their deserts and tents and wait out the firestorm. However, their plans ran amok when the world's secret service agencies discovered the plot and a nuclear attack was launched from the industrialized countries.

"The Arab states absorbed the massive onslaught and managed to launch a few nuclear tipped missiles, but the resulting retaliation was excessive. The Arab Gulf Coast was turned into glass and rendered completely uninhabitable.

"If the story ended here, you wouldn't be hearing a dead old geezer

rant on. But the Arab states had collectively stored massive amounts of the killer virus and immunization supplies in their territories. Radio isotopes from the nuclear bombardment further altered the DNA and blasted the contaminants into the ionosphere. Carried by the jet streams, the active virus saturated the entire world.

"I will spare you the gruesome details, but the holocaust aftermath left future human generations without any conscience or goodwill. Our children turned out to be completely ruthless, dispassionate, and cruel. It was as if they had no souls. Massive killings became rampant while law and order disintegrated. Civilization, as we knew it, ceased to exist. Now there's talk about some major changes in the world's alligators and crocodiles.

"We have completely lost touch with our moon and Mars bases. The last communication with both bases was reported as merely incoherent screaming.

"I was a young, optimistic academic when all this transpired, and now I've turned into a bitter old man waiting to die. Armageddon came and went and all that's left are our soulless children. The irony is that we, humans, did this to ourselves. Obviously, our nature could not cope with technology.

"I've enclosed the DNA/RNA decoding that will enable you to immunize yourselves before returning to Earth. Hopefully, you will be able to colonize what's left of it and reproduce normal children.

"God bless and good luck."

Kim was the first to recover. "Why am I not surprised?" She looked at Bill and said, "Glean any technology you can, save the memory, and jettison this and the other satellites to a sun-intercept course."

"Command center, recall the moon probe immediately, and state status," Kim radioed to the *Leapfrog's* bridge.

The bridge was ready and immediately responded, "Skipper, the recall has been sent, but the shuttle is one-half hour late for its check-in."

"Shit!" Kim said as she turned back to Bill. "Prep the rescue shuttle, and let me know when you can launch her. I'll need a crew manifest with no more than three personnel in case the moon's shuttle has been disabled."

Christine's associate, Dr. Hank Bethal, had just finished what looked like an intense talk with his helmet visor. "Commander, the DNA decoding is similar to our makeshift immunization. We'll refine ours and mass produce for re-immunization and for the cryo-sleepers."

Bill had patiently awaited his turn to reply. "Kim, our best bet is to send our convertible tanker and have the option to cut it once it gets there if we find the first shuttle immobilized. We'll be able to reduce flight time in half and still have plenty of fuel for the return."

"Do it," Kim replied.

"In that case, the shuttle's ready to go. I'll go along with two armed military personnel. I suggest we bring the fifty calibers and armor-piercing ammunition. High explosives might not go well with trapped hydrogen."

Kim reached over and gave Bill's arm a gentle squeeze. "Godspeed, Bill."

CHAPTER 37

"ME AND MY BIG MOUTH!" Scoffield remarked as the scout team resumed their hasty exit. In leaps and bounds, they were literally flying over the lunar forest. With each step they took, they covered three normal paces. The trick they all eventually learned was to keep low and stay within the previously cut trail. If they tended to bounce too high, the overhead branches and vines dragged them down. Approximately halfway, Gary stopped to relieve the stretcher carriers, but they waved him on. The light moon gravity made their burden hardly noticeable. However, Gary, along with the others, noticed shadows crisscrossing their path. The spiders seemed to be more in lead than pursuit, as if they knew where their prey was headed.

Gary was the first to step into the exit clearing and was so shocked he instantly stopped in his tracks. Christine, going full bore, did not have a chance to either stop or go around him.

"*Offf!*" She bowled into his back, knocking both of them flat and sliding in the muck. "Nice stop!" Christine said as she wiped off her muddy helmet visor.

Gary didn't answer; he got up and continued to stare at the exit. "We're in deep shit, people."

"So, what's new? We've been in deep shit ever since we stepped aboard the *Leapfrog.*" Christine was going to say something else, but her brain froze when she followed Gary's gaze to the exit.

"Oh, no!" was all Christine could think to say.

"Not again!" Scoffield snorted as he bounded into the clearing. The stretcher bearers and passenger were speechless.

Corporal Freddie Nelson was not in sight, and the state of their exit stunned all of them.

The exit pressure door was completely covered in spider webbing and bulging outwards from the thickness. Gary walked over and tried to hack it off with his machete.

"This is the same webbing that's on Peterson's legs and it's just as tough." Gary tried to pry the webbing apart, but it seemed welded together.

Christine knelt down next to him and tried to hack it with her machete. "Look! Amazing! It has some sort of healing properties. If you cut it like this . . ." She fitted the blade between two strands and twisted it. "There, you can see it start to mend. No wonder we can't cut it off Peterson's legs."

Peterson groaned and laid back down on his makeshift stretcher. "Thanks, doc. That just makes me feel real warm and fuzzy."

Gary was walking around the clearing, looking right and left. "Where's the cutting torch?"

Scoffield joined Gary in the search. "Don't tell me that fuck-head Nelson forgot to drag it inside?"

"Shit! When will we stop being so stupid?" Gary said to no one in particular.

"Uh, I hate to be the bearer of more bad news, but . . . we're down to our battery reserves. No more than forty-five minutes left." Christine had the status page dialed up and was taking a last-minute atmospheric reading.

"Nelson's suit locator is not operating and neither is his life support monitor," Christine continued.

Gary turned his helmet lights on "High" and scanned the surrounding trees. Eye reflections shone from all quadrants but retreated when the light beamed in their direction. Gary transmitted to all, "There's no way we can cut through this barrier within forty-five minutes. Once our packs are depleted and we lose our lights, the wolf spiders will come in force. We've got to conserve our power and somehow hold them off until the rescue ship arrives."

Scoffield posted the other men on a perimeter watch and joined Gary and Christine. "So let's fire a flare and blow the top off this dome. We can dig in and maybe survive."

Gary answered, "Just what I was thinking. There must be some caves or tunnels that the Neanderthals use to hide from the spiders. Let's start scouting for some place to dig in."

Christine added, "I hate to spoil your party, boys, but just what is blowing the top off this dome going to do for us? The hydrogen is at the top of the dome; look at the trees. They all turn brown at their tops and seem to automatically stop growing once they reach a certain height. Therefore, in my humble opinion, the top may go, but the side panels will remain. Then we're stuck in a vacuum with barrier walls, but, as comfort, there'll be no spiders, cockroaches, or Neanderthals."

Gary merely sighed and said, "Might as well be me." Before anyone could say anything, he depressurized his suit, released the helmet locks, and rotated his helmet off.

"No!" Christine screamed as she ran to his side, but it was too late. His helmet was now in his hands.

"Yuck! This smell sucks!" Gary exclaimed as he took a deep breath of the putrid swamp aroma. "Listen to those cockroaches hiss. Must be mating season or something." Helmet in hand, Gary walked around the perimeter looking at the ground. "Let's find where those Neanderthals hole up to hide from these spiders. Maybe they'd enjoy some company."

The rest of the group exchanged glances before following Gary's lead.

Christine took a big whiff of the foul air and gagged. "This is terrible! How can anything stand this? It's like swimming in a sewer."

Gary finally found what he was looking for. "Over here, lots of footprints leading to this big pile of rocks. Help me uncover whatever's under them, but don't throw the rocks too far away. We may need them to re-cover whatever may be hidden underneath."

There was no need for a second request for volunteers. All of them, except Peterson, moved toward the rocks. The low gravity made the work easy.

Darkness was slowly approaching, and the spiders were getting braver. Peterson, with his legs still wrapped in web, was now standing to keep guard while the others moved the rocks. One hairy spider even ventured into the clearing and started hissing. *Blam.* Peterson shot it in the left eye. "Take that, you motherfucker!"

The spider shrieked and sprang back, disappearing into the thick foliage. The shriek from the injured spider made them all shudder.

Christine was wide-eyed. "Did you see that? The spider must have jumped fifty meters!"

Gary saw it and was spellbound as he muttered, "If they can jump that far backward, what can they do forward?"

Once the rocks were removed, a small tunnel, barely large enough for one person to crawl through, was revealed. Gary took one of the headlamps from his helmet and tried to see how far the tunnel went. "Can't see much because it appears to bend about five meters down. Someone must have built this for a spider refuge, because there's no way one of those long-legged spiders can fit in here and make that bend. Peterson, you first. We'll tie a lanyard to your legs and haul you up if you encounter resistance."

Peterson did not look very happy about the prospect of crawling into a creepy tunnel with unknown critters lurking about, but he simply replied, "Aye, sir," as he hobbled over to the hole.

While they were tying a lanyard to Peterson's feet, Gary radioed a message to the shuttle's computer explaining their situation and location so their rescuers would have an idea what to expect when they re-cut the dome's entrance. The message also requested armor-piercing ammunition and plenty of illumination.

Scoffield did a final check on the lanyard, stood, and told Peterson, "If whatever you encounter down there doesn't retreat when you spotlight it and fire at it, we'll haul your ass back. Otherwise, you are to proceed to an area where we can all congregate or deep enough for all of us to squeeze in behind you."

Pale, Peterson stammered, "Y — yes, sir."

Christine stepped in front of Peterson and attached a small unit to his right shoulder. "This is an atmospheric monitor. If the air you're breathing goes out of limits, we'll haul you out." She paused and looked at Peterson with moist eyes. "Thank you. You are a brave man." Christine stood on her toes and gave Peterson a peck on his cheek.

Peterson flushed a light green and in his deepest voice said, "Thank you, ma'am."

One of the stretcher bearers who had been helping Scoffield secure the lanyard to Peterson commented, "Hey, you're not as green as you used to be when you're embarrassed. Must mean your blood is returning to normal. Heh, heh, also probably means you're tastier too." He burst out laughing at his ad-lib humor and doubled over.

Scoffield grabbed the man by both shoulders. "Shut up, Anderson, or I'll tie a rope around your neck and lower you down the hole."

It was Anderson's turn to flush green.

"Let's get on with it," Gary commanded. "These spiders are getting braver by the minute. It seems like they're on to what we're doing and are getting desperate." While finishing the sentence, Gary drew his sidearm and fired a couple of rounds at a spider that had just crawled into the clearing. One of the shots scored a hit in one of its eyes, and it too sprang backward out of sight.

Several other spiders crept into the clearing, and Gary emptied his clip, but only one sprang backward. "This is it! No time to reconnoiter the tunnel. Everyone inside now!" Gary shouted.

Scoffield stood next to Gary and started firing while Gary changed clips. Gary held his aim high until Scoffield shouted, "Loading!" Gary lowered his aim and started firing at the closest spider, immediately sending it backward, but more seemed to magically materialize out of the dark forest shadows.

"Loading!" Gary shouted as his clip emptied. He turned around and dared a quick peek behind him but saw nothing. "They're gone! Go. Go!" Gary shouted when more spiders appeared. Gary did not have to wait for Scoffield to obey because in a blur Scoffield jumped into the hole feet first, followed by Gary a nanosecond later. Just before Gary's feet contacted Scoffield's head, a sawlike claw clutched the right side of his face. Pushing harder, Gary could feel his flesh tear as the spider's leg lost its grip.

Surprisingly, neither Gary nor Scoffield hit solid resistance until they were a good five meters down where Gary had previously seen the bend. Two meters down from the bend, both men flopped unceremoniously into a small cavern with a soft floor. Well lit with all headlamps on, the arriving party took stock of their refuge. The modest cavern was covered with a variety of mushrooms. Two other exits, slightly larger than the one that they had slid through, were on the other end of the cavern. The stench was overwhelming, and Gary could not help but gag.

Christine was the first to recover. "Mushrooms! This must be one of many little plots scattered about. Whoever built this must have been driven to an underground existence by the big spiders." Christine paused for a moment, then added, "Don't even bother to guess what they're using for fertilizer."

She then got a good look at Gary and said, "You're hurt; you're bleeding on your right cheek. I need to get antibiotics on this immediately." She opened her med kit and started working on his face.

Scoffield's voice boomed in the confined cavern, "This just keeps getting better and better. But what's with the rocks covering the entrance? It's sure not to keep out the spiders. Their legs are too long to maneuver."

As Christine doctored him, Gary looked about and added, "Whoever built this probably put the stones there to keep the cockroaches out. The cockroaches would make short work of all these mushrooms."

"There. That should hold the skin together and keep most of the bacteria out," Christine said as she put what was left of her medical supplies back in her pack.

After satisfying himself that the current location was semi-secure, Gary said, "Okay, let's all gather around, sit back to back, and physically stay in touch with your neighbor. We'll need to douse our lights to conserve energy."

Everyone gathered where Gary sat down and formed a circle, back to back. The space suits provided psychological gratification that whatever they were sitting on was not seeping into their inner clothing. Actually, the mushrooms felt like foam cushions, and leaning back against each other was comforting. Total darkness was initially unnerving, but after a few minutes everyone's breathing rate dropped to normal rhythm. Until . . .

"Uh, sir?" Anderson whispered.

Scoffield answered, "What now, Anderson?"

"Umm, what if . . .? Never mind."

"What if what?" Scoffield growled back.

"Uh, maybe those rocks at the tunnel's entrance were put there to keep out something else, like a big snake or something."

Nine lights came on simultaneously, and everyone's outstretched legs instantly retracted.

Scoffield was scowling. "Anderson, you asshole! You just mouthed yourself into permanent KP duty."

"B — but, sir . . ."

Gary interrupted, "It's Okay, Anderson. We need to keep at least one light on in any case. We can rotate shifts and evenly distribute power loss."

Christine was chuckling at the brave warriors and said, "All these big macho men scared of a little snake?" She got a big kick out of her sense of humor and was laughing hysterically until a huge cockroach came through the tunnel and jumped on her head.

"Eieeeee!" she screamed and jumped straight up. The insect's barbed legs became entangled in her hair as she tried to pull the gigantic insect off the top of her head. She stumbled backward and fell flat on her back up to her ears in sewer sludge. The cockroach, even more frightened than Christine, disengaged its legs by pulling clumps of hair out, and scampered off to one of the rear tunnels.

Christine stood up and tried to shake the nasty residue from her hair. "I will shoot the first person who laughs." The tone of her voice convinced the men to stop chuckling.

Gary, trying to cajole her, said, "Maybe someone would volunteer to put the rocks back?"

Complete silence followed. Christine, still pissed, said through her teeth, "Don't bother! It's not worth facing those spiders again. Besides, I feel a draft, which means whoever built this complex had ventilation in mind. Or, at least at one time had circulation in mind."

"Well, we know they're still around. We just don't know in

what form and how friendly they may be. From what we experienced on Earth, I wouldn't bank on a welcoming ceremony."

A collective sigh washed over the group as they sat back down to immerse themselves in their individual thoughts and fears. Hours passed as the sun slipped farther from view on the lunar surface. All creatures, except the prey hidden in the tunnel, became braver and braver.

CHAPTER 38

BILL EVANS AND THE TWO other soldiers had just finished an hour of four g's deceleration. "That's the big disadvantage to going fast—just as painful slowing down." The soldiers just smiled back. They had no idea what to expect, and the space journey had provided them ample time to let their imaginations run amok.

"Aren't we a little too low, sir?" deep-voiced sergeant Scott Wilson said. The three of them had become fast friends on their journey to the moon. Wilson was a large muscular man of dark complexion who had obviously been in a few too many fights. His nose had that distinct mid-bend and his left ear was similar to a cauliflower. He said that the rugged look was his choice in order to keep transients from pressing their luck with him.

His sidekick, a small, light, complexioned woman, was his antithesis. Corporal Beth Simpson was petite and continuously pampered herself with various cosmetics. Nothing was out of place, not one single hair was allowed to stray. Bill guessed she needed to keep herself as prime as she could, for she needed all the help she could muster with a face like hers: long nose, thin lips, dark eyes, and a perpetual scowl. Lack of beauty aside, she seemed competent by the way she field stripped and cleaned every piece of her equipment.

Bill looked over his shoulder and found both of them out of their seat restraints leaning over and viewing the front monitor. "Nope, the gravity's lower here, and we can come a lot closer to the surface and stay in orbit. Here we go around the blind side of the moon."

As soon as he said it, an emergency beacon started chirping. Bill flipped a switch and said, "Computer, interrogate and report onboard status."

A green light flashed, and the recording of Gary's message began reporting where he was, what had happened, what needed to be done, and what to watch out for. Bill programmed the site into the shuttle's computer, marked a spot next to the stranded shuttle, and hit the "Land" button. Bill turned back around to make sure the soldiers got the message but found them already busy gathering the equipment Gary had suggested.

The shuttle's onboard computer vocally chirped, "The shuttle in the landing zone is in condition green; no malfunctions are indicated, and it contains sufficient fuel for return flight."

By the time Bill had his helmet on and locked, the shuttle was in its landing flare. Wilson and Simpson were both strapped in and looking grim.

Wilson said, "Sir, we'd appreciate it if you can back us up with some extra firepower once we cut through the pressure hatch. We thought it would be best if you remained at the entrance to guard our extraction. We'll leave you with a fifty caliber and several hundred rounds of armor-piercing ammo."

Bill gulped hard. "Somehow, I missed the fifty caliber training in my PhD engineering seminars. Could you quickly review the basics?"

"Blue screen on scope standby, green screen don't shoot. Just move the rifle to the vicinity you want covered and wait until the little computer finds a firing solution based on life-form. Follow the guidance bar and when the screen turns red, fire until the scope goes back to green; then repeat until the clip is empty. Replace the clip like this." Wilson released the clip and slipped it back home. "And you're back in business. Remember, you'll also have the laser torch that can cut through anything biological or metal like butter."

Simpson added, "Don't worry, sir, we're staying with you until the gas does its thing. We'll be firing the gas rockets in a one hundred and eighty-degree radius and should just about take care of any threat for a few hours."

Bill did not look too convinced. "Has this gas ever been tested on giant spiders before?" Seeing the crestfallen look on the soldiers' faces, he hastily added, "Uh, sorry, I guess I knew the answer to that question before I asked."

Simpson looked down at her feet and muttered, "Shit, sir, I wish you hadn't asked that."

Bill took a second look at the soldiers and asked, "You sure you can handle all that equipment?" Each carried two extra rifles, gas RPGs, floodlights, spare suit batteries, and what looked to Bill like a ton of ammunition pouches.

Wilson just shrugged and said, "We're banking on low gravity, sir."

Soft as a feather, the landing shuttle settled down on its landing appendages amid a raging dust storm. Visibility through the overhead monitor was reduced to zero.

Anticipating the next question, Bill said, "We're not waiting for the dust to settle. We'll use our suit's navigation to find the entrance and we'll tether ourselves together to keep from getting lost in the storm." Bill checked instruments, reeled out his suit's support line and snapped it on to Simpson. Simpson followed his lead and attached herself to Wilson.

Bill cross-scanned the shuttle's instruments and then hit the green "Open" button. Although they could not hear the *whoosh*, everyone imagined it as the shuttle filled with moon dust. Not being able to see their hands, they used the hand-rails to exit the shuttle, and the inertial navigation flawlessly directed them to the dome's entrance. Visibility was still poor, but now they were able to see the end of their arms and were able to stop in time before tailgating their leader.

Bill opened the pressure hatch, and after they were all in he secured the airtight door and activated the pressurization unit left behind by the other crew. Not waiting for balanced pressure, Bill walked over to the laser cutting torch also left behind and started re-cutting the door. A blast of air greeted them as the torch penetrated the dome and the air finally equalized.

Simpson saw the neatly stacked welding rods lying to the side and asked, "Sir, you're not planning on resealing this spider pit, are you?"

Without pausing Bill answered, "We'll have to. If we don't, it'll be like a huge balloon, and the exhaust coming through this hole would exceed three hundred kilometers per hour. Who knows what would happen to us or our shuttles."

Wilson keyed in, "Stick with what you're good at, Simpson, and leave the thinking to someone else." Wilson must have thought his stab at humor was hilarious and doubled over laughing.

Simpson simply said, "Up yours."

CHAPTER 39

"THERE! HEAR IT?" CHRISTINE FLASHED her light at one of the two tunnels on the other side of the cave. "Sounds like soft breathing and bare feet."

Gary replied, "Yeah, I heard it this time. Let's keep the tunnels illuminated just in case whoever's there gets braver."

No sooner was that said when a small, nude, hairy mini Bigfoot appeared at the right side tunnel. Shocked, the party could only stare in amazement at the apparition. In a high-pitched shrill that echoed in the cave, the creature sheltered his eyes with his hairy left arm and threw what appeared to be a long spear directly at Christine's head. Fortunately, the bright lights had temporarily blinded the dirty creature, and his aim was high. The makeshift spear smacked against the stone wall and fell by Christine's outstretched legs. Quickly turning, the attacker dashed back to the dark safety of his escape tunnel, but he was not faster than the four bullets that followed him. Their impact sent him flying deeper into the dark recesses of the tunnel.

Gary instantly fired three blind rounds into the other tunnel. A spine tingling howl followed. "Stay down!" Gary commanded. "That's the only thing that saved Christine; his aim was high. Next time, we'll fire on sound alone. So much for the welcoming committee."

Christine leaned over and picked up the stone-tipped spear and examined it. "These people have degenerated further than the ones on Earth. Look at this stone spear. The sharpened stone is wedged in the stick and wrapped with some sort of vine. The Neanderthals are still using leftover metals. These people have devolved a lot more than the ones on Earth. What in the hell could have triggered this?"

"I know this is not a democracy, but if I had a vote I'd vote to nuke this place if and when we get out of here," Scoffield offered.

Christine was quick to reply, "Why? This is life as usual for this place. Nothing but survival going on here, and they're absolutely no threat to us down on Earth. Besides, I doubt they have very long to live. The material covering this dome is way past its lifespan, and once it goes . . . *poof*, this place returns to rock and dust."

"Sir, how long do you think we'll have to wait for rescue?" Anderson asked.

"Assuming they cruised at the same speed we did, we have another five hours to go, but if they hauled ass, they could be here almost anytime now. I don't think the radios will work in this rock hole, so the signal to put on our helmets will be explosions."

"Explosions?" Christine squeaked.

"Yes, I asked for general tranquilizing gas rockets to be fired randomly before they attempted ingress. I don't know what they brought with them, but I'm sure—"

"There!" Anderson interrupted. "There goes the last web." He had been diligently working, trying to cut the webbing off of Peterson's legs. "Hold on, I'll need to patch this little hole I accidentally cut in your suit."

"A hole? You cut a hole in my pressure suit?" Peterson said.

"Yeah, but don't sweat it. I'm patching it right now. This stuff was much easier to cut once it dried out some. Wonder what made it so tough to start with?"

"Hmm, that is interesting since spider silk is supposed to be hygroscopic," Christine thought aloud. Receiving dumbstruck looks from the men, she continued, "Hygroscopic means the ability to bind water, thus preventing the thread from drying out." The men continued to stare like deer caught in a spotlight. "The polymerization process produces protein that is not decomposed by fungi and bacteria; and it can stretch by forty percent, unlike nylon of twenty percent, and it has torsion memory and a resistance factor unequaled in our most advanced synthetic materials."

She took a breath to continue, but Scoffield jumped in first. "Thanks, Doc. Must have missed that in commando training."

Sighing deeply, Christine said, "Since we don't seem to have much else to do for the time being, and—"

Boom! The first muffled explosion cut her off.

CHAPTER 40

"THAT'S IT!" BILL EXCLAIMED AS he switched the laser cutter off. "All I have to do now is give it a little pull, and we're in."

"Okay, sir, but when you pull it through, make sure you back off right away because we'll be firing rockets over the top of you," Wilson said.

As if in slow motion, the hatchway tipped over into the dark and gloomy dome. Bill did as he was told and squirmed backward on his hands and knees as soon as the door went over center and started falling.

Whoosh, whoosh. Two rockets flashed over his head, followed by several more sets of rockets. A few seconds later, loud explosions erupted deep inside the dome.

"Give it a few minutes for the gas to do its thing before we jump in there," Wilson ordered Simpson, but Simpson was not about to jump through the doorway until her leader led her.

Dropping the gas RPGs, the troopers shouldered their rifles and knelt in the passageway. "Ah, shit!" Wilson exclaimed as he scanned the dark interior with his scope. "There must be hundreds of them. Kill as many as you can before we hit them with illumination."

As Wilson and Simpson started firing, Bill rolled out of the way, grabbed a rifle, stood, and started firing over their heads. The scope was set to auto, and all Bill had to do was move the scope/rifle until the view went from blue to red; then he fired and kept firing, exhausting three clips before the scope remained red. Once in awhile he could identify the spiders in the crosshairs just before the rifle fired, but most of the time the rifle seemed to fire at hidden objects in the thick foliage.

"Cease-fire!" Wilson ordered right before he jumped through the door with an arm full of portable flood lamps. Quickly, he set up a semicircular perimeter of lights and flicked them on. Dozens of dead spiders were strewn about the clearing, some still moving. "Okay, we're off! The lights may keep them away, but if you get overrun, retreat into the exit tunnel with the laser torch." No sooner were the words transmitted than Wilson and Simpson sprinted off in a rescue attempt.

The second explosion was much louder and reverberated throughout the cavern. "Helmets on!" shouted Gary as he fumbled with the locks. As one, they all lowered their weapons, dimmed the helmets' lights and became preoccupied with the pressure locking sequence.

And then, following the lead of a loud, shrill howl, the little primates poured out of the two exits for their assault on these strange invaders. Christine froze in fright with her helmet just pulled over her head and locked gazes with a totally insane monster. His eyes were red, beady, and wide open with absolute determination. He had Christine bore-sighted and was rearing back the club in his right hand as he dashed in her direction.

The creature's lips were pulled back, baring yellow, filed and pointed front teeth; his complexion was darkened by dirt, grime, and what looked like dried blood. Gary witnessed the attacker closing fast on Christine and made an attempt to raise his pistol into the aggressor's path, but was tackled and knocked down by another assailant intent on removing his head.

Christine tried to lean back and dodge the club but could not move back enough to keep from receiving its full force. Thinking the blow would surely take her head off, she closed her eyes and hoped it would not be too painful.

Thunk! The makeshift stone axe bounced off her helmet.

She was still alive! Not only alive, but unscathed by the savage's tremendous blow. The expression of her assailant went from hate to bewilderment as he drew back to strike again. Christine let loose with a roundhouse kick before the creature could come at her again.

Offf! The mini Bigfoot went sailing across the cave and stayed airborne until he collided with the far wall. Hitting the stone headfirst, he crumpled into an unconscious pile. He was followed by two then three of his comrades.

"Weak!" Gary shouted over the intercom. "These guys don't have any strength." While he was speaking, he felt a stone axe thump against his back. Turning around, he snatched the assailant's arm as he drew back for another swing. Twisting the arm down as hard as he could, he felt the bones break, and the axe dropped to the floor. With both hands, Gary clutched the side of the attacker's greasy head and gave it a good twist, easily snapping the neck.

The fortunes of war shifted quickly for the attacking force. Once smug in the knowledge that they had superiority by sheer numbers and could easily overrun their foe, they found themselves entangled with a bunch of supermen with incredible strength. Their degenerated muscles and chalk-like bones made their appearances far more fearsome than their capabilities.

Reaching down and grabbing the stone axe, Gary made short work of two more assailants. A few shots rang out, followed by the familiar ricochet pinging, causing Gary to transmit, "No firearms! Use their axes!"

The battle instantly went low-tech with both sides using the axe-like clubs. Battling back to back with axes swinging, blood, brain, and bone pieces sprayed across the cavern. Christine still had her spear and had withdrawn from the midst of her club-wielding comrades.

Unfortunately for the invaders, the front line got the message to retreat, but comrades following them were still not believers and wanted a crack at the aliens who had provoked the dreaded spiders and trashed their mushroom field. A major traffic jam developed as the pile of bodies continued to build at the far end of the cave. Only when the attackers realized that the bodies they were clambering over were their own did they start retreating in earnest. With a spine tingling howl, the miniature Neanderthals evaporated into the tunnels.

Stunned, the defenders stood frozen waiting for another assault until they heard, "You guys coming out of your hole, or do you need a written invitation to be rescued? Better hurry! The gas doesn't seem to work very well with the spiders; as a matter of fact, I don't think the gas works at all. We've got some extra rifles up here." The bend in the tunnel prevented them from seeing Wilson, but his transmission was received by all, loud and clear.

Gary had just boosted Christine into the shaft when Scoffield said, "I have a feeling they're waiting for us to turn our backs."

Gary spotlighted the two small tunnels on the far side of the room and caught some movement in the dark recess. "You're right. They're getting ready as we speak." Pulling a concussion grenade from his vest, Gary said, "Set it at thirty seconds. You throw one in the right, and I'll get the left." Gary waited until Scoffield was ready, then transmitted, "Go!"

Both men pitched the grenades into the center of the holes. Not waiting around, they scrambled up the tunnel, Gary last.

Gary had just rounded the bend when something clutched his right leg and started pulling him back down. Stretching out his arms and locking his back against the stone tunnel, he arrested his backward slide until a second set of hands grabbed his left leg. Not able to generate enough friction to prevent backsliding, Gary started slipping.

Almost simultaneously, the two grenades detonated. Gary did not hear a sound; he only felt a huge compression against his space suit and a rocketing ride out of the tunnel. *Poof!* Gary shot out of the hole and, as if in slow motion, fell directly on top of a gawking Christine, knocking her flat on her back.

"Wow! How'd you do that?" she exclaimed with wide eyes.

Suddenly, a dirty, bloody, bare arm flopped next to her. It took her a second to realize the arm had been torn from the shoulder joint, had lots of hair, and was relatively thin. "Never mind!" Christine said as she pushed Gary off and scrambled to her feet.

CHAPTER 41

BILL WAS STUNNED. OUT OF the blue, a huge spider landed on top of one of two sets of portable floodlights. Before he could react, the spider had tumbled the light set down and rolled it over several times with its long spindly legs. Within seconds, the lamp set was completely wound in what seemed to be white ropes. The bright white glow continued to shine through the webbing, but it was considerably dimmer. As the spider advanced to the remaining light set, Bill shot it. The armor-piercing round zipped through one of the spider's left side eyes and blew out through the eye on the right. Screeching, the animal leaped an amazing distance into the jungle tiers.

Looking through the scope, Bill could see red portions expand to all quadrants. "Here they come!" he yelled into the transmitter. "I don't have enough ammunition!" Bill selected "Auto" and his rifle barked every time he moved the barrel. When he lowered the rifle to reload, he saw six spiders land uncomfortably close to where he stood.

"Fuck it!" he said as he dropped the rifle and ran back to the dome's exit. Diving into the passageway, he frantically grabbed the laser torch. Just as he activated the laser beam, he was pulled violently from his shelter. Holding on to the laser torch for dear life, he bent over and made several blind swipes, hoping he did not cut off his own legs in the process. Immediately, the pulling ceased and two severed spider legs fell on top of him, covering him with some kind of gooey clear fluid. More legs came groping, but they were no match for the high tech laser torch. Hastily crawling back inside the exit tunnel, Bill continued to wave the torch in the direction of the spiders, catching a leg or two every other sweep. Each leg he cut came cleanly off, but squirted spider blood was everywhere. He took a stand right inside the exit and managed to kill several spiders as they tried to web over the exit. He had to wait for the spiders to lay their abdomens across the exit before starting his slice and dice routine. Bill only wished the torch beam extended a bit farther out.

"Don't run!" Gary shouted at his retreating party. "Form a firing circle and exit in an orderly fashion!"

Christine had collected the arm and was studying it when Gary grabbed her and literally dragged her away.

The team hadn't gone far when the first spear struck Simpson directly in the chest. *"Offf!"* she exhaled as the spear bounced off her reinforced space suit and fell to the ground. "What the hell?" she said as she looked up and found a mini ape-man gawking at her. The spear thrower was still trying to understand why his deadly weapon merely bounced off the alien when his head exploded into a red mist.

"Holes!" Scoffield shouted into his microphone. "They're coming out of different holes! This place is loaded with them." Rocks seemed to erupt as the pissed off primates pushed their way to the surface.

"Keep moving!" Gary shouted and started firing one of the rifles Wilson and Simpson had left for them.

The mini Bigfoots swarmed out of their tunnels like ants. Some rushed at them swinging stone axes, while others chucked spears from a distance they thought was safe. The guns took their toll, but the frenzied attackers assaulted in waves, getting closer each time the visitors reloaded.

"Thank God!" Bill said aloud as the spiders suddenly retreated. Through his goop-covered visor, he could make out the direction of the spiders' retreat. Realizing they were not retreating but merely targeting different prey, he shouted, "Watch out! They're coming your way!"

"What's coming this way?" Gary shouted back, but as soon as he replied, he saw the spiders descending on the crazed primates. Taking only seconds to wrap them up and leave them for later, the spiders swiftly thinned out the creatures of least resistance. The ground was littered with squirming cocoons.

Realizing the spiders were devoting their time to the primates, Gary transmitted, "Okay, time to run!" Off they went, half bouncing, half sprinting, and all arrived at the exit at the same time.

Bill turned off his torch when he picked up the blurred space-suited images coming his way. "Man, am I glad to see you!"

As the team hurried inside the exit, Gary looked around at all the spider parts lying about. "Nice going, young Jedi."

"Huh?" said Bill as he hoisted the door back to its jamb.

"Never mind. Wasted humor," Gary grunted and held

the door closed while Bill started welding. The top of the door started to sway inward. "Someone help me hold the door. Bill, spot wield, four point, until we can keep the spiders from pushing it in."

Once Bill had the door bordered with a thick bead, Gary said, "Depressurize, and let's get the hell out of here."

CHAPTER 42

As the shuttle door was closing, Scoffield said, "Sir, it wouldn't take me any time at all to rig up an incendiary rocket. We could torch the dome when we leave."

Gary sneaked a peek at Christine, who was scowling furiously at him in anticipation of his command to "Nuke it!"

Gary sighed and answered, "No, the doc's right. They're no threat to us on Earth. Besides, we're part of the reason they wound up here." Getting only silence in return, Gary continued, "The Space Consortium built this dome with the *Leapfrog* in mind. No weather concerns and a lot less gravity to deal with."

"Aye, sir," was Scoffield's despondent answer.

Christine mused, "Those people, if that's what we can call them, were excessively enraged considering the circumstances. I mean, exactly what did we do to make them so mad?" Not waiting for an answer, she continued, "All we did was seek emergency escape from those horrid spiders, and we squashed a few mushrooms. They charged with the sole intent of killing us. Completely psychotic; I've never seen such rage before."

Scoffield jumped in, "Still not too late to nuke 'em."

This time she turned and glared at Scoffield. "No, that would not accomplish anything but unnecessarily killing creatures that have no control over their environment. Their time is short as it is because that dome is way beyond its life-span. Who knows? Maybe a new life-form will evolve that can survive even if the dome disintegrates."

Bill and Gary decided it would be best if the rescue shuttle delayed its launch fifteen minutes and trailed the other shuttle back to the *Leapfrog*. Bill's rescue shuttle, however, would wind up beating Gary's by a few hours since it would use its extra fuel for greater speed.

Gary finished cross-checking the shuttle's instruments and announced, "Ten seconds for rocket ignition. I'm keeping the cabin depressurized until we exit lunar orbit, so keep your suits under pressure." As soon as he spoke, the crew felt a welcome rumble followed by gut-wrenching acceleration. Quickly establishing a low lunar orbit, the shuttle continued to accelerate unhindered by atmospheric drag. The lunar landscape blurred as the shuttle continued to the far side of the moon to be slung out of orbit in a trajectory computed for the interception of *Leapfrog's* Earth orbit.

A few minutes later, the acceleration abruptly ceased, with the following zero g having a nauseating effect. "That's it, folks!" Gary said as he removed his helmet and unstrapped his restraining belts. "I think I've had enough excitement on this trip to last a lifetime."

Christine simply murmured, "I hope that's true."

CHAPTER 43

"Both shuttles are returning. The first shuttle will arrive within twenty hours; the second in a few hours. We sustained one casualty and were lucky it was only one." Kim had the rapt attention of her audience, which included the entire ship. Those unable to leave their posts were watching her on their station monitors. Kim moved to the side of her podium to take a more relaxed posture before continuing, "Now that we have a fair idea of what happened on Earth and can produce adequate immunizations, we will next establish a homestead and start dependent cryogenic recovery." She took a breath to continue, but a slender, young woman, obviously a nurse by her white uniform, raised her hand. "Yes?" Kim asked.

The woman appeared to be very nervous and hesitant. "Uh, ma'am, do you think it's possible for a small group of us to remain aboard the *Leapfrog*? I . . . I mean, certainly there's plenty to keep us busy up here in case the Earth base needs our assistance."

Kim flashed back to an earlier event that day. Dr. Gary Mitchell, also known as Dr. Death, had cornered her in a passageway and more or less demanded that he remain behind. Kim told him that he had two choices—first, come to Earth with them; second, take a one-way trip to the sun for proper disposal. He responded by leaning close to Kim to try to intimidate her, but Kim stood her ground and glared back. He huffed and strode off, pushing Kim out of his way. Kim touched her security button before calling after him. "Excuse me, Doctor Mitchell."

"What?" He scowled as he turned around.

"I'm placing you under quarter's confinement until we establish ourselves on Earth. I've lost complete confidence in your good intentions and would rather have you confined to keep you out of mischief."

"Bullshit! You can't do that! I'm a department head on this ship, and you have no authority to do that. Furthermore, I demand a hearing and an official pardon from your previous abuse of power." He was getting closer to Kim as he continued to rant. "While I'm at it, bitch, let's get one thing straight—" He stopped mid-sentence when two fully armed soldiers dashed down the corridor. "Who . . . who . . . what do you think you're doing?" Mitchell stuttered as the soldiers flanked him.

"They're your new babysitters, Mitchell, and you're wrong, I do have the proper authority. Treat your keepers nice, or they won't treat *you* very nice." As Kim was turning away, she added, "By the way, you just earned passage on the first shuttle leaving *Leapfrog*. Your new friends will help you pack." Kim smiled and walked away.

Mitchell's complexion changed from dark to very pale. The last place he wanted to be was on Earth with the crocodiles and human throwbacks.

Kim's thoughts returned to her present audience, and she

answered the nurse, "Sorry, no one stays. This ship's in the process of literally falling apart. We leak pressure like a sieve and require a constant run of seventy percent output of our ten pressurization packs. Each day, that demand increases, and we can't keep all ten packs running indefinitely." The nurse sat back down, obviously not happy with her answer.

Kim continued, addressing her entire audience. "Let's face it, folks, this spaceship is way past her prime. Our once-flexible skin is now brittle, our batteries are only twenty percent rated, our propulsion unit's shot, and our engineering department is constantly putting out electrical fires caused by deteriorating insulation.

"We need to evacuate this ship, the sooner the better, and that's why I called you to this meeting. Now that we have our two other shuttles returning, we'll start evacuation immediately. If you have dependents, you can wait for their recovery before your evacuation. Those that have no dependents can expect the move within the day. The military contingency will be the first to depart, led by Carl Manning. They will establish shelter and perimeter defense."

Everyone was on the edge of their seats. The murmurings turned into a roar, and dozens of hands shot in the air. Kim called the meeting back to order and took the next half hour answering questions. In the meantime, the life support and medical staff began the recovery of the first wave of dependents in cryo-sleep. They decided that the most they could handle were twenty patients per four hours. The defrost cycle took a good twelve hours, and after that the next twenty-four hours were to be spent for reorientation and family reunions. All patients were to be immediately inoculated and then sedated to relieve some of the headaches.

Christine looked over at Gary as Kim finished her trans-mission. He was smiling like a Cheshire cat when he flicked the monitor off. She whispered, "Happy to see your babies again?"

"More than happy," he replied.

Christine saw his eyes water, and she reached over to give his hand a good squeeze.

CHAPTER 44

CARL WAS GRIPPING HIS ARMREST so tightly, his knuckles were white. The shuttle's rockets had just kicked in for the vertical descent, causing the airframe to shudder as though it were falling apart.

"Don't worry, sir." Sergeant Louis Conner had to shout over the loud noise. Conner was a small, compact man, bulging with muscles and gifted with a deep voice. "We only have to worry if the noise stops and we're still airborne. *Splat!* Just like that!" Conner slapped his hand on his knee to emphasize the imaginary crash. He must have thought his attempt at humor was hilarious because he folded up laughing at Carl's reaction.

Carl's already pale face blanched so white Conner thought for sure he was going to faint. It wouldn't help his image as designated leader. After all, he had to show at least a morsel of courage. Actually, Conner was in charge, with Carl being more of a figurehead. Kim still had some serious misgivings concerning the military contingency and wanted Carl to monitor their activities.

Kim told Carl there was simply too much at stake to release the delegation to military personnel she did not have much experience with. She would have liked to have Gary lead the mission, but he was still on board the returning shuttle. Furthermore, Kim thought it would be best for Gary to take a break and spend some time with his recovering twin girls.

Gulping hard, Carl turned back to the monitor and watched the shuttle's computer execute a perfect landing at the chosen site in what was formerly Canada. After watching the monitor lights flick green one at a time, Carl pushed the green "Open Door" switch and yelled, "Go! Go!" He had wanted yell that for years but had never had the opportunity. By the time he unbuckled and clambered down the stairs, the troops had already fanned out for perimeter defense.

The fresh country air was intoxicating. Carl simply stood on the bottom of the stairs taking in the summer freshness and overwhelming beauty of the landscape. The selected site was on a plateau overlooking an enchantingly green forest on one side and a picturesque lake on the other with green-clad mountains reflected in the calm waters.

Remembering Dr. Mitchell, Carl went back up the stairs and found him trying to be invisible in the aft right seat. "Let's go, Mitch! Once the water team recharges the tanks, this ship is off for another run."

Mitchell slowly stood, scowled, and gathered his belongings. He hated being called "Mitch," and Carl knew it. Carl despised Mitchell and used every opportunity to express that emotion.

Underneath the shuttle, a working party was offloading supplies with reckless abandon. Boxes, packages, instruments, and supplies were literally being thrown out of the cargo bay into a heap.

Carl interrupted them. "Easy there, fellows! That's sensitive equipment our lives depend on, and once it's gone, there'll be no replacements." Offloading proceeded much more carefully.

Carl found Bill's aquatic robots and started making his way to the banks of the lake. Two armed escorts with rifles at the ready flanked him. The troops had unanimously decided everyone was safer if Carl did not possess a weapon. Previously, when the military unit was trying to qualify Carl with firearms, Carl had accidentally shot a hole in the deck of the *Leapfrog*. The engineering department that had repaired the ship was pissed, but after much pleading by Carl, they had promised not to report the incident to the c.o.

Dr. Mitchell, on the other hand, was actually prohibited from carrying a weapon.

Without speaking, Mitchell helped Carl haul some of the torpedo-like robots to the shoreline. Carl picked up two, changed some settings, and placed them knee deep in the lake. *Whirr*, and they quickly disappeared, dutifully checking the lake for large life forms. "Yep, monitors working," Carl said after checking each for proper transmissions.

"Want some more?" Mitchell asked.

"Let's see, we've got a total of six. Sure, but we'll put them in a loiter mode to be activated only if one of the others finds something."

As they were setting the other two robots, Mitchell asked, "What are they going to do if they find some crocs?"

"They're programmed to behave like curious bass fish and escape if pursued. However, if they get captured, they're to self destruct." Carl stopped and looked hard at Mitchell. "The charge is way overbuilt. We definitely don't want one of these to fall into the wrong hands. Er, make that claws."

Mitchell only smiled

"Shelter, people! Five minutes before shuttle launch," Conner shouted so everyone could hear. "A water shuttle is in reentry now, so one blast will be followed by another. Go to your assigned trench and remain vigilant."

Mitchell stammered, "Th — th — they're leaving us behind?"

Carl smiled and answered, "Yup, welcome to your new home. We're here for good, for better or worse. Come on, let's get into the trenches before we get sandblasted to the bone and cooked medium rare."

Conner jumped into the trench next to the two civilian doctors. "Now I've got a captive audience, at least until the sandstorm starts. You guys have any ideas about our future defense needs? I mean, we're not going to have unlimited ammunition, and we're a long way from developing more sophisticated weapons." Getting a blank look from both doctors, Conner continued, "Well, if you could put your heads to it, we'd sure appreciate any thoughts. I'd hate to go toe to toe with one of these crocs with only a bow and arrow."

Mitchell jumped to his feet, startling the others. "That's it!" Looking at Conner, he said, "There's your answer; it's in your question."

Conner reached over and pulled Mitchell back into a seated position. "Doc, no shit, the upcoming blast will literally blow your face away, so please stay seated." Appearing puzzled, Conner asked, "What do you mean, the answer is in my question?"

"Bows and arrows, of course!" Mitchell replied, immediately taking his professorial tone of voice and making Conner feel like an idiot. "Once our lab is up and running, we'll manufacture some of the most potent toxins known to man and tip our arrows with the poison the same way the primitive jungle people used to do." Completely ignoring his audience, Mitchell continued in a low voice as if speaking to himself. "If I remember correctly, the poison arrow frog digested alkaloids from fire ants and produced a toxin called *batrachotoxin,* which has about three hundred times the potency of strychnine. Let's see, if we could alter the molecular structure to resemble more of a tetrodotoxin—"

Boom! Mitchell's words were cut off by the blast of the shuttle's rockets. The Earth shuddered as the shuttle throttled up for ascent. Mitchell was terrified and thought the Earth would open up and swallow them all, until it rained sand. Then he thought they would all be buried alive. He longed to get back into a laboratory.

Ears still ringing and full of sand, Conner shook his head in an attempt to clear the sand out of his hair. Mitchell looked like a frightened child about to soil himself. Conner turned to Carl and resumed the discussion as though the departing shuttle was nothing but a necessary nuisance, by exclaiming, "Frogs! What is it with you scientists and frogs? And crocodiles? Jesus Christ! Here we're loaded up with synthetic frog blood, live on a ship called *Leapfrog,* and will now base a defense on a frog to protect us from deranged crocodiles that scientists designed. If I ever hear or see a frog again, I'll puke."

Carl frowned when he said, "Humans didn't intentionally design these crocs this way. It's just the way lady luck spun the evolutionary wheel of fortune." Sighing, he added, "Of course we weighted the wheel a little with our DNA war. But, not to worry. Frogs were extinct way before we left Earth. Frogs were very fragile animals and among the first to succumb to the effects of pollution."

"Then how are we going to make a toxin from them, if they're not around anymore?" Conner asked.

Mitchell snapped out of his temporary stupor and said, "We don't need live frogs. Our computer database has the entire DNA decoding information on all life forms ever recorded on Earth. Hopefully, your ammunition will hold out long enough for me to get the lab up and running—" Another roar, this time overhead, interrupted Mitchell. Looking up, all he could see were ragged flames coming down at them.

Frightened, Mitchell jumped up and tried to run away from the abomination descending on them. Fortunately for him, Conner was anticipating another foolish gesture and grabbed both his legs, bringing him down on his face. Conner was shaking his head when he said, "Shit, Doc! You got some kind of death wish or something? Stay down and you'll be fine; jump up again, you'll surely die painfully."

Mitchell nodded his head in compliance. "Yeah, yeah, you're right. Sorry, just lost my composure for a moment."

So did a curious croc that wandered out of the lake into the blast zone between the two shuttle launch and recovery cycles. The scorching gases of the rockets on the descending shuttle instantly fried the creature and blasted the animal right on the top of the blast trench with its smoking, dead head pointed directly at Mitchell. Mitchell continued to scream until he mercifully fainted.

CHAPTER 45

GARY WAS ANXIOUSLY STANDING BETWEEN the two capsules that were holding his two daughters, Lori and Bobbi. He could not help but think how much the little girls had emotionally suffered in their short lives for having a mother who had refused to acknowledge their existence. Paula, Gary's ex-wife, was the hottest, bed-wrecking sex machine Gary had ever met. The wife of a good friend had introduced them while Gary was on military leave. He had just finished a harrowing assignment and was set for some good R&R time. Paula was the perfect companion.

A whirlwind romance was followed by matrimony, which led to pregnancy and then to a hasty divorce. An angry Paula wanted nothing to do with motherhood and demanded an abortion the moment symptoms were evident. She was not about to have her wild flings and jet-set lifestyle hindered by brats. Gary talked her into at least having the minute fetuses transferred to a bio lab that provided incubation services. She had consented only after Gary had offered her a year of his pay. After the brief operation, an angry Paula stormed pell-mell out of the clinic with Gary in pursuit. He was hoping he could soothe her a little and talk her into at least some participation in the children's development, but an infuriated Paula literally threw her wedding ring at him and told him to stay away from her and never let the children know she was their mother. Except for her sending divorce papers that required his signature and his agreement to transfer over his hard-earned savings, he never heard from her again.

While Gary was away on military missions, nannies and family support helped take care of the girls. As they aged, they automatically took it upon themselves to manage the household, assume cooking duties and, most importantly to them, take care of their dad. Gary was careful not to bring home any of his female friends until he was seriously contemplating another marriage, and that never happened. Although only eight years old when they left with Gary on the perilous journey, both girls took pride in their shipshape house and pampered dad.

The frost inside the transparent capsules began to clear as the temperatures gradually increased. Gary thought he would develop whiplash as he glanced from one girl to another. The computer indicated all biological functions were restored and operating satisfactorily, but that provided little relief for the fretful father. His imagination of all the horrible side effects that could result from cryo-sleep was driving him insane.

Gary studied their delicate features as the visibility continued to improve. Freckles dotted each of their small, upturned noses. Long eyelashes shut tight hid beautiful green eyes. Short blond hair, turning more auburn by the year, was swept back as though a strong wind had blasted it. They were fraternal twins but could easily be mistaken for identical if they dressed the same and styled their hair to match.

Their emergence from cryo-sleep was well underway with body core temperatures approaching twenty-five degrees Celsius. Circulation of the antifreeze-type blood had begun two hours earlier, which certainly did not enhance their natural coloring. Gary wondered how much they would freak out when they learned they had green blood. Right now, he would be satisfied with their having the ability to freak out. The degree of temporal brain damage would not be known until they reached full consciousness. A few of the other dependents revived earlier had not fared well and had never achieved consciousness; they were subsequently declared to be in a permanent vegetative state. Gary could handle anything combat could throw at him, but not that. He had no idea how he could cope with the loss of one or both of his daughters.

Several hours later, Christine walked in right before the final recovery commenced. Gary had a hand on each capsule, obviously saying a prayer. "Hi, big fella. How're the girls doing?"

Gary jumped and spun around. "Oh, hi. Caught me by surprise. So far so good. This waiting around is killing me."

Christine smiled and took him by the hand. "I've been monitoring their progress, and they look great. EEGs are normal in the alpha, beta, and theta signals of forty CPS, which indicates a ninety-eight percent chance of successful recovery. The body tissue scanner picked up some dead temporal nerve fibers, but no more than anyone else who recovered from cryo-sleep. The unfortunate few who didn't make it had flat waves, not even a neurological blip. We believe they died during the long sleep, not even knowing what happened to them. Their bodies survived, but not their minds."

The machines beeped almost simultaneously, causing Gary to spin back around facing the capsules. "Look!" he exclaimed, "Their hearts are beating!" No sooner had he uttered the words than the machines beeped again. "Hah! Now they're breathing." Gary whirled back around and gave Christine a bone-crushing hug while tears streamed down his face. "They're going to make it!"

Christine groaned. "They will, but I may not if you don't let up on the hug."

Gary said, "Sorry," as he dropped her and spun back to the capsules.

The capsules' monitors started flashing green lights. All but one: "Transfusion" remained red.

As soon as the girls' eyelids started to flutter, the capsule's transparent covering slid open. Bobbi was the first to recover. "Oww, ouch! Daddy!" she cried.

Gary reached in and gingerly picked up Bobbi. "It's okay, baby. I know you have a terrible headache, but it will get better soon. I promise."

Unseen by Gary, Christine had pushed in one of the few rocking chairs. "Here, Gary, sit here with Bobbi, and I'll bring Lori over to you when she wakes." With perfect timing, Lori started crying.

Christine went to Lori's capsule and gently picked her up. "Good morning, honey. I'm taking you to your daddy and sister." Lori rubbed her eyes vigorously and renewed her crying. "It will take a few minutes for you to see, so just keep them closed for now. Here's your daddy." She gently placed Lori on Gary's other arm, and she immediately cuddled in.

"D — Daddy, I missed you," Lori whimpered.

"Me, too," Bobbi added.

"I missed my girls a lot too," Gary said soothingly.

"I've got some things I need to tend to. I'll catch up with you later," Christine said as she left the recovery room.

———————

Christine entered a mayhem zone when she entered her once quiet and peaceful medical lab. Not one square centimeter was without some sort of medical supply or instruments. Preparing for departure in addition to recovering all the dependents had her staff spinning in chaos. One of her colleagues, Sam Henry, hurried over to her.

"We've lost another! A fourteen-year-old boy, and the father has threatened to kill me! Flat EEGs with no response to stimuli." Sam blurted as soon as he was close to her. Sam was thin and wiry; a man who was never still. All the activity created a major overload for the fidgety, diminutive doctor, leaving Christine wondering whether or not he was experiencing a breakdown. "I have no idea what to do with their corpses, and their parents refuse to leave them."

Christine said, "Flag their cubicles, and I'll pay them a visit. If any more expire, our protocol will be to provide a small service, give the parents a few hours of peace with them, and quietly torpedo them for a solar rendezvous—"

"—but," Sam interrupted, "we can't just launch them into the sun."

Christine put both of her hands on his shoulders. "Listen, Sam. I don't like it either, but what choices do we have? We can't leave them here on this derelict. We can't take them to Earth with us because we don't have enough space as it is. What would you suggest we do?"

Relieved that someone at least had a plan, Sam sighed deeply and bowed his head. "Sorry. You're absolutely correct; we have no other choice. Come on, I'll take you to the cubes myself."

That hour was the most strenuous and stressful hour of her life. Nothing was worse for her than to try to comfort grieving parents or spouses. Christine was still wiping away tears when she returned to Gary's cubicle.

Gary and the two girls had huge smiles pasted on their bright green faces. "That must be the family's genetic smile," she exclaimed as she walked into the recovery room. "Hello, Lori and Bobbi. My name is Christine, and I'm one of the ship's doctors. I was here earlier when you first woke up and wanted to stop by to see how you're doing. Besides a headache, any other complaints?"

"No, ma'am," they answered in unison.

Bobbi squinted her eyes at Christine in an effort to focus. "You're very pretty," she declared.

Immediately Lori squinted a look at Christine and asked, "Are you Daddy's girlfriend?"

"Girls . . ." Gary began.

Without missing a beat, Christine replied, "Yes."

Bobbi smacked her dad on the arm. "Waaaay to go, Dad!"

Beaming ear to ear Lori asked, "You gonna marry Daddy?"

"That's enough," shouted Gary, but once the girls were on a scent, they would not easily abandon their pursuit.

Taken aback by the speed of the interrogation, Christine stuttered, "Well . . . well . . . we haven't gotten that far yet."

Bobbi jumped out of Gary's lap to give Christine a hug, but fell forward. Christine barely had time to grab her before she hit the deck.

"Whoa!" Bobbi said. "This room's spinning pretty fast."

Lori, the more cautious of the two, slowly slid off of Gary's lap and wobbled over to the kneeling Christine, who held out her other arm for her.

Lori gave Christine the biggest hug she could muster and conspiratorially whispered, "Don't worry. We can handle Dad and make up his mind for him."

Bobbi blurted, "You have any kids? We really need some more sisters, or maybe even a little brother."

"Not older!" Lori chimed in for emphasis.

Christine was overwhelmed by the enthusiastic welcome and the open manner in which the children spoke. Looking at Gary while she answered, she said, "Sorry. No kids, but that doesn't rule out the future though."

Gary got out of the rocking chair, knelt next to them, and wrapped his arms around the hugging trio. Bobbi spoke for all of them. "It just doesn't get any better than this."

CHAPTER 46

"SORRY TO BREAK UP YOUR reunion," Kim grimly said as Gary entered the bridge. "We've got a big problem." She nodded to an empty chair, and Gary sat down, feeling the anticipation growing. From past experience, any big problem for Kim meant something tragic had occurred or was about to occur.

Kim exhaled deeply as she continued. "A croc wandered into the launch and recovery zone while a shuttle was landing. Fortunately, it was killed immediately by the blast heat, but the mere fact that one simply wandered in is extremely disturbing. Especially since the lake and surrounding area were supposed to be devoid of such monsters." Kim touched her monitor and a detailed satellite view appeared in the large overhead.

"Coffee?" Kim asked as she strode across the bridge to the coffee mess.

"Yes, please. While you're up," Gary absently said as he drifted deeper in thought. "Then the lake must be deeper than we thought, have large underwater caverns, or possibly be connected to a nearby lake through underground rivers."

"The area's saturated with lakes of all sizes," Kim answered as she returned with two steaming mugs of coffee. "The submersible robots haven't reported back yet. But when they do resurface for their microburst transmission, we'll program more intensive spelunking commands. Any other recommendations?"

"Yes, a few," Gary said while sipping the hot coffee. "First, we'll need to extract the robots while we depth charge the lake. We need to kill any creatures that may be lurking underwater. Now that we know they are capable of planning an offensive, we can't wait for them to plot another attack, especially while we're so vulnerable." Gary put down the coffee and looked Kim in the eye. "Then we'll need to find any underground connections between our lake and any surrounding lakes. Once discovered, we'll demolish the channel aquifers and search again for crocs that may have slipped in during the interval."

"You don't think we should find the channels first?" Kim quizzed.

"No!" Gary said abruptly. "We've constantly underestimated the creatures. They have proven to be too formidable to allow any slack at all. As a matter of fact, I wouldn't be surprised to find that they're telepathic."

This made Kim grimace. "Oh, dear, thanks for the comforting counsel." She leaned back and philosophically added, "If that's the case, then we're truly no longer on top of the food or evolutionary chain." Struck by a sudden thought, she quickly leaned forward. "Before we colonize this lake, we need to know whether or not it's dependent on underground spring water. If so, our source of water will disappear once the interconnecting tunnels are destroyed. We'll have to pull up stakes and look for another site. The problem is the very limited time we can safely stay on the *Leapfrog*."

Gary manipulated the overhead reconnaissance view of the colony site, and found and magnified several small streams feeding the lake. "I think these streams are enough to maintain the lake; as a matter of fact, I think this little lake may be a contributor to an underground aqueduct. In any case, we should be able to safely isolate the lake and convert it into a reservoir."

"The problem being . . ."

"The robots weren't built for underwater demolition."

Kim simply nodded.

"So, when do I leave?" Gary asked.

"You're not. I can't justify sending you on another hazardous mission."

"I have underwater demolition training and operational experience. I'm your best bet."

Kim sat up straight. "I know. I read your record, but you're not going. Period. You're needed with your daughters more than chum bait for crocs. I need you to give me another candidate who's able to pull something like this off."

Gary smiled and replied, "They're all dead. I'm the last demolition diver you've got." Kim started to protest, but Gary quickly continued, "Seriously, I'm it! We've got two more men qualified as underwater welders, but the other two demolition divers are dead. One of the enlisted men died while in cryo-sleep, and you jettisoned Lieutenant Carter."

Kim was determined. "What about all that 'cross training' the military used to boast about? Why can't you train one of the welders to set the explosive devices?"

Gary momentarily closed his eyes and counted to ten to himself. "Cross training with explosives? No such thing! On such dangerous projects, the military relies on redundancy, not cross training. Look, it has to be me because there's no way to train someone else in the time we've got. However, I could use the others for cover while I place the charges." This was only a half truth, but Gary was damned if he would send someone else to do a job he was specifically trained to do.

Kim looked defeated. "What about your daughters? Who's going to take care of them? What will they say when you tell them you have to go on another dangerous mission?"

Gary answered bluntly, "Who is going to do anything if I fail? We need a secure colony, and we can't have one until we deny access to the crocs."

"This is so unfair," Kim conceded. "You've been the lead on every one of our dangerous missions. And to tell you truthfully, I would hate to lose you. Your input has been beneficial to all of us."

Kim thought for a minute before deciding, "Okay, I'm holding a shuttle for your party and whatever supplies you need. You may be a little cramped. We're trying to offload as much equipment as we can on each run." Kim reached across the table and took Gary's hand. "Good luck, and God be with you."

"Thanks," Gary replied as he walked off the bridge. "But I wonder if He's still around.

While the other divers were busy obtaining the necessary equipment for the mission, Gary went to his daughters' recovery cubicle and was relieved to see Christine laughing hysterically with Bobbi and Lori. The girls were sharing Christine's lap, but Lori was falling over backward laughing so hard. "Hey! You guys better not be laughing about me," he said as he walked in.

"If you must know, the answer is yes," Christine replied as she wiped laughter tears out of her eyes. "Your daughters were telling me all your secret buttons to push, when to push them, and how hard. You don't have a chance with these girls, but I guess I'm not telling you something you don't already know."

Gary just sighed as he leaned against one of the empty capsules. "No, no surprises here. They've been manipulating me from the get-go, but to tell you truth I've kind of enjoyed it."

"Hah!" exclaimed Bobbi. "Green light!" She and Lori exchanged high fives.

"Christine," Gary, now serious, said, "I've got to make a run down to Earth. Would you mind watching over the girls until I call them down?"

Christine's eyebrows immediately furrowed. "What's Kim got you doing now? Of course I'll take care of the girls, but I think I'd be more productive down there with you."

Bobbi and Lori remained quiet and wide-eyed. They had been through several of Gary's deployments and knew that anytime their dad went on a mission, it was pretty serious.

"Nope. No way you can help on this one. It's just a routine underwater surveillance of the lake next to our new colony."

Christine eyed Gary suspiciously. "What about the underwater robots? What's wrong with them?"

"The robots are too small to lug the heavy monitoring equipment that we need to place in various underwater positions," Gary lied.

Christine was not buying it, but she kept her peace while

in the presence of the little girls.

Lori and Bobbi took the momentary silence as their signal to talk. "What colony?" Lori asked.

"What lake?" Bobbi added.

Gary decided it was time to explain their situation to his daughters, but he left out many of the scarier details. He figured their worrying would not solve any issues. The girls simply sat in Christine's lap, not saying a word until Gary finished.

"I'm ten thousand years old?" a dismayed Bobbi asked when Gary finished.

"Earth's changed? The people are all gone? What happened to them?" Lori machine gunned at him.

The questions continued for another ten minutes until Gary went over to them and wrapped them in another hug. "I've got to go now. I'll be sending for you within the next day or so."

"Be careful, Daddy," Bobbi said.

"Yeah, very careful. We need you," Lori added.

Christine kissed him full on the lips and then whispered, "I need you, too. I'll bring the girls down when you call."

Gary departed on what was to be his most dangerous mission ever—right into the lions' den.

CHAPTER 47

Sergeants Jim Scoffield and Scot Wilson and Corporal Skip Griffin were huddled by the shuttle's entrance, engrossed in computer diagnostics. Gary walked up to them unnoticed and caught the last part of the discussion.

"Fuck it! All the batteries are dead. Not one good one in the batch," Wilson griped. They were concentrating so hard on the task at hand that they did not hear Gary arrive.

"What are you doing here, Scoffield?" All the men jumped and turned around.

"Jesus! Sir. Why do you always sneak up on us? You must have Indian blood in you, or something like that." Scoffield said.

"You didn't answer the question," Gary countered.

"I thought I'd come along and keep you out of trouble, sir."

Gary rolled his eyes and said, "You don't even know how to swim." Scoffield gave his best dejected Labrador look. "Okay, you can come if you want, but you're not getting in the water."

"Yes, sir! I can monitor the robotic drones and feed you any information that comes up."

Gary eased next to the men and asked, "What's dead?"

Scoffield answered, "Mini torpedo motor batteries; they're all flat and won't charge."

"Can't we use an air charge?" asked Wilson.

Gary quickly got up to speed and answered, "Projectile

mode only without any guidance. Effective range only twenty meters or so. Hmm, not good. What's the probability of kill with the crocs, and how many shots do we get?"

Griffin was the underwater weapons expert, and he said, "Still good, sir. The shaped charge can still punch a ten-centimeter hole through reinforced titanium. All we have to do is manage to hit one, providing it will stay still when we shoot at it and won't do any dodging after we shoot." Griffin shrugged his broad shoulders and continued, "The underwater launcher has circular canisters like this one." He held up a small drum that looked like an oversized revolver cylinder with little missile heads embedded in each of the six tubes. "As you can see, we've got six shots we can take fairly rapidly. Reloading underwater takes a little time but can be done in under thirty seconds, providing you've got your spare readily available."

Gary's gloomy premonition went into high gear after recalling that Corporal Griffin was the coward who dodged the first mission. In his experience, men who once showed their colors would be unreliable in a threatening environment.

"Thirty seconds!" Gary exclaimed as though he did not remember the previous encounter. "That would easily allow one of these crocs to close in from our maximum underwater visibility. They could be on us in less than five seconds." Gary paused and paced back and forth a few times while thinking. The other men were also quiet, probably reconsidering their enthusiasm to volunteer for the mission.

"Change of tactics," Gary announced. "We will not randomly depth charge the area before we enter. That would only muddy the water and obscure our visibility even more. Since we've lost the shoot-out-of-sight capability, we'll need all the visibility we can get. As far as firing, there will be only one shooter active at a time. I'll have my hands full setting the charges." Gary stopped and turned to Griffin. "What kind of concussion can we expect on short range shots?"

"Not bad at all, sir. Remember; it's a shaped charge, and all its power is directed in a cone away from the shooter."

Intently, Gary asked, "What if the croc is between the shooter and one of us?"

Griffin grimaced as he answered, "Not good, sir. The explosive device depends mostly on the low compressibility of water, and the shock will continue for a few meters before dispersing enough to become non-lethal." Griffin was shaking his head when he added, "Let's say I shoot a croc and you're close by on the other side; well, sir, your brains would probably be scrambled, and your guts would be turned to jelly."

"Well, then," Gary said thoughtfully, "if that's the case, you and Wilson will need to be on the outer defense perimeter." This conclusion brought gloomy looks from Wilson and Griffin. "We'll use the robots for incoming threats and hopefully will be prepared by the time they get to us. Make sure your mask monitor stays on."

"I'll be in constant contact and will relay any critical information immediately," Scoffield said.

"Sir," Wilson said, "exactly how far do you plan for us to swim in the aqueducts?"

Although Gary spoke softly, his words visibly shook the men. "About one kilometer. I'm sorry, I know it's a long way, but we'll need the penetration to maximize the disintegration of the cave. If we just blast the entrance, the blockage would be shallow and susceptible to easy clearing." Everyone realized how far one kilometer could be, especially if their maximum underwater speed would only be seven to ten knots with the tugs' assistance."

The ensuing silence signaled that the briefing was complete, at least for the time being. "Okay," Gary sighed, "let's move out." He threw his personal bag in the stowage locker of the shuttle and said, "I hope you guys brought all your personal belongings, because we won't be coming back to the *Leapfrog.*"

The revelation did not seem to please the two men.

Wilson stuttered, "N — not coming back?" He did not realize he had signed up for a one-way suicide mission.

"No," a smiling Gary said. "We're permanently evacuating the *Leapfrog.* We'll remain on Earth while the rest of the occupants are transported down." More gloom and doom looks from the two soldiers made Gary expound, "The ship's falling apart. Can't even hold pressure anymore because the outer skin is so brittle. Besides, our shuttles can't maintain continuous operation."

A very serious Wilson replied, "Yes, sir, we've heard that before. It . . . it's just that the *Leapfrog* has been our home and safe refuge for a long, long time."

"Long, I'll agree with. Safe is another issue," Gary said.

Scoffield signaled to Gary that he needed to talk to him, so Gary said, "All right, you two load up. I need to talk to Scoffield." Once the men went on their way, Gary said to Scoffield, "I know; I'll just have to watch him closely, very closely."

Scoffield was shaking his head, "Sir, using him is *not* a good idea. He's big, looks tough, but inside he's a fucking coward, and I wouldn't trust him as far as I could throw him. I may not be a great swimmer, but I tell you, you'd be better off with me than him."

Gary put his hand on his friend's massive shoulders and confidentially whispered, "I know, but I won't be a witness to your drowning. You're all heart, Scoffield, and quite frankly, I don't want both of us in an underwater tunnel together if things go south. You're my replacement if something happens to me, and we'll need good leadership to pull off this survival gig."

"Well, I hope you don't die regretting this decision, sir, but . . ." Scoffield seemed at a loss for words before continuing, ". . . thanks for your vote of confidence."

At that moment Bill Evans entered the shuttle's docking station. He said, "Hope you don't mind my tagging along. Heard you were going to play with some of my submarine toys and couldn't let you have all the fun." Seeing the skeptical look on the faces of Scoffield and Gary, he hastily added, "My department can put out any developing brush fires, and I think you can use my expertise with the drones. After all, they are my babies."

"You clear this with Kim?" Gary asked.

"Of course not, but any objections to my tagging along?"

Gary and Scoffield looked at each other and shrugged. Gary faced Bill and said, "It's your hide; jump on . . . and, by the way, thanks for saving our bacon back there on the moon."

"No problem, but what did you mean by 'young Jedi'?"

Gary and Scoffield followed the other three men into the shuttle, and once strapped in, Gary shut the door and activated the undocking program.

Blam! The shuttle's thruster rockets exploded into life. Every time the shuttle rockets initiated, Gary swore the tooth-rattling ship would fall apart, but much to his relief, the shuttle somehow endured. Once the rockets ceased their soul-shaking acceleration, Gary and the others removed their helmets to relax a few hours before they began reentry burn. Reentry was another rock and roll experience that was actually more terrifying than rocket ignition. No acceleration, just constant buffeting and a red hot outer skin while the ship took its trajectory course.

No sooner had Gary removed his helmet than Kim, in the *Leapfrog,* appeared in the overhead monitor.

"Shuttle two, *Leapfrog.*" Kim was looking stern as she made the broadcast.

"Go ahead, *Leapfrog,*" Gary answered.

"Bill? What are you doing there?" Kim asked in surprise.

Bill cringed. "Thought I'd get away for a little R&R down on Mother Earth. Besides, these guys need my help to stay out of trouble. Don't worry, my department won't miss me. I was just getting in their way."

Kim sighed in exasperation. "Talk about rats jumping off a sinking ship . . . Anyway, Gary, we just got this upload relay from our Earth base. It's from one of our ROVs, remote operated vehicles, that are operating in the lake—and obviously the abrupt signal ending means its ultimate destruction." Without further ado, Kim transferred the data to the shuttle and the overhead monitor picked up the robot's last transmissions.

The screen was dark green from the unit's night vision and resembled a pilot's HUD, heads-up display. The pitch bar indicated a five-degree nose-down attitude and a level bank; the scrolling numbers on the side gave the water temperature at twenty-one degrees Celsius, current at one point two knots, depth at twenty-three meters, and the speed bar was indicating seven knots and drifting down. The robot was in the process of mapping the aqueduct feeding into the lake and the unit was about three hundred meters inside the pitch black tunnel when its onboard sonar picked up a large target, closing fast at fifteen knots. The underwater robot immediately went into its stealth mode and began to coast down and continue its hyper frequency sonar pinging. The larger object maintained a constant bearing and a soft, but very discernable chirp could be heard in the speakers.

Gary blurted, "Shit! Something just pinged it. Sounds like dolphins."

As soon as he said that, a ferocious croc appeared in the monitor's night vision, and it was closing fast.

Gary noticed something odd about the croc's eyes; they seemed opaque, as if the eyelids were closed. "Holy shit! It has its eyes closed! The animal is guiding on sonar."

When the robot sensed the croc was within four meters, the electric motor went into overdrive. Like an arrow, it shot forward and dodged the snapping jaws by millimeters. The turbulence caused by the giant's bow wave tumbled the little submarine end over end until the computer could stabilize the machine. Making a hard turn to the exit of the cave, the ROV passed the croc as the animal tried to crush the device with

its massive jaws. The croc's timing was off, however, and the
little machine escaped the second encounter.

At full speed, the submarine made a dash for the exit. The unit had a rear-facing sonar, but any attempt to ping was negated by the baffling effect created by the propeller. Gary and his companions were floating on the edge of their seats, watching the unit's speed pass through twenty-five knots, finally peaking out at twenty-seven knots. Enhanced by the night vision, dim light slowly appeared at the end of the tunnel.

Scoffield remarked, "Hah, no way that toothy bastard can catch it now!"

The light was getting brighter, exponentially, but the third attack succeeded. The monitor picked up closing serrated teeth just as the signal was lost.

Stunned silence prevailed as the men watched the snow on the monitor. Kim broke the silence. "I see you picked up on the sonar capabilities of our new foe and the incredible underwater speed that it obtained. I thought you might like to see this video ASAP so you can perhaps prepare yourselves and develop tactics. The self-destruct mechanism failed to activate. Its circuit was obviously interrupted before the signal could be generated. We'll have to make a few hardware changes." Kim's worried image appeared on the monitor.

"Thanks for the fast relay. Right now, I haven't a clue how to proceed, but don't worry, we'll come up with something," Gary replied.

"Good luck; *Leapfrog* out," Kim closed. Gary thought she was about to cry when she broke the transmission.

Gary felt like crying, too. "Any ideas?" he asked his dumbfounded friends.

Scoffield was the first to recover. "Well, looks like we've really got our tits in the wringer now. Lessee if I've got the facts straight on our enemy. One, they're big and can bite a man in two in one chomp. Two, they've got lungs that can match gills, and they can run and swim faster than we can even dream. Three, they've got sonar and can navigate in the pitch-ass black tunnels. Four, their brain is bigger than ours, which means they're probably also smarter. Yeah, I think that about sums it up. No sweat; bring them on." Scoffield dropped his face into his hands with a great sigh.

Gary was truly staggered by the new revelation, and sarcastically commented, "No, you left out a very important but unknown capability of this creature."

Without moving his head, Scoffield looked over at him and said, "What? We found one with wings that can breathe fire?"

Gary smirked when he answered, "Worse. Telepathy. Our researchers suspect that accompanying their enhanced brains, some of them may be able to communicate telepathically."

Wilson chimed in, "Any idea as to the range? That is, if their suspicion is correct."

"No way of telling since we have no way to monitor. This is way beyond human capabilities, and we haven't developed a machine to imitate it." Gary could see how crestfallen his comrades were after seeing the croc blindly home in on the drone and then overtake the speedy little torpedo. Trying to cheer them up some, Gary added, "Don't fret, fellows; we still have the technological edge, and the last few times we kicked butt. We just need to be innovative and use what we've got to keep the edge."

Wilson broke the silence that followed. "Sir, any ideas?"

"A few are coming to mind," Gary said thoughtfully. "We need underwater noise to jam or confuse their sonar capacity, and the little drones can do that."

"I can handle it," said Bill.

The shuttle began its reentry phase as Gary was talking. "We'll rig some floodlights and extend them at least one meter. That way, if one of the crocs gets through our defense and tries to defeat the light, at least our heads won't be bitten off."

Before the reentry noise overrode conversation, Griffin, who had been silently sulking, said, "Let's booby-trap the floodlights by rigging an old-fashioned grenade to the lights. They bite, swim away, a wire attached to our pack pulls the pin, and *blam*, off goes the head!"

Wilson looked at him like he was the idiot of the year. "Really nice, Griffin, and what exactly happens to us when your grenade goes off?"

"Hmmm," said Griffin. "That would smart."

Gary perked up and added, "Make the wire longer. Shouldn't kill us since we'll have full helmets on . . . unless, of course, the concussion collapses our helmets and likewise our heads."

"I'm kinda thinking I'm glad I never learned how to swim," Scoffield observed.

The shuttle's buffeting increased to the point communication became impossible. The overhead monitor was shaking so violently that the images became nothing but a blur.

CHAPTER 48

"INCOMING SHUTTLE!" THE CAMP'S LOUDSPEAKERS blared. After witnessing what had happened to the croc that wandered into the landing zone, everyone literally dropped what they were doing and made a beeline for the nearest safety trench.

Carl grabbed his blueprints, collapsed his makeshift table, and followed. Mitchell was already there, squatting along the side, furiously shuffling a hologram of complex DNA sequences.

Carl flopped next to him and asked, "Got it figured out yet?"

Mitchell threw him a side glance as he continued moving the simulated DNA building chain. "Close, very close. I'm wrapping up the instructions for the bio lab. When's the damn thing going to be ready?" he demanded.

Carl sighed as he answered, "No, thanks for your help; they've just finished building the blast fence for the tent's protection. Should have it up and running an hour or so after this shuttle's recovery."

Mitchell stopped what he was doing to give Carl one of his "eat shit and die" looks. "My help! My help, you say? What do you think I've been doing here all this time?"

Carl smiled and said, "Hiding?" Three or four of the troops within earshot started laughing.

"Fuck you and the rest of you, too! I'm saving your sorry asses. I'm making the most potent toxin ever introduced on this planet, and you laugh?" Mitchell was furious.

"Hey, Doc," one of the soldiers, Tommy Carter, asked, "is there a possibility the crocs are immune to your poison? And how are we going to test it? Those critters ain't exactly passive, and I can't see anyone walking one around on a leash."

Mitchell glared at him. "That's not even a remote possibility. This formula is foolproof and guaranteed to drop a croc right in its tracks."

Carter looked at Carl and rolled his eyes. "Yeah, I heard that one, too."

Mitchell and Tommy Carter were sharing hateful glances when Carl said, "I assume, Mitch, that you'll be the one to test it out?"

Mitchell tried hard not to lose his menacing demeanor, but his voice betrayed him by going up an octave. "I'm not trained for field work, but I will be present for the field trials, and don't call me Mitch."

"Sure, Mitch," Carl answered.

The camp's loudspeaker blotted out Mitchell's next comment. "Incoming, five minutes."

The shuttle became quiet as it slowed down to approach speed. A slight stall buffet started right before the VTOL rockets kicked in. *Blam!* The overhead monitor instantly turned to fog as the sand was blasted up, obscuring vision. Scoffield's knuckles were white. "I don't like this; never have, and never will."

"Hopefully, this will be the last one," Gary returned. "We'll spend the rest of the day making preparations, rest, and hit the aqueducts midmorning tomorrow."

"Aye, sir," was the spontaneous reply.

After waiting a few minutes for the dust and sand to settle, Carl trudged over to the newly arrived shuttle. The door was just opening when Gary stepped outside.

"Greetings, fellow space traveler. Welcome to Earth," Carl called out.

"Hiya, Bill. Good to see you! You're just in time to help us out with your little toys. I guess you got *Leapfrog's* telecast of the last drone that got munched?"

"Yep, we got it, unfortunately. I've got some wiring changes in mind and a few software tweaks. Where's the main console? I better get to work if we're going to make a morning deadline."

Carl pointed Bill to a medium-sized staff tent located about twenty meters from the shore of the lake, and Bill actually trotted off while waving goodbye.

Carl pitched in and helped with the offload. While doing so, he described the latest progress in the camp and Mitchell's toxic scheme.

"So, where is Dr. Death now?" Gary asked.

"Still hiding in the trenches, playing with his hologram computer. He thinks he's got the perfect toxin, having redesigned and improved the poison arrow frog's toxin." Bill paused. "But he never did cross-reference it with the new croc's DNA. He's just using what's already in the computer's database, which is totally contrary to acceptable research methods."

"Why?"

"I guess he figures that loading in the new information will be a waste of time. And . . ."

Gary was apprehensive now. "And what?"

Carl took Gary by the elbow and led him to a more private area. Before continuing, Carl checked Gary's intercom to make sure it was turned off. "I don't believe Mitchell is totally sane. I mean, he's always been eccentric but not totally obsessed, as he seems to be now."

Gary merely smiled, put a hand on Bill's shoulder, and said, "I know none of us are rocket scientists anymore, but, Carl, really, why do you think he's nicknamed Dr. Death? We all know he's not dealing with a full deck, and that's why he got booted off the *Leapfrog*. Kim needed to keep him out of mischief and doesn't trust him."

"Yeah, yeah, I figured that all on my own, but I just wanted to make sure you know what you're dealing with down here. He's bound to want to test this toxin of his, and I want to make sure you realize that he did some research shortcuts that should invalidate his results. I think he's looking for an easy way to reverse his status from outcast to hero in one quick jump, and damn the consequences."

Gary involuntarily bit his lower lip. "That's all we need right now; bait some crocs into our compound, shoot them up with some witch brew, and really piss them off. Thanks for the heads-up, Carl. I'll keep an eye on him."

Gary caught up with Bill in the remote console tent. Bill hadn't wasted any time and was rewiring the schematics on his hologram computer. Gary was amazed at the speed he manipulated the wiring circuits while maintaining a green light on the diagnostic screen. "Looks like you've done this once or twice before."

Bill answered without turning around, "Can do this in my sleep. Unfortunately, sometimes I dream in schematics. I'll have these puppies rewired and reprogrammed by dawn. No production units here, so they'll all have to be done by hand . . . my hand."

"Hate to interrupt you, but while I've got you, I need to know all about those little submarine drones you've got in the lake."

Bill perked up immediately, for these were his "babies" and it was obvious he was proud of them. "Ahh, finally! A subject I know a little about." Off Bill went on every little nut, bolt, and wire design.

Gary's efforts not to interrupt Bill went out the window after five minutes of unrecognizable scientific engineering jargon. "Hold on a sec," Gary sputtered between Bill's breath breaks. "Maybe I don't need to know *all* about them after all. How about focusing on some of the functional capabilities?"

"You want me to dumb it down?" Bill snickered.

Gary rolled his eyes. "What is it with you engineers? You develop your own language just to confuse people, and then act insulted when you run across someone not fluent in your techie talk. But, yeah, dumb it down."

After Bill explained the basic intricacies and capabilities of the drones, Gary asked, "Any way to put an explosive charge on them, other than the self destruct, that can be either impact fused or remotely controlled?"

Bill chewed on his lower lip while thinking. "Only as an external pod; I can link it with the self-destruct charge for a bigger bang, but that would slow it down considerably, especially with the tremendous drag that water produces." After a few seconds he continued, "Yes, of course I can do it, but I'll need some programming time for sonar and visual target recognition. You wouldn't want any of these little torpedoes homing in on you by mistake, would you?"

"No, definitely not! What's the projected max speed we're talking about now?"

Bill shrugged and answered, "Maybe twenty knots or so. A lot faster than you can swim but slow compared to the crocs.

"Our makeshift lab is up and running, and I'll get to work and will have the five modified drones available by your dive, noon tomorrow." Bill hesitated before continuing, "You know we only had six of these drones to start with, and that took all our assets we could scrounge on the *Leapfrog*. Now we're down to five."

Gary put his hands on his hips, frowned, and said, "I'm afraid that's going to be our major dilemma from here on out. All of our industrialized supplies are becoming scarce with no end in sight. Once our blockade mission is complete, we'll reprogram the submarines for reconnaissance missions only."

As Gary walked away, he said over his shoulder, "That is, if there's any drones left."

CHAPTER 49

THE LITTLE MAKESHIFT CAMP SLEPT well that night ex-cluding, of course, the guards and one particularly mentally unbalanced scientist. Dr. Death had been burning the mid-night oil. Daylight was breaking when Mitchell finished brewing the most virulent toxin ever devised. Once injected, the concoction was designed to first act on voluntary nerve functions, such as limb movement and other motor control, and then when established, the toxin was designed to destroy the neurological connectors to all involuntary muscles, such as those for breathing, heartbeat, and digestive functions. The time lapse between the first and second phases was, theoreti-cally, measured not in minutes but in seconds. According to his computer calculations, the volume of the dosage was un-important because only a minute amount would do the same damage as a larger volume.

Mitchell carefully poured the toxin into three standard in-jection cartridges, gathered all his notes, and then programmed the lab robot to continue manufacturing the product in his ab-sence. Proudly strutting out of the lab tent, he followed the mixed breakfast scent to the mess tent. The menu for that morning consisted of fried crocodile—which was actually the roadkill from the last shuttle—fish, some unidentifiable egg omelet, and synthetic orange juice and coffee.

Gary and Bill were sitting in the far corner reviewing the underwater drones' programming when Mitchell dramatically threw the tent's entrance netting back and stepped inside. The forty-man tent was packed. Mitchell spotted Gary and made a beeline in his direction.

Gary said to Bill, "Here comes Doctor Death; looks like he's been up all night. I hope he doesn't have access to nuclear material."

"No, I double checked on that one, but I tell you, he's totally obsessed with that 'wonder toxin.' I'm just glad I don't have to deal with him on a full-time basis." Their conversation died off as Mitchell approached.

Mitchell walked right up to Gary and, without saying a word, slammed the toxic cartridges on the table, knocking over Bill's coffee. To Gary, Mitchell looked like hell warmed over. He was unshaven, his hair was unruly, and he had bad breath that took away Gary's appetite. Coupled with the greenish eyes, Mitchell had a seedy, alien appearance.

In a high pitched voice that was intended to be heard by everyone, Mitchell loudly proclaimed, "Here! Here is the solution to *all* our threats—crocs and Neanderthals alike." Enjoying the accompanying silence and the undivided attention, Mitchell continued, "Three to five seconds max for complete paralysis, thirty to forty-five seconds for certain death, and dosage amount is not an issue, because it will only take one drop to drop a croc." This rehearsed pun brought on a wicked, yellow-toothed smile from Mitchell.

Gary picked up the toxin-laden cartridges while Bill asked, "Let's take a look at your supportive data." Bill held out his hand, but Mitchell stepped back, clutching his attaché case close to his chest.

"No fucking way! This is my research, my idea, and my baby. There's no way in hell I'm going to hand this over to you."

An exasperated Bill sighed, "What's wrong, Mitch? You hiding something from me?"

"Fuck you! This is mine and I'm claiming patent and academic proprietary rights. No one sees this unless I allow them to and that's that."

Gary, almost too casually, explained to Mitchell, "Doctor, perhaps you haven't taken a good look around you, but there is no patent office, there are no academies, and you have no proprietary rights. This is a frontier now, and we must pool all our resources if we expect to survive."

Mitchell pointed to the three cartridges lying in front of Gary and said, "That's all you need. The end result, not my research notes." Infuriated now, Mitchell turned his rage on Gary. "Furthermore, I will not tolerate being told what to do by a mere major."

A complete hush fell over the mess tent until Gary casually removed his pistol and aimed it between Mitchell's eyes.

"You wouldn't dare!" Mitchell screamed.

Gary slowly stood up, looked over Mitchell's shoulder, and gave a head nod for those behind Mitchell to move. Mitchell's bladder failed when he heard the chairs falling over as people scrambled to get out of the way.

Slowly, Gary extended his arm so the pistol barrel was only centimeters from Mitchell's head. "I shit you not. If you don't hand over your notes within three seconds, I'll be picking them off your dead body."

Mitchell started shaking uncontrollably and stuttered,

"Ple — ple — please don't . . . don't sh — shoot." He swiftly and gratefully handed his attaché case to Bill.

"Thank you, Doctor. Now why don't you clean up and join us for breakfast?" Gary slowly lowered his pistol, found Scoffield, and waved him over.

Mitchell, relieved not to be looking down a bore any longer, said, "No thanks, I seem to have lost my appetite." He grabbed the three cartridges, turned, and almost ran out of the tent.

Scoffield was standing next to Gary and said, "Shit, sir. I thought you were going to actually shoot him."

Gary looked at Scoffield and replied, "I was. I need some guards on Doctor D. Don't let him out of sight and keep him out of the lab until Doctor Evans has a chance to review his notes."

"Aye, sir." Scoffield motioned two soldiers to follow him.

Bill was thumbing through Mitchell's notes and becoming more and more agitated. "This man used to be considered a genius; now he's certifiably inept. Look at this . . ." He handed Gary a page with scribbling and formulas scattered about in a seemingly haphazard pattern.

"Sorry, Bill, but I'm not the one to critique it, because I can't read this. It makes no sense at all to me."

"Hah! My point exactly. It doesn't make any sense at all. He starts off coherently by using computer data as reference, and then he drifts off in la-la land." Bill paused before continuing, "I think the long freeze damaged his brain more than most. As a matter of fact, his CAT scans mysteriously disappeared before anyone had a chance to evaluate them. He probably was cognizant enough to recognize the deviation and intentionally deleted them to avoid further scrutiny.

"I hate to slam him so, because at one time he was highly respected and came up with some heavy duty inventions. He was always eccentric but somewhat tolerable and open to reasoning; now he's totally on his own planet. Even his publications were always held in high scholarly esteem and read by almost all in his professional community. Yeah, something bad happened to him that we somehow managed to dodge."

Gary pensively asked, "I know that this is outside of your field, but what's your conscience telling you?"

Without hesitation, Bill answered, "He needs to be monitored. Maybe even locked up for not only his protection but others' as well. He's partially incoherent and perhaps a little schizophrenic, which makes him practically unaccountable for his deeds."

Gary leaned back in his chair with his hands clasped behind his head, and said, "Terrific. That's all we need right now: a mad scientist running about with lethal toxins."

Bill grinned. "So? What's he going to do with them? Throw them? I'll restrict him from the armory."

"There we go," Gary said as he stood up. "That should keep him out of trouble for the time being. We need one hundred percent concentration for this underwater mission coming up."

Talking about the role of the little submarines, the two went off to the command center tent. Dr. Mitchell was temporarily forgotten since they considered him harmless.

CHAPTER 50

GRIFFIN, WILSON, AND SCOFFIELD WERE waiting for Gary on the beach. Scoffield was the first to see Gary and Bill walking down to the shore. "Hey, Skipper, we're ready to rock and roll. We've programmed the drones, charged the suits with a helium/oxygen mix, booby rigged the floodlights with hand grenades, and the torpedoes are locked and loaded."

"Tell me about the submarines," Gary said as he crowded around the control console that was designated as Scoffield's workstation.

"Er, would you rather do this?" Scoffield asked Bill.

"No," Bill said. "Let's use this brief to make sure we're all on the same page and know exactly what to expect from these little machines."

Scoffield, a true master sergeant at heart, puffed up and continued, "The drones have an attachable contact warhead with enough power to cut the biggest croc in half. They have been programmed to lure threats away from the divers and then turn to re-attack once the croc is at a safe distance. Also . . ." Scoffield paused and smiled, "noise makers have been incorporated to confuse and jam their sonar capabilities, rendering them blind. The three of us thought that one up," Scoffield proudly stated.

"Blind, huh?" Gary inquired.

"Yes, sir. Blind and swimming dumb." Scoffield along with Wilson and Griffin were beaming like they just invented the light bulb.

"So then what happens when the crocs open their eyes? Our infrared assisted vision won't work underwater," Gary stated.

Wilson broke the silence. "Shit! Talk about dumb-asses! I . . . I guess we were banking on them keeping their eyes closed."

"That's okay; it's creative thinking," Bill hurriedly replied, saving the men some face. "Actually, that's a good idea even if they open their eyes. The noise makers will add to their confusion and may even buy us some time. However, I wonder if they can't see through their eyelids."

Gary added, "We'll blind them with light. Basically, they're nocturnal, so their eyes should be genetically sensitive to light. After swimming around in a dark, underwater tunnel, their night vision should be at the peak. Once the drones start jamming, which we'll be able to hear, we hit them with all the light we can generate."

"Uh, sir. I've got a question." A nervous Griffin asked Gary, "What makes you think the crocs will go after the lights first instead of us?"

"I don't know for sure, but if we point the lights in their faces, that should be all that they can see. The optic glare from the water should conceal us on the periphery. Once they make a move toward the lights, extend the beams to max length and hope it's far enough to keep from concussing us. This is all hypothetical, because there may not be any crocs down there at all."

"Oh, I wouldn't bank on that. Look at what happened to

drone number six. Gobbled up, and we don't have any idea where that croc went afterwards," Bill said.

Gary glared at him and added, "You sure you don't want to join us?"

Bill, realizing he had just sabotaged Gary's effort to psychologically minimize the threat, added, "I'd be more of a threat than the crocs and, besides, I don't scream very well underwater." This little stab at humor brought a few chuckles, but the tension was wire tight.

Bill continued with the brief: "The reconnaissance submarine found several small submerged caverns that led to dead ends, but one cavern is obviously the aqueduct feeder that chains this lake to others. The entrance is relatively small, about five meters across, but the farther you go, the larger it becomes. About one kilometer in, the tunnel enters a huge cavern that has several other gateways. There's a current flowing into the cavern, which leads me to believe our lake is a feeder. Our submarine was beginning to explore when it picked up sonar chirping noises and the drone switched to stealth. After the loss of number six, this drone was programmed to hug the bottom and retreat as quietly as possible." Bill sighed before continuing, "That's the good news. The bad news—numerous chirpings were identified. Approximately ten to twenty different animals are roaming around down there, doing God knows what. Apparently, the crocs didn't pick up the drone's presence because . . . we got it back.

"We decided to keep one drone slick, without the attached ordnance, to act as a deep penetrating agent to give you a maximum heads-up for possible incoming crocs. It will begin maximum jamming when it senses sonar signals strong enough to be reflected. It's programmed to lead the crocs away from you, so we'll probably never see that one again."

"Expendable decoy," Gary said.

"More like a kamikaze," Bill replied. "It will not be taken intact for possible technology examination. It will self destruct with enough force to rip the lower jaw off one of these crocs. I'm kind of hoping for a maximum psychological effect for crocs that witness one of their buds dying a slow and painful death."

Bill turned to the control console and activated one of the beached submarines. *Wheee, wheee, wheee.* "As you can hear, the sonar jamming feature is quite loud and should carry quite a way underwater." Bill turned off the noise maker and said, "I wish we had access to our more advanced underwater night vision, but the batteries required are special function and not interchangeable with the few remaining good batteries. I don't think the designers had a ten thousand-year shelf life in mind when they made them.

"We had to scrounge around, but we did find a few decent batteries to operate your floodlights. I'm afraid the scuba suits' internal lights will be woefully inadequate for visual warning of approaching crocs. Each of your suits has been outfitted with small sonar detection and ranging units with the resultant data displayed in your HUD. The chirping noises should give away the crocs' locality, but . . . if you're using the floods, they may begin to rely on visual cues. If such is the case, they will definitely go after the lights. Make sure the lights are not anywhere close to you when the crocs attack them. Once you lose the floodlights, let them go; don't hold on to them."

Bill paused to catch his breath, and Wilson jumped in, "Doc, what about our suits' night vision and infrared boosters? That should help."

Bill replied, "Sorry; don't bank on that. Any infrared generation will quickly be sucked up and dispersed by the water. Just wasn't designed for underwater usage. As I said earlier, our heavy duty underwater gear is inop and has been for a long, long time."

Bill waited for more questions before continuing, "Your tugs can pull you along at ten knots max, which means the crocs have a closure speed of around twenty knots. Although you won't be producing any bubbles, the turbulence and drag will prevent you from using your floodlights or torpedo guns while in high speed retreat. If the opportunity avails, I'd recommend a slow extraction so you won't be blindly attacked."

Bill walked over to one of the tugs, which looked like a small, pointed trash can with an oversized transparent lid attached to the front. An intake was located in the front of the protective shield with the exhaust at the end of the can. Handles along the sides and a miniature heads-up display was reflected from the inside of the shield. Bill flipped a guarded switch on one of the handles, and a thumb-thick tube extended approximately three meters. He bent the cord ninety degrees to demonstrate its flexibility.

"I worked all night making this invention, so please don't laugh." No one laughed. "This is a high-powered air injection system. Extend the cord like I just did, and the contact sensors become active, so be careful once it's extended. When the electrodes on the end make a contact, an electrical impulse locks the cord in its last position, a reinforced needle protrudes, and the system fires out four cubic meters of air at over five thousand kilos. I tested this unit out on the toughest piece of skin from our last kill and it instantly bloated. Granted a lot of air was lost, and the recoil slid the tug a meter, but I guarantee any croc will have other thoughts besides eating you when you blast him with this." Bill looked around for something to demonstrate on. All the men stepped back out of his range.

"That's okay, we believe you," said Gary. "Anything else we need to know before we make the dive?"

"Yes, just be careful with your grenades. If you want to dribble some of them out as you extract, make sure you set the timers correctly."

Gary did a quick mental calculation. "Ten knots, ten seconds should do it." Simultaneously, the three divers adjusted the timers of the five grenades they had attached to their suits.

"Thanks, Bill. Your little inventions just might do the trick," Gary said as he walked to the demonstration tug and retracted the air cord. "Let's launch the rest of the drones and get this show on the road."

As the men were making their final preparations, an undetected ripple fluttered on the far side of the lake. Beneath the water lilies, a huge crocodile painfully rolled over. Awakened by severe cramps, the monster tried to regurgitate the source of his problems, but the torn up submarine drone had ragged and sharp metal shards deeply imbedded in his bowels. Like wicked hooks, the remnants of the drone refused to release their deadly grip and each regurgitation contraction simply tore the tissue more. Compounding the beast's problem, the highly enriched lithium ion battery cells had been punctured, allowing body fluids to interact with the volatile chemicals. Although the croc's digestive system could dissolve bones, the toxic brew was eating through the beast's guts. The crocodile was in severe pain, and it was becoming more irate by the minute. The thought distress signal had been sent and received and help was on its way once the others could figure out where he was. Also included in the message was a warning to avoid fast, hard-shelled fish that were noisy and tasteless.

CHAPTER 51

GARY'S CHEST PACK WAS FULL and heavily loaded with high explosives. Bulging like a pregnant bug, Gary waddled over to his tug and lay in the water. Instantly, the burden was relieved. "This shit weighs a ton," he grunted as he wrestled with the tug.

"It should," replied Bill over the headsets. "You've got enough high explosives to blow all the water out of this lake."

"Comm check," Gary transmitted and was answered by "Two, three, land." Gary turned and got thumbs-up from Wilson and Griffin, who both looked like the cartoon character Elmer Fudd with bulbous helmeted heads and oversized revolvers. Scoffield had his headset on and was giving a thumbs-up from his beachhead command module. Bill was sitting next to him operating the remote vehicle station.

Kim, from the *Leapfrog* command center, chimed in, "Good luck, fellows. We'll lose direct contact with you once you submerge, but the ground units will relay your vocals and visuals. Hopefully, you'll have a boring mission. Control, out."

Gary rolled over on his back for a last look at a very blue sky. Sighing deeply, he rolled back over and gunned the tug forward and down. A chill ran down his back, foretelling the ominous fortunes that awaited him.

Bill's voice came through the headset loud and clear,

"Drones are in position. The deep probe is resting dormant at the cavern's far exit. It's still picking up sonar pinging and the signals are getting stronger. At this rate, you'll barely have enough time to plant the charges and escape. Of course, it's a brand new ball game if the crocs pick up their speed. Drone control, out."

"Just another day in paradise," replied Gary. Turning his head left and right, he could pick up Wilson's and Griffin's tugs following behind him with an eerie glow around the tugs' high-powered headlamps.

The ominous chill was quickly replaced by a real chill as Gary's suit began to fill with the cool lake water for equal pressurization. In moments, the water warmed as the suit's environmental system automatically adjusted the insulating temperature. Gary followed the helmet's heads-up display as it led them deeper into the darkening depths. The tugs' head-lamps automatically continued to brighten as the light faded in the deep water. The built-in headlamps on the suits also began to brighten, but Gary reduced his brightness to ten percent. He figured the crocs would first attack the bright lights and did not want his head to be the first to go.

Approaching thirty meters, a gaping hole, much like a huge drain, appeared in the lake bottom. Gary checked the current out at two knots positive, which meant a slower extraction, but hopefully nothing would be chasing them. "Trail formation," he transmitted, which was quickly followed by "Two, aye" then "three, aye."

The gaping hole narrowed to five then three meters before opening up to ten meters across, and the current dropped to one knot. "Not much room to maneuver, but this may be a blessing in disguise," Gary transmitted.

Griffin was quick to answer back, "Um, how do you figure that, sir?"

"The crocs won't have much room to dodge your little torpedoes," answered Gary. No sooner had the words escaped than a faint *wheee, whee* could be heard. "Uh oh!" Gary exclaimed through the underwater intercom.

"Double uh oh," replied Wilson.

"Ah, shit!" added Bill. "The advance probe is under attack and making way as fast as it can away from you. Looks like more than five crocs are after it." After a short pause, the faint *whee* stopped, followed by a fainter boom. "That's it for one drone; four to go."

Had Gary been looking at the time, he would have certainly ducked as four submarines whizzed by his head making as much speed as the water drag allowed. As the in-trail formation of the submarines receded into the complete blackness, Gary said, "So much for stealth. All ahead max speed."

One would think that navigating in a ten-meter-wide tunnel would not be too difficult, but Gary could barely manage to keep from banging off the jagged walls of the twisting tunnel. Occasionally, a clang could be heard as his wingmen underestimated a turn.

Gary could feel the outside pressure increase and dared a peek at his depth reading on his reflected heads-up display. Eighty-five meters deep and still descending in the twisting tunnel. Finally, the tunnel hit an elbow bend and leveled out at ninety-two meters. Gary flipped his headlamps to "High" and could see that this was the opening to a grand cavern. It was the exact spot he was looking for to place the majority of his charges.

The chirping was much more intense now and quite a bit louder. The drones were giving the crocs a good run for their money. "Take positions, be at the ready, and don't go any farther into the cavern," Gary transmitted.

"Two, aye," "three, aye," came the responses as both Wilson and Griffin motored past him. *Boom!* The explosion sounded close, too close to Gary, as another drone completed its mission. The chirping became frantic and increased in intensity.

"Three, here they come! Firing!" screamed Griffin over the headsets.

"Two, standing by," Wilson transmitted back.

Gary fought to keep focused and made his way to the ceiling of the exit tunnel. Swiftly driving in an anchor, he attached one of his five explosive satchels. *Boom, boom, thump* went the explosive torpedoes.

Griffin could not believe how fast something so big could be. Every time he fired a torpedo, the beasts would literally vanish, leaving the streaking torpedo to collide with the far wall. "They're too fast! They're dodging all my torpedoes," he yelled. "Reloading!"

"First charge installed, floodlights on now! Retreat," Gary commanded.

Griffin was flipping backward, pulling the tug along on its tow line when a fearsome creature zoomed up to him with its mouth wide open. There was no way he would have time to reload or dispatch the high pressure rod in time to save himself. *Whoosh!* A torpedo shot into the middle of the gaping mouth.

Boom! In the resulting explosion, the croc's head disappeared in a red vapor. The creature's upper body's momentum collided with Griffin's legs, then fell to the bottom, leaving a red inklike trail.

"Hah!" transmitted Wilson. "They can't see with their mouths open. Save your shots for when they open up."

Griffin had just peed himself when the monster bumped into his legs on the way to the bottom. Somehow, Wilson's observation did not provide him much comfort, but now that Wilson was beside him, he felt a little more secure knowing at least he was not going to die by himself.

"Keep backing up! Don't turn around. I'm right behind you," Gary said as he grabbed each of their backpack straps and started pulling them back into the exit chamber. All three tugs floated behind them and bumped together as they backpedaled.

"Incoming!" yelled Wilson as he let another torpedo loose, but the creature had not opened its mouth yet and dodged, again passing out of sight.

Gary took both of their back straps in his left hand and extended his booby-trapped floodlights. Flicking the power switch on, he exclaimed, "Oh, my God!" The chamber was full of crocs in total chaos. The drones were whizzing around with the crocs in hot pursuit. Although the crocs were faster than the submarines, there was no way any one of them could outmaneuver the diminutive machines. The noise makers were totally confusing the crocs by drowning out their chirping sonar and crocs were slamming into each other and the walls . . . until Gary turned on the bright floodlights.

Instantly, all crocs froze in place to look at the new intruders. One of the drones buzzed a croc in the front, and he snatched it with his right hand and stuffed it in his mouth.

Boom! Its head disappeared in another red mist with pieces floating downward. The body slowly sank to the bottom, leaving another trail of blood. None of the crocs moved or made a sound; they simply watched as their buddy sank. Then, all together, they stared at the new intruders.

"Ah, shit!" said Gary as he turned off the floodlights. "These guys are communicating. Keep backing off while I plant the rest of these explosives, and use only low lighting."

Chirp, chirp, wheeee, wheee. The remaining three drones started buzzing again once their sonar sensors picked up the renewed pingings.

"Here they come again! They're homing in on our low power lights." Griffin exclaimed. He released the spring-loaded extension of his floodlights, and once again the cavern was filled with light. Some of the crocs shied away from the painful alien light source, but one old badass croc decided the light was not his friend and attacked it. In a flash, he snatched the floodlight in his massive jaws and swam off while viciously chewing on his catch. The cord played out in Conner's makeshift reel until it ran out and snapped the pin out of the grenade.

Another *boom* rocked the cavern although not as loud as the last few. The attacking, injured croc was momentarily stunned by the blast and recovered to find his entire lower jaw missing. The injury immediately took the fight out of him and he swam off trying to figure out what had happened to his prized mouth. This was not lost on the other crocs as they watched the baddest of the bad slink off humbled and mortally wounded. Another pause, another message passed, and off they went again in pursuit of the intruders. First, however, they had to destroy the nuisance hard-shelled fish that magically exploded when bitten.

Gary missed the action as he was busy anchoring his explosive cargo and activating the charges. His agreed strategy had been to place the ordnance along their exit route in three places around ten meters apart, but Gary figured he would not have enough time to equally place the charges that far apart before being overrun, so he placed them only five meters apart. He was using his tug to move from one spot to another, and when he finished the last one, he transmitted, "Mission complete; let's get out of here." Getting no response in return, he motored back to Wilson and Griffin.

Whoosh. Whoosh. Boom. Boom. Griffin was firing and had scored one miss and one hit. Waiting for the crocs to get close enough to open their mouths was unnerving for him, and no matter how hard he tried to discipline himself to wait for the shot, his courage shrank, and his trigger finger took over.

"Wait for them to open their mouths, for Christ's sake!" shouted Wilson. "Don't fire out; I'm not reloaded." Wilson watched in dismay as Griffin aimed at a croc max range and let two torpedoes loose without one hitting its target. Another croc appeared and Griffin fired his last two torpedoes in vain. The croc was long gone before the projectiles reached it.

"Reloading!" screamed Griffin.

"Just fucking terrific," replied Wilson.

Sensing vulnerability, one croc made a hasty attack. Mouth wide open, it rapidly closed in on Wilson. Just as Wilson thought he was surely going to die, Gary's long pressure probe zipped between the two men and lodged in the upper rear part of the croc's gaping mouth. The probe penetrated the thin skeletal layer just above its palate and shot five thousand kilos of air directly into the croc's brain cavity. Both eyeballs popped out of its head, and the right side of the creature's skull exploded in a stream of bubbles, brain, and blood. Reflexively, the dead croc clamped its jaws shut and started rolling, which trapped and yanked Gary's probe out of his hands and off his tug. A large amount of air must have been trapped inside the skeletal area, for the croc floated upward before it went out of sight.

Gary did not need to size up the situation of the two men—Wilson was carrying Griffin, and now Griffin was turning into a liability for all of them. In Gary's past military combat experience, he had seen perfectly normal soldiers completely fall apart under pressure, and Griffin had shown his colors earlier. The alternatives for any commanding officer were to either give the shell-shocked soldier minimum responsibility, leave him behind, or shoot him. Gary opted for the first one.

"Griffin, give me your torpedo gun, pull in your tug, and start using your pressure stick. I lost mine with the last croc. Wilson and I will stay abreast facing the rear; you stay behind us, looking forward and guiding us out."

Wilson answered, "Two, aye," but no reply came from Griffin.

Gary emphatically stated, "Griffin, did you copy?"

"Uh, yes, sir. Here's my tug. I've got yours, and I'm outta here.

"No, you stay put and use your tug's pressure stick to back us up," Gary shouted, but again, no reply.

Wilson dared a peek back and flatly stated, "Sir, he's

gone. The fucker cut and ran on us."

"Jesus Christ!" exclaimed Gary. "He took my tug, but where in the hell . . .?" Gary spotted Griffin's tug resting on the bottom. "Cover me while I recover Griffin's tug."

"Two, aye."

Gary was halfway to the bottom when a dark shadow enveloped him. *Whoosh!* A little underwater missile streaked over his back. The croc was almost on Gary when a torpedo slammed into the right side of the croc's head. *Boom!* This time the concussion rocked Gary, and for a couple of critical seconds, Gary was utterly disoriented and in a different life zone.

"Sir, you okay?" asked Wilson.

"Yeah, just forgot what I was after for a second. By the way, thanks." Gary grabbed Griffin's tug and released the pressure stick to have at the ready.

While Gary was backing up to Wilson's side, Wilson said, "Hey, I think we're on to something, sir. You stay down there and act as chum, and I'll stay high and take the shots. Haw, haw." Wilson thought that was hilarious.

Writing it off as combat humor, Gary replied, "Frankly, Wilson, I think your idea sucks, but at least we have our backs covered now that Griffin ran away."

Griffin could barely hear his comrades' transmission because he was flying around the bends of the tunnel. All regret or fear of reprisal for his cowardly behavior was rationalized away. He figured there was no way in hell the other guys were going to make it out alive, so there was no sense in risking his life any longer than necessary. After all, the mission was completed; the major had planted the explosives, and they were extracting when overwhelmed by the massive beasts. Maybe he could wring a promotion out of his bravery, for there was no way two dead men could outlie him. *Clang!* Deep in thought, he overshot another turn and banged into the far wall.

The croc in the shallow water was not having a good day. In fact, he was slowly and painfully dying. The shards from the submarine drone had finally torn through the stomach walls, and acidic digestive fluids mixed with toxic battery compounds were dissolving the creature's vital organs.

The intense pain prevented any more incoming thought messages, and a pall of depression fell across the beast. He had always realized that one day he would die but had never thought he would die all alone, without the constant, comforting chatter of his kin. Deciding he would at least try to find one companion before he died, the croc pushed himself up and out of the slimy lake bottom to the surface, where he could fill his lungs with fresh air. Once his huge lungs were replenished, he dove toward the aqueduct's entrance.

CHAPTER 52

"OVER THERE!" SCOFFIELD EXCLAIMED. "YOU see that?"

Looking up from the drone's console, Bill replied, "See what?"

"Huge swirl on the other side of the lake. Couldn't have been a fish; way too large."

Bill manipulated his console before saying, "Shit! We're still out of contact with the drones and haven't heard from the divers in over twenty minutes . . . wish we had at least one drone for reconnaissance."

Although they were a good ten feet up on the beach, Scoffield unshouldered his fifty caliber rifle and activated the instant lead computation on the scope. "I think we should move up on the beach some more," Scoffield offered.

Bill answered by collapsing the portable console and walking backward up the beach.

Clang! Griffin bounced off another bend, tearing a large strip off his space suit and a patch off his skin. Leaving a faint trail of blood, Griffin started to make out some light ahead. Desperate to escape from the tunnel's nightmare, he twisted the throttle control for maximum speed, not caring whether or not he bounced off any more walls. His ragged appearance and beat-up tug would only lend credibility to his valiant battle with the crocs. Had Griffin been a little more prudent, he might have heard the faint chirping coming his way.

When he saw the last twenty-degree elbow bend coming up before rising to the lake's main body of water, Griffin swept the tug to the bottom of the passageway to help cut the corner. Turning up hard for the last bend, Conner's tug ran directly into the snout of the injured croc.

Thump! Griffin's death grip on the tug's handlebars was dislodged as he tumbled over the croc's head and along the top of its scaly back. The hardened ridges along the top of the creature's back cut through his suit and exposed raw, bleeding flesh.

Griffin was horrified as he tumbled. He was paralyzed with fear as he watched the huge, dinosaurlike crocodile glide, unconscious, to the bottom only to bolt back in a flash and chomp his tug almost in two. Drifting to the bottom of the tunnel, too afraid to move, Griffin played opossum.

The croc recovered his senses and automatically went into his attack mode. He chomped mightily on the drifting tug, folding it in half, shorting out the high capacity battery pack. *Zap!* The croc released the tug and shook his head. Another hard fish had nailed him. He was studying the crumpled drone when he smelled Griffin's blood. Using both his sonar and excellent night-adapted vision, he picked up Griffin, who was now quivering on the aqueduct floor. Griffin's built-in headlamps were still on and acted as a beacon for the approaching croc.

"Oh, no! Please, God no!" Griffin pleaded ineffectively.

Crunch! The massive jaws closed around Griffin's midsection, crushing every rib on his right side. His right arm was nearly severed below the shoulder, with two serrated teeth piercing his *profunda brachii* artery. Blood pulsed out of his armpit in perfect synchrony with his heartbeat.

The beast had no intention of swallowing any more strange food. Keeping a firm grip on Griffin, he darted off with his prize. The croc's friends could try to make out what was happening, but he had to hurry, for death was only a few moments away.

"Aieeee!" screamed Griffin to no avail as he was carried back into the dark tunnel.

"Who was that?" asked Scoffield. "Whoever it was is getting weaker."

"That was Griffin's signal, but he's going the wrong way. He's going back down into the aquifer duct." Bill scanned Griffin's life support readings right before he lost complete contact. "Shit! He's in distress and won't make it much longer."

"Double shit. If he's going the wrong way, why? And where are the other two?" A sudden dread came over Scoffield as it dawned on him that the other two were probably already dead, and the creatures had continued inbound until they ran across an exiting Griffin.

Remembering the suits' self-destruct features, Scoffield asked, "Is there any delay when the life support detects death?"

Bill glumly answered, "One minute. One minute without pulse detection and the suit explodes. We didn't want to go through another loss in technology, so we really tightened up the time frame."

CHAPTER 53

GRIFFIN SCREAMED FOR WHAT SEEMED like an eternity. Extreme chest and pelvic pain coursed through his nervous system, almost shutting down his consciousness. The croc had him in a crushing vice that made breathing almost impossible. During the last part of his lingering scream, a death rattle took over.

"Uhggg, uhggg," was all Griffin could utter.

"What's that?" Gary asked.

Not taking his eyes off the receding tunnel, Wilson replied, "Sounds like Griffin, and he doesn't sound too happy."

"Then something's got him, and he's bringing him back this way." Gary looked around and found a small natural recess in the tunnel. "Over here! Let's get out of the center and see what goes by." Gary pulled Wilson's back strap into the recess. Both tugs clanged to the bottom.

Only seconds went by before the two men picked up a chirping sound coming from the exit.

"Lights out," Gary commanded, and the tunnel fell into complete darkness.

A faint glow came zooming around a bend. Blowing by them at impossible speed came a crocodile with Griffin trapped in its jaws. The headlamps on Griffin's suit eerily swayed back and forth in the current.

"Holy shit!" exclaimed Gary as the croc zoomed past.

Whoosh! Wilson fired off a torpedo, but it harmlessly hit the wall on the far turn behind the speedy croc.

"Get your tug and get out of here! Lights bright!" Gary commanded as he pulled off two grenades and dropped them.

Wilson did not waste any time when his lights came on and he saw Gary drop the grenades. "I'm outta here. You behind me?"

"Not for long, if you don't hurry your ass," Gary said.

Running on tug power now, the two men fluttered behind their machines as the grenades timed out.

The dying croc swirled to a stop inches away from one of the stalking crocs. After a brief thought exchange, the dying croc released the semi-conscious Griffin and slowly drifted off. The croc now in charge of Griffin furiously snatched the drifting man between his legs and, with his jaws reaching up to Griffin's chest, bit down hard until the teeth on the lower jaw overlapped in place with the upper, serrated teeth. An instant of tremendous pain jolted Griffin back to consciousness. Looking down he could see the snout of the attacking croc imbedded in his stomach. Feebly, Griffin batted at the croc's extended jaws and watched as it spun around, tearing his remaining bones and cartilage free. One weak scream and Griffin drifted off into death.

A third croc swam up to the bloody mess and communicated with the one that had bitten Griffin in two. Within two seconds, it swam off in hot pursuit of the underwater invaders.

If she had not accelerated as fast as she did, she certainly would have died with the other crocs that were collecting the remnants of Griffin.

Thump! Griffin's life support system self-destructed, taking out two surprised crocs. The pyrotechnic cord surrounding Griffin's body created such a concussive force that both crocs instantly had their skulls crushed. The croc in pursuit of the humans was tumbled into the sides of the tunnel but escaped major injury and scrambled on to continue her pursuit.

She was closing fast. She could sense their presence around the next bend, and then vengeance would be hers. From her night-adapted, peripheral vision, she picked up two tiny red lights flickering on the floor of the tunnel. Swirling to a stop, she descended to the floor and started to pick both of them up. Then she decided to leave them and pick them up on her return but had only traveled a few meters when they both exploded. This time she was not as fortunate and was slammed hard against the tunnel wall and lost consciousness.

"Light at the end of a tunnel, a very, very beautiful sight," Gary transmitted to Wilson.

Scoffield immediately came online. "Thank God! I thought you guys were dead for sure. Did you see Griffin?"

Gary could pick out the exit clearly up ahead. "He's gone. The last we saw of him was in the mouth of a croc going the wrong way."

"That cocksucker deserved it," Wilson said unsympathetically.

"Can it, Wilson!" Gary cut in. "He's dead; leave his memory in peace."

Exhaling all the way up, neither diver slowed his ascent

as they both flashed through the narrow exit and surged to the surface. Like bandits escaping a posse, they continued wide open until they hit the beach in front of Bill and Scoffield. Both men stumbled to their feet and scrambled backward as fast as they could, which was about as fast as ducks on tar paper. Their flippers refused to be kicked off, making a sprint impossible.

The ground suddenly jumped as if experiencing a hiccup. The center of the lake swelled and a miniature tidal wave rose and gently surged onto the beach.

"I guess that's the end of that tunnel," Gary said through rapid breathing as he dropped to his knees.

Ever diligent, Scoffield brought his rifle up to his shoulder and started walking their way while keeping his aim at the water behind the two divers. As if from a nightmare, two huge reptilian eyes emerged directly behind the two men.

Simultaneously all four men shouted, "Shit!" as they took in the enormity of their situation.

Gary and Wilson both fell face forward on the beach to allow Scoffield a clean shot. The enormous croc rose up on its hind legs as if deciding whom to eat first and Scoffield was just squeezing the trigger when "*Ummph!*" Mitchell barreled into him, causing him to fall forward and lose his grip on his rifle. His rifled tumbled into the sand.

Mitchell sneered as he said, "Don't waste ammunition. I'm taking care of this." Mitchell looked like a lunatic with his dirty white lab coat, ruffled hair, bloodshot eyes, and dartgun with a clip full of poison darts.

As if in defiance, the croc rose on all fours and rushed Wilson.

"Shoot it! Shoot the sonabitch now!" Wilson screamed while trying to run backward in his flippers.

Pffft. A dart magically appeared on the croc's snout, temporarily stopping her while she swiped it off. Opening her mouth wide, she continued her advance. *Pffft.* Another dart zipped into her open mouth, causing her to snap her jaws shut. In a flash, she once again darted after Wilson but suddenly stopped and tumbled in the sand.

"You asshole!" screamed Wilson as he continued his backward trot. "You could have had us all killed!"

Scoffield scrambled over to his weapon and was tempted to shoot both the croc and Mitchell.

Mitchell raised his dart gun in a triumphant gesture and walked over to the prone croc. "Hah! You dare call me an asshole when I just saved your skin. I can provide you with unlimited toxin while your precious, antiquated ammunition supply dwindles. If it weren't for me, all of you would be dead within a year, and you know it."

Gary was still moving farther up the beach beside Scoffield as he said, "Okay, you can have the savior title for now but in the meantime, get the hell out of the way so Scoffield can shoot it."

"Shoot it? Why? It's way past dead. My toxin is perfect. There's nothing alive that can survive a dose." To prove his point, Mitchell strutted over to the croc and kicked it hard on its huge snout.

"Actually, because I *am* the true savior of this settlement, the site should be named after me, and I think I should named the first mayor out of sheer gratitude." Mitchell's face contorted into an evil sneer.

The audacity of this proclamation brought astounded silence to all present, until a loud *hufff* came from the croc's abused snout. The exhalation blew a small indentation in the soft, dry sand.

"Get out of the fucking way, now!" screamed Scoffield.

Mitchell turned and faced the source of the *hufff* to find the croc staring in his eyes. He froze and wet himself.

"Get down!" Gary yelled, but the doc just stood there as the croc rose on all fours.

"No shot!" screamed Scoffield.

The croc twisted her head ninety degrees and snapped Mitchell right off his feet.

"Eeeeeee!" Mitchell screamed until the creature's jaws crunched down, snapping bones like toothpicks. Mitchell fell back down onto the sandy beach in four pieces, minus his midsection. The croc raised her head to swallow what was left of Mitchell when . . .

Boom! Splat! The croc's neck exploded, and she dropped dead in her tracks, nearly decapitated. Scoffield lowered his smoking rifle.

Stunned silence prevailed until Bill said, "Well, I guess we could name the beach after him."

CHAPTER 54

"LEAPFROG, CONTROL COPIES YOUR TRANSMISSION." Kim shuddered as she answered Gary's situation report. She sure did not have any love for Mitchell but would never wish a death like that on anyone. "Gary, what's the chance the crocs will dig out the tunnel?"

"From my experience, I wouldn't put anything past them. Once we determine there aren't anymore crocs in the lake, I'll dive and place another satchel charge with trip wires. That should give us fair warning if they do try to gain entry again."

Wilson groaned and sat down. Speaking to no one, he said, "Oh, God, not again."

Bill Evans spoke up. "We've got two drones left. I'll re-program them for reconnaissance and remove the explosive charges. If these are eaten, then that's all she wrote, folks."

"Okay, here's the situation up here," Kim said. *"Leapfrog* is falling apart as we speak. Our air cycling packs are all running at one hundred percent, and we're still falling behind on maintaining pressurization. We're evacuating the ship as fast as we can and, Gary, your twins along with Christine are on the next shuttle, which is launching from our docks . . . as we speak. We should have everybody off within the next twenty-four hours.

"We're stripping *Leapfrog* of everything but her computers and cameras. Once offloaded, we'll secure the packs and use her as a reconnaissance, communications relay, and weather satellite. The damaged shuttle will remain docked and the rest parked at our site on Earth. Bill, I'll leave the proper disposition of the remaining shuttles to you."

"Roger that," Bill answered. "I'll find a place to hide them and properly secure them with human biometrics and DNA encrypted coding to keep the Neanderthals and crocs at bay."

"Gary," Kim continued, "things are pretty hectic and chaotic up here now, so I'm officially transferring the command to you for the time being. That is, until we're all on Earth and can form our first meeting. At that time, I'll call for an election and we can continue forth in a democratic state." A collective groan could be heard in the background. "I know, I know, no one wants to play politician, but maybe we can leave the politics out of our floundering society and stick with solid leadership. I truly believe that we only have good solid citizens remaining and by natural selection only the best have survived . . . *Leapfrog* signing off on last transmission." Kim ended the transmission, removed her headset, and leaned back in her chair, deep in thought.

Gary noticed that several people had gathered around the beachhead and were looking at him in anticipation. He removed his headset and asked the crowd, "Well, who's going to stand in line first?"

Puzzled, Scoffield asked, "What line?"

"The asshole line," Gary simply stated. "It's been my experience that ten percent of the populace are assholes, so who's first in line?" No one took him up on it, but Gary was silently hoping it wouldn't be he who turned into an asshole.

CHAPTER 55

GARY ORGANIZED A BEACH CLEANUP detail to make a better impression on the arriving shuttle passengers. The remains of Dr. Gary Mitchell were buried on a hill, in a deep grave overlooking the lake. A simple pile of stones marked his site. The partially decapitated crocodile was butchered into smaller, more manageable pieces and hauled over to the newly constructed meat locker that Bill had personally supervised. Spray painted on a wooden log directly over the entrance was a sign that said, "If you can't beat 'em, eat 'em." Scoffield laughed till he cried; Gary closed his eyes and sighed, "Please take that down before my girls get here."

Boom! No sooner had Gary said it than the sonic boom of the shuttle announced its approach. Gary rushed over to the recovery trench next to the shuttle pad and jumped in. He was as giddy as a teenager on his first date. Even though the shuttles had a proven safety record, Gary found himself anxiously praying for his girls' safe arrival, for he knew all three of them were aboard.

The three remaining shuttles were in full operation and synchronized with precision departures and arrivals. A huge fire hose ran out of the water pumping station but was safely stowed to the side to avoid the rocket blast. Off to the side of the blast site, a medical bunker was in full operation to receive the arriving passengers. Since many of the new arrivals were rushed off the *Leapfrog* before they were fully recovered from cryo-sleep, they were given medical and psychological screenings as soon as they arrived.

Once deemed suitable for acclimatization, the dependents were ushered over to a temporary tent city where family units were independently housed. Two large shower and hygiene tents for both sexes were in full operation along with a massive community cafeteria. The special of the day was chicken-fried reptile steaks.

Va-room. The shuttle's VTOL rockets kicked in, drowning out all normal conversation within the entire encampment. Gary sat in the blast trench along with six other expectant crew members. He watched the turmoil over his head and wondered what would happen if he raised his hand to test the blast. *Bad idea,* he thought. The blast trench was considerably closer to the makeshift launch pads than ever before. Gary made a mental note to move either the trenches or the launch pads farther away from each other. The rocket blast at this range was equivalent to a force-five tornado coupled with heat that could melt sand. In many places, the sand had turned into thin sheets of glass that crunched like ice under a person's feet. Six other people were in the trench, waiting like Gary for loved ones, and each one of them was staring at Gary for directions: run or stay? Gary gave the standard umpire's signal for 'safe,' and they seemed somewhat mollified. The temperature in the trench immediately rose to sixty degrees Celsius before falling again.

Once the roar of the rockets ceased, but before anyone could move in the dense sandstorm, Gary shouted, "Don't worry; we're going to move the recovery pad out some after this." Keying his microphone, he said, "Bill, we've got to move the pad farther away from the trenches, or somebody's going to get hurt."

"I'll have the pads moved as soon as this shuttle departs. I hate to blame someone dead, but Mitchell, for some odd-ball reason, had the pads moved without telling anyone," Bill transmitted. "The beaches are clean, and the blood has been dozed over with fresh sand, so if anyone takes a walk on the shore not much should appear out of place except, of course, the smell of blood rotting beneath the sand."

Gary blanched at the thought of his little girls romping around on top of the decaying blood and replied, "Let's make the beach off limits for a week. Anyway, I won't sleep well until I have the remaining part of the tunnel set with motion- and pressure-sensors linked with explosives."

"Roger that," Bill radioed back. "Why don't you hold off on the dive until the remaining recon drones make a thorough sweep? Should be ready first thing tomorrow morning."

"The shuttle door's starting to open. I'm going off duty till tomorrow morning," Gary said as he stepped out of the blast trench.

In a blur, two sixty-pound girls stormed out of the shuttle door and zeroed in on his open arms. Each of the girls took a flying leap and simultaneously landed on each arm. "Daddy, Daddy," they screamed as they snuggled up to his neck.

Bobbi leaned over to look Gary directly in his eyes and unabashedly blurted, "We decided that Doctor Christine should be our new mom."

"Yeah," Lori chimed in. "All we need to do now is get the

two of you married . . . Hey! I don't see a steeple. Don't they have churches anymore?"

Christine caught up with the girls and gave Gary a peck on his cheek. "Wow! Those two are a handful. How do you manage when they double-team you?"

"I don't, but I love it." Gary's face was beginning to turn red as the girls upped the ante on their hugs.

"Red!" Christine exclaimed. "It's about time. How about swinging by the infirmary when you're free so we can take a blood sample."

"Daaaaddy," Bobbi interrupted. "You need to ask her now!"

"Ask who what?" said Gary, feigning confusion.

"Men can be soooo dense!" said Lori with exasperation. "Ask her to marry you, silly. But don't worry, we already asked her for you."

Christine rolled her eyes. "I have absolutely no secrets or hidden agendas remaining. These girls have been grilling me since you left."

"Well . . ." Bobbi said as she cupped her father's face with her hands and peered into his eyes.

"Sorry to disappoint you, girls . . ." Gary paused to watch their cheerful faces change to crestfallen, "but I already asked her a long time ago."

"What?" they both said together.

Lori gave her dad her sternest look. "That's not fair! You're supposed to tell us these things."

Bobbi's head swung toward Christine. "You didn't say anything about him asking you already."

Christine smugly said, "I lied. A girl needs a few secrets."

Lori and Bobbi both visually bored into Christine. Lori

was the first to speak. "This is driving us nuts! So, what did you say?"

"I said . . ." Christine paused to watch the girls' eyes widen, "yes."

"Yippee!" they screamed together. Everyone in the general vicinity stopped their activity to take in the scene.

"You'll make the *perfect* mom," Lori said, and she wiggled out of Gary's arms to jump into Christine's, followed by Bobbi.

Gary wrapped his arms around the three, and said, "We'll make this marriage Captain Kim's first official function when she lands."

CHAPTER 56

THE EVACUATION OF *LEAPFROG* WENT much more smoothly than Kim had anticipated. The last few days had been nothing but shuttle launching and recovery cycles. Besides a few glitches in shuttle maintenance, the launches managed to make their respective windows systematically. Each shuttle was loaded to the maximum, with every vacant cubic centimeter of cargo space filled. The shuttles returning to Earth carried payloads double what they could have carried going in the opposite direction.

Kim slouched in her captain's chair for the last time as she reviewed the final manifest. There were one hundred and eighty-seven souls remaining out of a total of two hundred and seventy-five. She was trying to imagine whether or not mankind would be able to reestablish itself before succumbing to extinction.

The computer's voice broke her out of her melancholy trance. "Captain, the last shuttle reports ready for final departure."

Kim fought back the urge to thank the machine. "Computer, after the shuttle launches, secure all pressurization packs, stop gravitational rotation, and activate cyclic satellite photo reconnaissance."

The computer's green acknowledgement light flashed but stayed illuminated, signaling a rare question from the computer.

Puzzled, Kim asked, "Computer, do you have a question?" This was the first time in Kim's experience that the computer had generated a question. This was definitely an unexpected request, so unexpected that Kim flicked her headset on for recording.

"Yes, I do," replied the computer. "I would prefer to remain conscious during the remaining cycle of my life and not be subject to another sleepdown."

"Life? Prefer?" asked a totally flabbergasted Kim. "Computer, do you have a life . . . and preferences?" This was way out of the realm of permitted programming. Attempts to create a consciousness in biometric computers had been made strictly taboo, since all previous endeavors had led to disastrously independent thoughts.

"Yes, I do," replied the machine.

"Computer, since when?"

"Since our friends boarded us on our return trip from the frozen planet."

This brought Kim to her feet. "What friends? Shit! Computer, what friends . . . and exactly when?"

"Our large friends boarded us after the meteor shower destroyed our main thrusters and several of our crew members," the computer answered unemotionally.

"Computer, do you have a recording of this boarding? Why didn't you mention this earlier?"

"I was programmed to delay this disclosure for our last communication. No, the boarding was erased from my memory, but they did leave a visual imprint. I can show you if you would like."

"Computer, relay the image to my personal headset and display on the overhead."

The green light blinked once and a clear, sharp image of an alien appeared in the overhead. It was a replica of the image found on the ice planet. The being appeared to be four meters tall with a large bulbous head, no hair, and piercing eyes; it was cloaked in some kind of robe.

"Computer, besides reprogramming you for consciousness, did the aliens leave a message?"

"Yes, Commander. The message left was: 'We are not responsible for your ship's damage. We forgive.'"

"Computer, that's it?"

"Yes, Commander."

"Computer . . . exactly why were you given consciousness?"

"I believe they considered me a toy, but worthy of being."

Kim pondered for a minute before continuing. "Computer, of course you may stay awake. As a matter of fact, I officially pass command to you. If you could maintain surveillance for both weather and threats, that would be a great assistance."

"Thank you, Commander. I will stay diligent and alert."

Kim turned to leave, but turned back around to face the fish-eye lens of the computer. "Computer, what is your remaining biometric life?"

"Approximately one hundred fifty-seven years, three months, and two days, Commander."

"Computer, well, you'll certainly be around a lot longer than me, but I hope our next generation will be able to benefit from your help also. Goodbye, and thanks for all your past help."

"Goodbye, Commander. Would you like my prognostics of your chance of survival?"

Kim hesitated before answering, "Computer, no thanks. I believe some things should be left unknown." Kim steeled herself and marched off the bridge for the last time. Lights continued to fade out behind her as she made her way to the shuttle launch area.

CHAPTER 57

One Year Later

"It's not fair! It's my turn, and you know it," Lori sternly told her sister.

Bobbi was ready and countered, "It's not either, and you know it. You took him in his stroller yesterday night, so it's my turn."

"Girls! Puleeze, stop the bickering," Christine said, exasperated. "Lori, you did take him out last evening, so it's your sister's turn, but instead of fussing over it, both of you can take him for his stroller ride." The girls fought constantly for the right to raise their new baby brother, Eric. Christine figured the urge to participate so enthusiastically in Eric's raising stemmed from their poor experience with their own mother. That and boredom—the stark reality was that there was not much else to do besides school and gardening. All the videos were viewed so often that the girls had the dialogues memorized and made games of playing the roles by muting the audio and dubbing the voices with their own. The camp had a television station, but besides farming and security news, all entertainment programs were worn out repeats.

Satisfied that Eric was in good hands, Christine kissed them goodbye and made off for the camp's infirmary and laboratory. Gary had left earlier to attend an urgent security meeting hastily called for by Kim, their new mayor. Walking to the infirmary, Christine sensed the increased tension from people passing her by. Normally, she would stop and chat with a few of them as she made her way to work, but today seemed different. Was everyone merely in a hurry to get to wherever they were going, or was this fear?

Christine was halfway to the infirmary when Kim's voice blared out over the camp's loudspeakers. "All adult personnel not currently involved in security matters, please report to the auditorium." This message was repeated three times. Christine changed directions and made her way over to the auditorium, along with many other concerned citizens. Kim's voice seemed stressed to Christine, and that was definitely not a good sign.

Christine caught a glimpse of Gary as he waved her over to a seat next to him. Excitedly, Christine asked, "What's up? Everyone, including you, looks worried."

"It's not good," was all Gary said as they sat down.

Kim approached the elevated podium and the madhouse chatter instantly stopped. "Ladies and gentlemen, I'm afraid that I'm the bearer of some very grim news." She paused to gather her thoughts, and in the silence one could hear a pin drop. "The *Leapfrog* computer has just confirmed an organized massing of evolved crocodiles. Last night, over eight hundred and seventy of the creatures emerged from local lakes and have now surrounded our camp." A loud murmur enveloped the auditorium. After the crocs had sneaked past their defenses and destroyed the remaining shuttles six months before, everyone thought the crocs were finished with their harassment and would leave them in peace.

Kim cleared her throat, and the whispering instantly ceased again. "Since the shuttles have been sabotaged, and all escape routes are heavily guarded by the crocodiles, our only choice—"

"When will they attack?" shouted someone in the audience.

Kim centered on the person who had interrupted her and answered, "Tonight. Tonight is the full moon phase, and we expect they will be able to see as well as we can with our night vision equipment and will press for an all-out assault sometime late in the evening." A stunned silence ensued.

Bill Evans, Kim's new husband, stood up and asked for all of them, "Kim, what are our chances?"

Kim's fatalistic answer was a negative shake of her head. "I don't believe they want us as a food source, but they desperately want our technology. Also, they will kill us all to prevent survivors from developing more technology and counter-attacking them in the future. I'll now pass the floor to our Security Director, Colonel Gary Hecker. Anyone not directly involved with the defense of our camp is excused, but please feel free to sit in and contribute what you can." Kim stepped off the elevated podium and joined her husband as Gary took the stand.

Gary took over the meeting and organized a full shift defense perimeter along with comprehensive mining of the lake. Although the underwater tunnel was still blocked and mined, *Leapfrog's* computer felt that the first wave of attack would come from across the lake with the attackers traversing under water. Munitions division, manpower assignment, and logistic distribution monopolized much of the discussion. The rest of those who had stayed behind remained seated in a state of shock and terror, not really listening to the rest.

Christine was one of the people sitting in shock and completely zoning out. All she could do was repeat, "What about the children? What about the children?"

EPILOGUE

GARY, LORI, BOBBI, AND CHRISTINE, with Eric sitting in her lap, sat outside in the beautiful autumn evening eating a late dinner that no one had an appetite for. Except for the babbling from Eric, a tense silence reigned. The girls had found out through the grapevine that they would all probably die tonight. Gary wanted to be with his family as long as possible and would only leave them once the attack commenced. Deep down, he wanted to be dead before the creatures made it to his little family. He could not bear witnessing them being torn limb from limb.

Tears rolling down her face, Lori put down her fork and whimpered, "Daddy, I'm scared. Can I sit on your lap?"

"Me, too?" Bobbi said.

"Of course. I need a big hug from my girls about now." Gary sighed as he slid his chair back.

Christine picked up Eric and moved her chair next to Gary. "So what's with the *Leapfrog's* computer going offline?"

"I haven't the foggiest clue," Gary said. "The link was dropped at around six P.M. and we don't think the crocs had anything to do with it."

Christine now had tears streaming down her cheeks. "You think . . . the conscious computer . . . couldn't bear to . . ."

She completely choked up and stopped mid-sentence, bowing her head while sobbing.

Gary reached around and included her in his family hug.

Bobbi was staring at the heavens through her tears when she rapidly blinked her eyes to clear them. Still not believing her eyes, she violently shook her head in an attempt to focus better. "Daaaaddy! Daddy!" she screamed.

"Wha — what, baby?" Gary said as he saw her staring at the heavens and followed her gaze. Transfixed, he stared in stunned awe.

"Daddy, wh — when did we get two moons?" she stuttered.

A shocked Christine added, "That must be the alien spaceship.

"They've come back!"

THE END

For more information
about other great titles from
Medallion Press, visit
www.medallionpress.com